*For Cheryl, my mermaid.
Always.*

CEMETERY BEACH

AJ BAILEY ADVENTURE SERIES - BOOK 17

NICHOLAS HARVEY

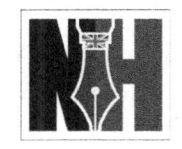

Copyright © 2025 by Harvey Books, LLC

All rights reserved. This book or any portion thereof may not be reproduced or used in any manner whatsoever without the express written permission of the publisher except for the use of brief quotations in a book review.

Printed in the United States of America

First Printing, 2025

ISBN-13: 978-1-959627-29-6

Cover design by David Berens

Author photograph by Lift Your Eyes Photography

This is a work of fiction. Names, characters, businesses, places, events and incidents are either the products of the author's imagination or used in a fictitious manner unless noted otherwise. Any resemblance to actual persons, living or dead, or actual events is purely coincidental. Several characters in the story generously gave permission to use their names in a fictional manner.

1

AUGUST 1ST, 1969

Luna had never seen anything like the incredible sea of humanity before her. Sixty thousand people swaying and singing along to every word. The air, thick with heat and humidity, caused sweat to soak her flimsy white blouse, leaving the cotton transparent as it clung to her skin. Not that Luna noticed or cared. Singing before the biggest crowd of her young career, she was lost in the moment, completely absorbed in a mixture of awe and desire to give them her best performance.

Stacks of amplifiers on the stage behind the band blasted every note and melody across the Atlantic City Race Track in New Jersey. The same stage on which iconic names like Joni Mitchell, Santana, Procol Harum and Jefferson Airplane had preceded 'new sensation' Luna and the Lanterns, as they'd been introduced. The Byrds would be up next, and Janis Joplin, Joe Cocker, and Three Dog Night would be amongst the stars playing tomorrow, the last day of the Atlantic City Pop Festival.

Luna felt connected with the crowd, as though she could reach every dancing, singing soul and they could feel her heart racing, full of love for the moment. As she reached the final chorus, Luna glanced across at Rollo, their lead guitarist, producer, and her boyfriend for the past year. He fleetingly caught her eye before launching into a guitar solo to wrap up the song. Rollo loved this moment, and she eased a few steps back to let him take centre stage. The crowd pumped their arms in the air as he ad-libbed a crazy run of notes, sweat glimmering from his toned, shirtless chest.

On drums, Trina kept a looping beat while Rollo continued in a rising crescendo. It went on and on until there was nothing more than a wall of electric sound and distortion filling the air, and with a subtle nod he ripped a final note while Trina landed an explosive drum and cymbal sequence to end their set. The crowd went wild, cheering and whooping as the band met at the front of the stage, joined hands, and took a bow. Luna blew them kisses and was about to leave with the other three, when what began as a murmur from a group of fans soon became a unanimous chant. Luna, Luna, Luna!

Speechless, she knew this evening would live in her heart forever. An indelible memory to be savoured in the moments when her seemingly perfect life of blossoming stardom lost its shine.

"I love you!" she said into the microphone as she clipped it to the stand and waved goodbye.

"They love you too," came Roger McGuinn's voice over the speakers as he took the mic.

The lead singer for The Byrds turned and smiled at Luna as she left the stage to the continued chants of her name.

"That has to feel amazing," a male reporter shouted to be heard over the noise.

Luna beamed and nodded, struggling to summon any words. Trina threw her arms around their singer.

"You were sensational, babe. That was freakin' incredible."

The two young women jumped up and down and screamed.

"Less than two weeks ago we had the first lunar landing on the moon," the reporter yelled. "And tonight Luna just landed big time in New Jersey."

Trina released her embrace. "Too bloody right, eh? This girl is far out."

Luna shook her head, blushing, although there was no way to tell beneath the glow from exertion and heat.

"This is the best night of my life," she enthused in her London accent, which mostly disappeared when she sang. "The crowd is fab. I couldn't be more chuffed."

"You were supposed to warm them up for The Byrds, but I think you stole the show," the reporter said, leaning in close. "I'm Jacob with *Rolling Stone*. Can I have some time with you? I'd like to write a feature piece about your performance here and what's coming next."

Luna couldn't believe her ears. "Too bloody right," came out of her mouth before she had a chance to refine her answer.

"Is now okay?" Jacob asked.

"Don't you want to hear The Byrds?" Luna asked.

Jacob shook his head and grinned. "No, man. They're old news. You're what the music fans want now. That crowd wasn't lying."

Luna laughed and blushed again, certain her cheeks were glowing like a traffic light. "Cool. The dressing rooms are in the buildings over there. Is that okay?"

"Lead the way," Jacob said, and Trina linked arms with Luna as the two headed through the makeshift backstage tents.

"What's going on?" Luna heard Rollo ask.

In the crowd and deafening noise, she'd almost marched right by him.

"Jacob's from *Rolling Stone*. He wants to interview us, babe."

Rollo nodded. "Hi, Jacob."

Immediately, the whole vibe changed. The two men clearly knew each other, and Luna could sense the animosity. At least from her boyfriend. Rollo was thirty-three, fourteen years older than her, and he'd been in the music business since he'd left school.

"You know I was just doing my job, man," Jacob said, offering his hand.

Rollo didn't accept it, taking a drag of his cigarette instead.

Jacob shrugged his shoulders. "Are you going to tell me the *Haze* album was your finest work, Rollo? I told it as I saw it, man."

"'Juvenile' – that's how you told it, you bloody prick," Rollo snapped.

"C'mon babe, he wants to do an interview with us now," Luna said, trying to defuse what had turned ugly in a hurry and was killing her post-performance elation. "Can you let it go? He loved our set tonight."

Rollo looked her over, and she immediately felt self-conscious in her flimsy top, which she guessed was revealing more than he approved of. His judgemental stare made her shiver despite the oppressive summer heat.

"Let it go?" he repeated low enough that she doubted anyone else had heard him above the sound of The Byrds and 60,000 fans. Rollo turned back to Jacob. "Don't screw me again, man."

Jacob held up both his hands as though surrendering. "You guys put on an incredible set tonight. I just wanna capture the moment. Keep this wave rolling for you."

Trina winked at Luna. "Come on, then. I need a bloody drink," she announced and took her friend by the arm. "We can interview while we celebrate."

Luna allowed herself to be pulled towards the race track buildings but checked over her shoulder to make sure Rollo was following. She breathed a sigh of relief when he fell in step behind the reporter, although his expression hadn't softened. She quickly turned when Trina shouted their bass player's name.

"Panda! Come on, lad, we're being interviewed for *Rolling Stone*."

"No way," the tall, skinny young Londoner breathed in his laid-back tone. "That's pretty fab. I just took a hit, man, is that okay? Can't guarantee I'll make any sense in about ten minutes."

Trina looped Panda's arm and towed her two bandmates along. "You never make any sense, you lanky streak of piss."

They all laughed, and Luna felt her elation from the show slowly returning.

"With *Time and Light* being such a success for a debut album," Jacob began as they all crammed into a small office space which had been converted into a dressing room for the festival, "how do you plan to follow that up?"

He was looking at Luna, but Rollo answered.

"With a second album," he said flatly.

Jacob laughed, but Luna knew he'd tire of the battle if this was how Rollo chose to handle what she saw as an incredible opportunity. *Rolling Stone* magazine had quickly established itself as the leading music publication in America, and their album had hit as big in the US as it had in Europe.

"When can fans expect to hear songs from the second album?" Jacob soldiered on. "I noticed you didn't play any new material tonight."

Rollo exhaled a stream of cigarette smoke. "They'll hear it when the album releases. It'll be worth the wait."

"No sophomore slump for you guys?" Jacob probed.

Rollo shook his head.

"What's sophomore?"

Luna was glad Trina asked. She didn't know either.

Jacob laughed, then realised they were serious. "It's the word for second year in school. You know, after freshman. In music it's the follow-up album."

"Oh," Luna grimaced. "I've never heard that term before. But I don't think our new album will slump. It's really cool."

"So you've already recorded it?" Jacob said, pouncing on her comment.

"Most of…" Luna began, but Rollo cut her off.

"Some of the songs," he said firmly. "We're still working on it."

Jacob nodded and sat forward on the threadbare sofa he was sharing with Trina and Panda. "Where are you recording? I hadn't heard you'd started."

"We're floating, man," Panda said, staring off at something only he could see on the ceiling. "It's wild man. Truly rock 'n' rolling."

"We've kept the studio quiet," Rollo quickly intervened as Trina laughed and Luna looked at her boyfriend in concern. She knew how badly he didn't want his new studio project getting out before he was ready. "We're actually recording in a few different locations."

Luna smiled. He wasn't lying.

"And are you writing the songs again for the new album, Luna?" Jacob asked.

She glanced at the frown on Rollo's face. She wanted to say yes, but that would be risky.

"Your biggest hits from *Time and Light* were songs you wrote, Luna," Jacob continued as she hesitated. "Surely you guys took note of that?"

She forced a smile. "Co-wrote. We all contribute, but it's Rollo's amazing music and production that makes our sound. I just make a contribution with the lyrics," Luna lied.

Jacob looked at her and smiled. "Really?"

Trina scoffed, and Luna frowned at her.

"The new album will be better than *Time and Light*," Rollo said, rising from the equally threadbare armchair in the room. "It'll establish our sound and the fact we're here for the long haul, not some flash-in-the-pan one-album wonder."

He beckoned to Luna in the other armchair and she reluctantly stood, straightening her short skirt down her thighs and checking the buttons on her top.

"I'd love to ask a few more questions, Rollo," Jacob protested. "This isn't much to fill out an interview piece."

"No, it doesn't have a title yet," Rollo replied. "Yes, it'll be complete well before the end of the year. No, I can't say when the label will actually release it. And yes, every song will be an original tune written by me and the band."

"Aren't you a member of the band?" Jacob immediately asked.

"By us," Rollo corrected. "Now, we gotta split."

"Thank you," Luna called out as Rollo tugged her hand through the door into the smoke filled hallway. "Come on, Rollo, we need interviews like that," she urged, but he practically dragged her down the hall until he found a door leading out the back of the building.

Pushing through, they both stumbled into an employee car park. The noise of the ongoing concert echoed in the air from the opposite side of the building.

"You have no bloody clue what we need and don't need, Louise," Rollo fumed. "Give them an inch and parasites like that wanker will bleed you dry. You understand?"

He shook her arm and his vice-like grip dug into her flesh.

"I'm sorry," she muttered, knowing deep down that she shouldn't be apologising.

He'd been in the business his entire working life. She'd been a nobody playing pubs in London with Trina and Panda until a year ago. Rollo had discovered them and taken Luna and the Lanterns from obscurity to the top of the charts, so she always deferred to his experience. But this felt like a personal grievance standing in the way of the band landing themselves an amazing article. She said nothing more. Luna had learned in the past weeks to let things go. The Rollo she'd been enthralled with had disappeared somewhere along the line on their American tour. All she could do was hope that the man she'd looked up to would return, and soon.

2

GRAND CAYMAN – PRESENT DAY

Annabelle Jayne Bailey opened up the throttle until the needle reached 9,000 rpm and the twin-cylinder Ducati engine sang as only a finely tuned piece of Italian engineering mastery can. Shifting to third, the sleek Multistrada 950 adventure motorcycle flew down the two-lane island road, swiftly surpassing 80 mph before AJ backed off, letting the wind, engine, and tyre resistance slowly curtail her speed.

"Oh, sod it!" she wheezed under her full-face helmet as she flashed by the white police car tucked behind a stand of casuarina trees.

Carefully downshifting to second, she let the gear-braking further slow her pace, avoiding the obvious brake light flashing on, but it didn't matter. It was too late. In her mirrors, AJ saw the Royal Cayman Islands Police Service car pull out and immediately switch its lights and siren on.

Muttering and swearing, she indicated, then pulled to the side of West Bay Road in front of the cemetery, opposite the fire station. As a crow flies, she was no more than 200 yards from her little cottage, although more like a mile by road. As usual, she was late, and hoped she'd know the copper. Maybe she could talk her way out of a ticket, but she was pretty sure the speed limit was 40 mph, and she'd been close to double that. Her beloved Ducati didn't like going anywhere slowly.

Slipping her helmet off, AJ continued muttering and complaining to herself while she switched off the bike and used the key to unlock the seat and retrieve her paperwork stored underneath. She was already sweating in the humid Caribbean air without the wind rushing through her armoured Gore-Tex jacket and trousers and over her leather boots.

"Dat was a tiny bit over da speed limit, miss," came a local man's voice, which AJ recognised.

She turned to see Constable Jacob Tibbetts grinning at her. Next to him was a tall, lean, young female constable with long blonde hair and a stern expression.

"You're busted, big time," the woman said flatly in a Scandinavian accent from behind her dark sunglasses.

AJ rolled her eyes and extended both arms to accept the handcuffs. "Fair cop, governor," she said in accentuated Cockney. "You nicked me, proper. I'll do my porridge."

Jacob laughed and looked at his partner. "What dat she say?"

"No idea," the female constable replied.

"You two are no fun," AJ chuckled. "Reg would have been in stitches."

"Probably not," the blonde responded.

"On the inside, he would have," AJ insisted. "Well Nora, what was I doing?" she asked her close friend, who was more like a younger sister than a woman thirteen years her junior, born in a different country.

"Seventy-six. Not bad," Nora replied and finally grinned.

"I'd slowed a bit before I passed you," AJ admitted. "It's too tempting leaving the roundabout when there's no one in front of you."

"Lucky it was us, AJ," Jacob said. "Be hard talkin' your way outta dat."

"Well, you scared the daylights out of me, so I doubt I'll do it again for at least a week or two, if that makes you feel better."

Jacob laughed. "Slow down, miss. You bin officially warned."

"Absolutely, officer," AJ replied with a broad smile. She turned to Nora. "Dinner's at seven."

"I told you I can't make it," Nora frowned.

"I know, but that doesn't matter. I need you to be there. Not a chance I'm facing another evening with my parents without bringing a distraction along."

"I'm shit at conversation," Nora pointed out. Which AJ knew to be a fact.

"Yeah, but you're bringing Jazzy with you. The kid'll keep them entertained for hours."

"I feel like one of those things at a circus," Nora replied.

"A clown?" Jacob offered.

"No. The animal that claps the clangy things together with the music. A circus cat."

"I think you mean a circus monkey," AJ laughed.

"Okay. Then I'm not your circus monkey."

"Technically, Jazzy will be the circus monkey," AJ said. "You're more like the ringmaster. But I didn't say that."

"But you just said that," Nora responded in her usual literal Norwegian interpretation of everything.

"You said it first," AJ countered and stuck her tongue out at her friend.

They grinned at each other.

"Can we get back to work now?" Jacob asked.

"Bye, Jacob, and thank you for my warning," AJ said, picking up her helmet. "I'll see you at seven, Nora."

"*Nei*, you won't," Nora replied as she walked away.

AJ laughed to herself as she fired the Ducati back up. Checking for traffic, she eased back onto the road and resisted popping a wheelie as she accelerated away.

Parking by the tall wooden fence along Boggy Sands Road, the cul-de-sac behind large homes fronting the famed Seven Mile

Beach, AJ slipped through the gate while she took off her helmet and jacket.

"Hi dear," her mother said, looking over her shoulder from the patio.

Beryl Bailey and her husband Bob were sitting on chairs outside AJ's tiny cottage in the grounds of the large, modern house.

"You must be cooking in all that gear, love," her father said as AJ leaned over and kissed his forehead. "Get the part you needed?"

"Took three places, but I found something that'll work," AJ replied, opening the sliding glass door to go inside. "And I got pulled over on the way home, the cheeky buggers."

Both her parents turned in their seats.

"Were you riding like a bloody lunatic?" Beryl asked.

"Did they give you a ticket?" was Bob's question.

Their responses struck AJ as being both typical and amusing. Her mother assumed AJ had been in the wrong, and her dad was more concerned with the consequences and how it would affect his daughter. She'd find it more amusing if her mother wasn't right more often than not.

"Not entirely looney, and no. It was Nora and Jacob."

"Are we finally to meet this Nora girl we've heard so much about?" Beryl asked. "And you said she fosters a teenager? Will the girl be with her?"

"Yes, and yes. Tonight."

AJ slid the door closed behind her and was glad to wriggle out of her motorcycle trousers. She took the stainless-steel screws she'd bought at the hardware store and dropped the paper bag on her little dining table for two on her way to the fridge. Relieved there was still one coffee-flavoured energy drink left, she popped the top and took a swig. Her morning had been hectic.

AJ loved having her parents visit, especially as it had been years since they'd flown over from the UK, but there were stresses which arrived with them. Her father had long ago accepted that their only child was not destined for a corporate path. Perpetually almost retiring, Bob still worked hard and couldn't find a way to pass his company along to a new owner. His plan A had been his daughter taking over the reins, but he'd come to terms with the fact that wasn't on the cards, and seemed to have a hard time settling on a plan B.

Her mother had spent her life as a barrister with a reputation for winning her cases and was still convinced AJ was going through a 'phase'. Despite AJ having worked in the scuba diving industry for over a decade, moving to Grand Cayman to pursue her love of the ocean and building a successful business, Mermaid Divers. Beryl couldn't accept that her daughter wasn't doing 'more' with her life. AJ tried her best to recognise her mother's projection of her own version of success stemmed from a desire for her daughter to be happy, but it wasn't easy. Beryl had a way of judging without saying a word.

Guzzling more of the drink, AJ poked her head out the door.

"Shall we go for a dive?"

"I was hoping we would," Bob replied, getting up from his chair. "I can't wait."

"Are we going out on the boat?" Beryl asked, rising more slowly.

"Nope," AJ replied. "We're going out right here."

She pointed beyond the white picket garden fence to the calm ocean beyond, with the early afternoon sun high overhead and the breeze rustling the surface of the turquoise water.

"Through all the sand?" Beryl questioned.

AJ laughed. "Unless you can talk dad into carrying you over it."

Twenty minutes later, AJ had changed into purple Mermaid Diver leggings and rashguard, which brought out the purple-highlighted streaks in her shoulder-length blonde hair, and had carried three scuba tanks from her van to the gate leading to the beach. Making two more trips, she lugged down her dive gear and a couple of rental sets for her parents. Her dad was the first to join her, changed into board shorts and rashguard, ready to go. They began assembling the buoyancy control devices, or BCDs, the vestlike apparatus which strapped to the diver and held the 80 cubic-foot air tanks on their backs.

"I can't believe how much has changed since we were last here," Bob said, as he finished his rig and moved on to assembling his wife's. "So much new construction."

"Yeah," AJ agreed. "For a while it was really bothering me, but then I realised the island was still an amazing place to live and progress happens everywhere. There was no stopping it, so I decided not to let it get me down."

"Is it progress, or simply change?"

"Depends who you ask," AJ said with a laugh. "I feel bad for the locals who can't afford to live anymore in the areas they grew up. My little place here would rent for four times what I pay if the Flemings ever kicked me out."

"Which they'll never do," Bob said. "They know they can trust you to watch the house."

"They're very generous," AJ replied as she double-checked her Dive Rite backplate and wing set-up she used whenever she wasn't teaching a dive course. "I'm an idiot for not raising the rent more on my condo, but it doesn't seem fair. My tenant has been in there for over five years now."

Bob began checking over the rigs he'd just assembled. "That's got to be getting close to paid off by now."

"Made the last payment six months ago," AJ replied proudly.

She'd used the cash she'd earned from selling her story of discovering the wreck of a long-lost German U-boat in Cayman waters a few years back to put a deposit on a small condo. Her goal had been to make extra payments on the mortgage whenever she could and she applied the net profit from rent straight towards the principal. Making the last payment had been a very satisfying day.

"Good for you, hon," her dad said.

They heard the slider close and saw Beryl walking towards them.

"We're all set and ready to go," Bob declared, and Beryl nodded.

AJ often wondered how her parents' marriage had endured

when so many fail, but she was happy they'd maintained their joy with each other. It was understated, and rarely flowery or vocalised, but there to see for anyone who paid attention. Her mother settled a hand on Bob's shoulder, which was her way of showing appreciation.

"Is the tide way in?" Beryl asked.

"It's the slight ebb between high tides," AJ replied. "But that's how much beach we've lost. The storms along with the rising seas have shifted the sands. Seven Mile Beach is no longer anywhere near seven miles long now."

"That's not good," Bob said, lifting his rig to his shoulder, which was now heavy with the tank.

"Less sand for us to walk through, I suppose," Beryl commented. "But sad to see."

AJ picked her rig up by the tank valve and opened the gate. Bob grabbed his wife's rig in the same manner and followed. AJ led them along the beach under the shade of the sea grapes and silver thatch palms lining the front of the neighbouring home. When she reached a pathway on her left which led to the road, she turned towards the water.

"Remind me what this dive site is called," Beryl asked.

AJ pointed over her shoulder. "Cemetery Beach," she said, indicating the beachfront graveyard next to which she'd been pulled over an hour earlier.

"Lovely," her mother commented, but couldn't hide a slight smile. "How creepy."

"Don't worry, Mum," AJ said, sliding her fin straps over her wrists and walking into the water. "The dead stay up there. They won't bother us."

3

Luna cracked an eye open and wondered what time it was. The hotel room was dim, but sunlight leaked past the edges of the curtains. Next to her, Rollo's steady breaths told her he was still asleep, and she carefully slipped from the covers. Hurrying to the bathroom, she closed the door before turning on the light. She'd made the mistake before of walking around a hotel room naked only to discover bandmates, friends, or even total strangers scattered about the place.

Splashing water over her face, Luna felt the dull ache in her head from the night before. It wasn't drink or drugs, as she mostly avoided them both, but the after-effects of the pounding speakers and the roar of the crowd. She smiled at herself in the mirror. The headache was well worth it. Her joy quickly faded when she noticed the bruise on her arm.

This wasn't the first time. If he saw the marks he'd made on her fragile frame, he'd apologise and tell her how much he loved her. He'd blame it on his passion for what they made together. Say he was sorry for letting it get the better of him. But she'd heard it before. Luna would wear long sleeves, despite the summer heat, so he wouldn't see the damage he'd done. It was easier that way. No make-up sex and pretence that everything was fine. Her charade of loving a man who wanted to control her every move. Her every thought. This had become her new way of making their relationship work.

Luna had been completely besotted with Rollo after he'd approached her at her insignificant little gig at the pub. A few years earlier, he'd had chart success with The Velvet Rollo Band and had been instantly recognised by the patrons when he'd walked in. The fact that he'd stayed to listen to their whole set, then approached her afterwards, had been mind-blowing for the then eighteen-year-old. Things had moved swiftly from there. Rollo had insisted that she set aside her guitar to focus on fronting the band, and so the trio became a quartet. He suggested ways to rework the songs she'd written, which seemed at odds with his original enthusiasm.

"I thought you loved what we played?" she'd asked him. "Isn't that why you wanted to work with us?"

"I'm helping you turn potential into greatness," was his response. "I know what the labels want."

Luna had begun to doubt him after what felt like endlessly playing demo tapes for record executives at every company in London. Until one of them called Rollo back in. From there, it was hard to argue with his genius. Rollo landed them a two-album deal with Polydor, who had stars like John Mayall & the Bluesbreakers, Cream, The Who, Jimi Hendrix, Bee Gees, and Eric Clapton on their label. From there, life had become a whirlwind of rehearsals, recording, then radio shows and a tour to promote *Time and Light*.

The album was named after Trina's oil painting she'd created for the cover, and Luna wrote a track under the same name. Rollo rearranged the song, which became their first single and broke into the top ten in the UK. It hadn't been hard for the charismatic Rollo to coax young Luna into his bed not long after they'd met, and somewhere in the next few months as he reinvented the band, the two of them officially became an item. Enthralled, intoxicated, and bending to his every will, Louise Skye from a working-class home in Finchley couldn't believe she was becoming a household name across the country, and playing live on *Top of the Pops*.

But now, as she stared at the bruise on her arm and recalled Rollo's jealous denial that she was, in fact, a major contributor to their songs, she knew the shine had worn off her infatuation. *Had she ever truly loved the man?* It was hard to say. Certainly starstruck and awed, and for a while she'd assumed they were in love, but now she couldn't be sure. Although there was no question in her mind that she'd fallen in love with the attention and growing fame, which was an addictive drug.

Wrapping herself in a towel in case she stumbled across anyone else in the room, Luna turned off the light and left the bathroom. Fumbling as quietly as she could in the dark, she found a cotton skirt and a long-sleeved top in her suitcase. Quickly slipping them on, she took a room key and her purse from the bedside table, freezing when Rollo stirred for a moment. He turned over and continued sleeping, so she eased out of the room and took the lift down to reception.

From the busy coming and going of people in the lobby, she could tell it was past morning, and the clock behind the reception desk verified it was 11:35am. Far closer to lunchtime than dawn. Looking out the windows, Luna could see that Atlantic City was wide awake, with the busy street outside packed with cars and the pavement full of pedestrians. She retreated to a corner of the lobby where she found a coffee pot, and knowing she'd never drum up a decent cup of tea, settled for the American preference.

Wandering outside through revolving doors, bright sunshine, and already soaring heat struck her like a bucket of steamy water. Squinting, and wishing she'd remembered her sunglasses, the next assault came in the fashion of voices screaming her name.

"Luna! It's Luna over there!"

A group of a dozen or more music fans rushed towards her, and she didn't know whether to run away or prepare to defend herself. The young girls stopped short of charging into her and jostled for position as they held out magazines, programmes from the festival, and even her album to sign.

"Oh my goodness," Luna breathed. "I don't even have a pen."

"We do," every girl yelled at once, holding out a variety of writing implements.

"Thank you," she said, choosing a pen and beginning to sign anything they held in front of her. "Did you dig the concert last night?" she asked as she carefully added her well-practised signature to each item.

When she'd begun playing live gigs, Luna had filled a notebook with her own autograph, using her stage name she'd dreamed about for years. For hours she'd perfected just enough feminine swirl to the letters. The L was the hardest. She found it annoyingly tricky to create something aesthetically pleasing about a right-angled line. She'd practically bubbled over with excitement when someone finally asked for her to autograph a bar mat. Now that she signed hundreds of items at gigs and appearances, she wished she'd focused on making her autograph a little less fancy, and faster to write.

A sea of replies drowned out any individual comment, but it appeared those who had tickets had loved the show.

"Are you going to the festival tonight?" one girl asked her.

"I wish, but I can't," she replied, remembering they were leaving that day, but she couldn't recall at what time. "We're flying to Miami."

Groans of disappointment rippled through the gathering, which seemed to have grown since she'd started signing.

"Hey, you want another album from us, don't you?" she asked with a smile.

The enthusiastic cheers made her glow inside, but she needed to get back to the room. Their flight was sometime in the afternoon, that much she knew, and she didn't want to make them late. That was Panda's role. They were always waiting for her old school friend.

"Thank you," Luna said to the crowd, handing the pen to one of them. "I have to go. Thank you," she repeated, waving to them as she hurried through the revolving door where a member of the hotel staff stopped the crowd from following.

Softly opening the hotel room door, sunlight greeted her, so she knew Rollo must be up and the curtains drawn.

"Where have you been?" he asked sharply, glancing at his wristwatch as she entered.

He was wearing jeans, no shirt, and was drying his long brown hair with a towel. He'd shaved, which pronounced his full moustache. It tickled her face when they kissed. Rollo was a good-looking guy, and while not the tallest, he was in remarkably good shape and women went wild over him. They'd already been dating by the time she'd learned of his reputation for sleeping with a prodigious number of groupies, models, and famous actresses. She didn't care, as long as he didn't continue, now that they were seeing each other. Free love was the way of the modern world and although she hadn't subscribed to that dating method, he'd told her that was all in the past. Standing in the hotel room, looking at the man who millions of women would sell their grandmothers to sleep with, she couldn't help but wonder if one of them might lure him away. The idea didn't bother her nearly as much as she thought it should.

"I went downstairs for a cuppa," she replied. "What time are we flying?"

"Did you bring me one?" he asked in response and she realised she was empty handed. Which made her reason seem hollow and selfish for not bringing him a drink.

"All they have is coffee," Luna replied, heading for her suitcase to begin packing, glad she'd showered the night before.

"Two," Rollo said, and for a second Luna wasn't sure what he meant.

"We fly at two," he clarified. "Car picks us up at twelve-thirty."

"I'd better see if Panda and Trina are up," Luna replied, reaching for the phone on the bedside table.

Before she could lift the receiver, the telephone rang. It startled her, but she lifted the receiver.

"Hello?"

"May I speak with Rollo please?" a familiar cultured Englishman's voice asked.

"Hello David, this is Luna."

"My dear, how are you? How did the festival go?"

"Really well, I think, and we were interviewed for *Rolling Stone* last night," she enthused.

She didn't hear David's response as Rollo took the receiver from her and held it against his bare chest.

"Go make sure those two are ready. I'm not waiting on Panda again. You'll have to knock on their door."

He waited a beat before she began walking away and then spoke into the phone.

"Hey David, it's Rollo. What's cookin'?"

Luna could only hear one side of the conversation, but she didn't want to leave and miss it. She wrangled between the knowledge that Rollo would get mad if she didn't do what he'd said and her desire to know what was happening with their record label. David was the executive who'd signed them.

"It went fine," Rollo was saying. He paused and waved a hand at Luna to leave before continuing. "Same old problems we need to address, man, but we'll talk about that later."

Luna slowly sorted through clothes in her suitcase, using the thin pretence of changing as her reason for not immediately leaving the room.

"Yeah, we'll be back in Miami this afternoon, mate," Rollo said, forgetting about his girlfriend for the moment. "Straight back in the studio."

Luna picked out a sleeveless summer dress and dropped her skirt before remembering the bruise on her arm.

"C'mon, man," Rollo responded to whatever David had said. "It all takes time. You know what I'm dealing with."

Choosing another blouse, Luna wished she could hear what the other man was saying.

"I know what I said, David, but it's taking longer, alright? That's how this shit goes sometimes, man. It's art, not a factory punching out cans of bloody soup."

Luna took her top off, just in time before Rollo looked her way again while listening to David's response. She figured seeing her half naked would be enough to buy her a little more time. She smiled at him, but he wasn't looking at her face.

"I know when Christmas is, David," Rollo said into the phone, fighting to keep his anger in check. "I'm doing the best with what I have to deal with, man."

Slipping on the new blouse, Luna knew she needed to leave the room before the phone call was over. Her boyfriend was going to be in a foul mood.

"It has nothing to do with the studio!" Rollo ranted. "The studio works perfectly, man."

Luna hurried to the door. Rollo never shared any details with the rest of the band about their record deal or business issues, and she wasn't about to ask him when this call was over. He'd be steaming. Evident by the sound of the receiver being slammed down, which Luna could hear from the hallway. She ran to the next room and banged on the door, wondering what would happen if they couldn't meet the Christmas release deadline Polydor was clearly looking for.

And what Rollo had meant by 'You know what I'm dealing with'.

4

"How much weight did you put in my BCD?" Beryl asked as the three of them lay on their backs and kicked towards deeper water.

"Two more pounds than you think I did," AJ replied.

"You always think I need less weight than I actually need," her mother complained.

AJ rolled to one side and checked the depth of the gin-clear ocean below them. They were still over the gently sloping sand with occasional patches of small coral growth and old limestone. Ten or twelve feet above the sea floor, at a guess.

"You actually need far less than you think," AJ countered. "You're always overweighted once we've descended. It's just a bit of anxiety beforehand."

The ballast weight was to overcome the air in the diver's lungs and any other pockets which acted like a balloon, resisting the descent. Once the water pressure increased with depth and crushed the excess air away, then less weight was required to compensate and the diver put air in the wing of their BCD to maintain neutral buoyancy. Learning to dive with less ballast was a progression which came with experience and comfort in the environment.

"I'm not nervous," Beryl said defensively.

"I said anxious, not nervous, Mum."

"You know the more you natter, the more you'll huff and puff and then you won't be able to descend 'cos you're holding too much air in your lungs," Bob pointed out.

"Firstly, the man on blood pressure medication should worry about his own inner workings," Beryl responded, "and secondly, I don't get anxious or nervous. I focus."

"You're taking blood pressure meds, Dad?" AJ asked. "Since when?"

"A few years now. It's nothing to worry about, just getting older stuff."

AJ was stunned for a few moments and they kicked in silence. Her parents may live a continent away, but they were still her rock in more ways than perhaps she'd realised. An anchor, still living in her childhood home where she could run to at any time. Not that she had, or probably ever would, but simply knowing they were always there gave a stability, support, and confidence to her life. This news was a reminder that their world was moving along just as AJ's had. The idea that the bedrock of her existence wouldn't always be there was one she hadn't considered in her insular bubble of life on the island. She was used to them constantly fretting and worrying about her, but not the other way around.

"Should we stop kicking when we hit Venezuela?" Beryl asked. "I thought we were going for a relaxing dive, not a trans-ocean swim."

AJ rolled to her side again and looked down. A larger coral head was around twenty feet below them, and a shadow against the lighter sand slightly farther out let her know they were nearing the shallow band of reef.

"We can drop here," AJ said. "We're almost at the reef."

She unclipped her compass from a D-ring on her harness and aimed the lubber line at the cemetery in the distance. Rotated the bezel until zero degrees faced north, AJ then read the degrees at the lubber line. She repeated the figure in her head seven times to ensure she'd remember it.

Turning in the water, she tried to spot the marker buoy she was looking for. The swells were a foot high at most, but the morning's ocean breeze had become its usual afternoon wind, and the rippled surface made it harder to detect many details.

"I'll see if I can get us to the *Doc Polson* wreck," she said, unable to spot the Department of Environment's buoy – these were affixed to all dive sites around the island. "But it'll be a bit of a guess."

Based on nothing more than experience in the waters, AJ aimed the lubber line in the direction she expected the wreck to be and took another reading.

"Great. Haven't seen the *Doc Polson* in far too long," Bob said, raising his inflator line in preparation to dump the air from his BCD to descend.

"Do we get a dive briefing?" Beryl asked. "Seeing as you've swum us out into the middle of the Caribbean Sea where we may or may not find the dive site before swimming miles home." She smirked and AJ laughed, almost falling for her mother's extra-dry humour.

"Follow me, so if we're lost, we're all lost together," AJ replied. "Let me know when you get down to 1500 psi, and don't pester the locals. How's that?"

"I feel slightly short-changed on the details, but that's what you get for free," Beryl quipped.

"Fine. Little known fact," AJ added. "On almost all the dive maps and guides, the wreck is spelt P-O-U-L-S-O-N, but that's incorrect. The doctor it was named after was a Scottish character of Scandinavian descent, and the spelling should be P-O-L-S-O-N. He helped get the first hyperbaric chamber here to the island back in the early seventies."

"You've told us that before," Beryl said.

"Every time we've ever dived the wreck," Bob agreed.

AJ put her regulator in her mouth, raised her inflation line above her shoulder, and hit the release button. Air escaped, and she dropped below the surface, frowning at her parents as she disappeared.

The world outside disappeared as though she'd donned a pair of headphones, and all she could hear was her own rhythmic breathing and the bubbles exhausting into the water during her exhales. Pausing a few feet above the sand, AJ watched as first her father and then her mother descended to join her. She gave them a few moments to reacclimatise with being submerged and to figure out their buoyancy. Once they'd both settled down, AJ held up an okay sign as a question and they both responded with the same hand signal in reply.

Taking a look back at the coral outcrop she'd seen from the surface, AJ gave herself a moment to remember its distinct features. Noticing exposed limestone, she registered the results of the shifting sands over the past year. New coral hadn't had a chance to take hold yet. She hoped to return to the same spot and use her compass heading to bring them out in front of the cemetery. Providing they still had air in their tanks, she'd save them the surface swim and finish the dive underwater. Spinning around 180 degrees and wishing she'd taken a refresher look at her Reef Smart Dive Guide for the site, she set off on her best guess heading towards the wreck. They often dived the *Doc Polson*, but from her Newton custom 36-foot dive boat, not from shore. She'd only made the dive from the beach once before, but avoided telling her mother that little gem.

In a few fin strokes, AJ reached the edges of the shallow reef and the underwater world burst into vibrant life. At only 20 feet down, the water was yet to rob all the colours of the spectrum, and orange and yellow hues burst from sponges and coral growth. Small fish from a hundred different species flitted about, moving from the divers' paths as they approached. AJ spotted the long antennae of a lobster probing the area in front of the hole in which it hid.

Keeping to her heading, AJ tried her best not to be distracted by the scenery, which became more prolific as they moved across the sprawling coral reef structure. Without any current or surge, maintaining a compass heading was relatively easy, except for when she detoured to follow a sea turtle or point out a lemon ray to her parents. Cayman's west-side shallow reef was a mass of coral fingers running somewhat perpendicular to the beach. But after thousands of years of growth, with new coral fighting the old for their view of the life-giving sun, those fingers had become more broken and angular, with odd-shaped channels and troughs in between. Every time AJ skipped over a finger to hang out with a fun critter, she created an offset, so her heading was now slightly off. Except her heading was a guess from experience rather than an accurate number, so she didn't worry too much about it. Luck would need to have a participating role for her to find the *Doc Polson*, anyway.

Steadily, they headed deeper, and at 40 feet, AJ knew if she didn't see something she recognised soon, then they'd need to think about turning around. The wreck sat in the sandy patch between the shallow and deep reefs, which ran parallel to Seven Mile Beach. The pattern of the reef on the land side of the wreck had a distinctive series of troughs between the fingers, which AJ now kept her eye out for.

A metallic tapping resonated through the water, and she turned to see her father knocking a stainless-steel carabiner against the bottom of his aluminium tank. He pointed to the north, where a five-foot nurse shark swam lazily over the reef in AJ's direction. With the lens effect of a mask underwater, the fish looked closer to ten feet long, but AJ was used to the illusion, and as it neared, the fish assumed its actual proportions. Curious, the shark cruised by, made a wide circle around the divers to be sure they weren't hiding a speared lionfish, then continued its patrol of the reef.

Bob clapped his hands together and held up an okay sign. AJ laughed into her regulator, which wrinkled her cheeks and made her mask leak. She loved seeing her dad so excited. It was easy to forget the thrill when she was used to seeing a nurse shark on four or five dives a week, but for her parents, like most visitors, it was truly a memorable moment when they only dived one week every year. AJ held up an okay sign to her mother, who returned the same signal and chuckled again. It was too soon in the trip for her mum to let down her tough lady guard and show excitement at seeing something as mundane as a shark.

Turning and checking her compass, AJ kicked again, and hadn't gone far when a hint of recognition made her pause. Changing direction a few degrees to the west, she began following the spine of a coral finger. On both sides, similar fingers curved ahead and pretty soon, she spotted sand to the south. With a pang of pride, she finned to her left, over the ridge to the stretch of sand where an ominous dark shadow loomed.

Rolling onto her back like an otter, she continued finning towards the wreck of the *Doc Polson* while she looked back at her parents. Even her mother was smiling behind her mask.

The wreck was an old 80-foot-long cable-laying vessel, sunk as an artificial reef in 1981. Decades immersed in seawater had rotted much of the deck plating away, but covered the structure in a fantastic array of coral growth. Taking out her underwater torch, AJ played the beam across the sponges and fans sprouting from the bridge and the big cable reel on the forward deck. The artificial light brought the coral's true colours to life as though a child had used every crayon in the set to decorate the old boat.

AJ dipped through a large hole in the bow decking and waited a few beats for her father and then her mother to follow. A school of yellowtail snappers moved to the far side of the room, and AJ gently finned towards the stern. When she'd first seen the wreck many years ago on a trip with her parents – during which she'd fallen in love with scuba diving – she recalled only small holes allowing pinpricks of light inside. Years of erosion since then had opened the little cracks into gaping holes, and she didn't even need her torch to navigate the rooms to the stern.

Emerging through the rear decking, she again waited for her parents, and they both came out tapping the Shearwater Tern dive computers she'd given them. AJ checked her own Teric. She still had over 1800 psi, so she knew there was plenty of air amongst them to return to the beach. They'd head straight back without the sightseeing detours and delays.

Leaving the *Doc Polson* behind and using a reciprocal compass heading, AJ kicked smoothly away, floating over the reef and soaking in the perfect conditions. Every year seemed to get more unpredictable with the weather. Bigger storms came earlier and showed up later than usual during hurricane season, and a nor'wester last winter had caused enormous damage on the west side. She'd been keeping her fingers crossed for calm seas while her parents visited, and her wish had certainly come true.

After fifteen minutes of gentle swimming, the paler tone of the sand appeared beyond the reef, and their depth was now only 20 feet. The navigation was basically simple from there, as shallower meant closer to shore, but as it gently sloped, it was easy to swim at an angle and hit the beach a quarter mile from where they'd entered. As AJ finned over the edge of the large reef structure, she spotted the smaller coral head where they'd descended. Her navigation had been spot on. Her dad would rave about her prowess later, and she'd blush, knowing luck had played at least a small part in her success. But for now, AJ moved to the coral head and adjusted her compass heading to the figure she'd noted earlier.

Finning forward, she took a moment to look back and check on her ducklings following along, and quickly stopped. Certain her eyes were playing tricks, AJ almost shrugged off what she thought she'd seen, but the more she stared at the coral head, the more she needed to take a closer look. Swimming back, she paused over the patch of exposed limestone she'd noticed before. There was now no question in her mind that the base of the coral head had long been buried in sand. Otherwise, a diver before her would certainly have noticed the weathered and aged human skull she was staring at.

5

Luna awoke to the dull drone of the diesel engines on *Soundwave*. Heavily soundproofed, like everything which made noise on the yacht, the barely perceptible tone was more of a subtle vibration than anything audible. She rolled over to discover she was alone in the master berth. From above the spiral staircase leading up to what was once the main salon, guitar chords Luna instantly recognised drifted melodically her way.

Throwing off the covers, she used the 'head' as the crew called it, then took a mini-dress she loved from her wardrobe. A glance in the mirror to check her hair reminded Luna of the bruise still dark blue on her upper arm. She returned the sleeveless dress and chose a V-neck crochet sweater instead. Despite the tropical Florida summer heat, the studio was always chilly so the wool would feel good. Donning denim shorts, she went upstairs, where Rollo greeted her with a smile.

"I've figured out the bridge on 'Wanted'. Listen."

He played the piece she'd heard from the bedroom and Luna closed her eyes, stitching the new part into the song she'd originally written. The new bridge worked, and she smiled, reminding herself that Rollo was still one of the best producers and musicians in rock music.

"That's perfect, babe. I'm going to get a cuppa. Want one?"

Rollo shook his head, jotting notes down on a pad he had next to him.

"Where are we?" she asked, walking towards the forward door leading to the galley. In the conversion from luxury yacht to floating recording studio, the windows had been removed from the salon in favour of sound insulation.

Rollo shrugged his shoulders. "However far we made it out of Miami overnight."

Luna let him be and left the studio.

"Morning," she called up to whoever was on the bridge as she continued to the galley, where a window on either side showed her nothing but bright blue skies and deep blue ocean. She found it gorgeous, but slightly unnerving to be surrounded by water as far as her eyes could see. The 105-foot-long yacht smoothly rode the calm seas, barely rocking in any direction, so she turned on the kettle and left it to boil.

Returning to the short steps leading up to the bridge built a half-level above the main deck, she was greeted warmly by Captain Garrison.

"Good morning, miss. I trust you slept well?" he asked.

Luna liked the older man. He was formal in a typical English gentry sort of way, but had an air of efficiency and experience about him, and a warmth. Like a beloved uncle.

"I didn't even know we'd left port," she laughed in reply. "I'm fixing a cuppa if you'd like one?"

"I'm fine, thank you, miss. I took over from Mr Dumfries a few hours ago, so I'm full to the brim with tea."

"Where are we going again?" Luna asked. Rollo had told them, but the name wouldn't stick in her mind.

"Grand Cayman, miss, but we have to sail around Cuba to get there."

"Have you been to Grand Cayman before, Captain?"

He shook his head. "No, miss. Close by a few times, but I've never had cause to dock there."

Exactly why they were going there was still unclear to Luna, as Rollo had been typically dismissive when asked. 'It'll be an amazing place to record,' had been the only reason he'd given.

"Where are we now?" Luna asked, able to see more from the bridge, although it was still the same endless ocean.

"About to pass Key West over there off the starboard side," the captain replied.

Luna moved closer to the window and squinted to focus on the horizon. Now he mentioned it she could see the tops of a handful of structures.

"We're about six miles off the coastline and the Keys are only a few feet above sea level," Garrison explained. "You should be able to pick out the taller buildings."

"I see them now," Luna replied. "I wish we had time to stop there."

"It's a unique and fun place," the captain said, but they both knew if it wasn't on Rollo's schedule, then they wouldn't be dropping in. They'd spent too many days in Miami sorting out provisions, paperwork, and an electrical problem with the power to the studio, so Rollo was already muttering about being behind. Although he seemed to be the only one who knew for what. They'd still managed to work in the studio some of the time at dock, so Luna figured they couldn't be too far behind whatever mystical timeline loomed. Rollo's mood had steadily declined with every new problem, and especially after a phone call he made each morning.

Luna heard the kettle boiling and scampered down the steps. She made herself a cup of tea and left the bag steeping in the mug as she returned to the studio. As she'd only ever been inside one other recording studio before, Luna's points of reference were slim. But, to her, their shipborne studio was relatively small but otherwise didn't seem to lack for anything. The mixing board was in a control room at the stern on the other side of a door next to a large window. Trina's drums were behind a partition of acoustic sound panels to stop her beats overpowering the entire room. Luna knew this because she'd asked.

Several comfortable couches gave them places to lounge in the long breaks while Rollo sorted a technical thing out or ruminated over a lyric or chord sequence while the others waited impatiently. The biggest difference from what Luna could tell was the low ceiling compared to the studio they'd recorded *Time and Light* in, the extra sandbags to hold things down, and the number of items screwed in place so they stayed put in heavier seas.

Rollo was still making notes, so Luna remained quiet until she heard footsteps on the spiral staircase.

"Trina, baby," she gushed as her friend appeared from below deck.

"Where are we?" Trina mumbled, looking like she was still half asleep.

"Key West," Luna replied. "I hear it's a hip town."

"Sounds hip," Trina replied, rubbing her eyes as she stood at the top of the stairwell. "Are we stopping for breakfast? I could eat breakfast in Key West. Wherever the bloody hell that is," she added with a grin.

Rollo was ignoring them both.

"What do you think, babe?" Luna ventured. "It's only a few miles off the…" She thought for a second. She was now facing the back of the yacht, which was called the stern. Luna turned around to face the bow, which she'd learned over the past six weeks was the pointy front part. She held her right hand out. "Starboard side!" she finished.

Rollo looked up. "What?"

"Can we drop by Key West for breakfast, babe? It's right there," she repeated, spinning around and pointing in what she hoped was still the correct direction.

"What for?" he frowned. "Stu will make us whatever we want onboard."

"Because we've never been to Key West, and it would be fun.

Can we please, babe? It'll only take an hour or so and we'll be back on our way."

"I've always wanted to go to Key bloody West, Rollo," Trina chimed in.

"You don't even know where it is," he pointed out, but his voice wasn't as harsh as he often could be, and Luna sensed they had a chance.

"Ernest Hemingway," Panda announced, as he plodded up the stairs.

"Ernest Hemingway?" Luna echoed. "The writer bloke?"

"Yeah," Panda said. "He used to spend his winters in Key West, man. The place is iconic."

They all turned to Rollo, who sighed. "We gotta work. We can't go dropping by every bloody island we see."

"But this isn't just any island, is it?" Luna persisted, doing her best sexy swagger his way. "This is Ernest Hemingway's Key West."

"Fine," he relented, much to her surprise, and she squealed with joy.

"I'll tell the captain!" Luna said, heading for the bridge.

By the time Captain Garrison had manoeuvred *Soundwave* around the island of Key West to a marina where he could safely dock the yacht, Luna knew Rollo was already regretting his decision. On the way in, he'd tried to get everyone focused on rehearsing the track he'd been working on, but they were all too distracted and excited.

Key West Bight seemed quite empty. Luna watched from the bridge as the captain skilfully guided the large yacht alongside a pier, directed by the harbourmaster. Sammy, the first mate, and Stu, a former British Navy cook, tied lines to large cleats on the pier, while the final member of the crew, Sally, the young stewardess, made sure the fenders were all in place.

The band stepped to the pier, where the harbourmaster watched as though he were witnessing an alien landing.

"Where's the best gaff for brekkie, mate?" Panda asked the man.

The harbourmaster, a middle-aged man with a thick beard, creased his brow and didn't respond.

"Breakfast?" Luna said.

The man's eyes lit up. "Right, sorry. Breakfast. Yes, there's a cafe over there in the wooden building. Or you can walk from here to Duval and take your pick."

"How long to leg it from here, then?" Panda asked.

The harbourmaster stared at the tall bassist and shook his head. "Where you from, lad?"

"Barnet."

"What language they speak there?"

Panda laughed. "English, mate."

"It don't sound like no English I heard before," the harbourmaster said. "Where's this Barnet place?"

"In London," Panda replied, lighting up a joint and exhaling a thick cloud of smoke.

"That's England," the man exclaimed, appearing confused. He frowned again at the joint. "If that's what I think it is, they'll lock you up for smoking that."

"You ain't gonna grass on me, are you?" Panda asked, without putting the joint out.

Trina borrowed it from him and took a drag.

"Cheers. We'll keep an eye out for the coppers," Luna said to the man. "Which way to this Duval place?"

"We don't have time," Rollo interrupted, already walking down the pier. "The cafe will do."

Luna shrugged. "Thank you for your help," she told the harbourmaster, then paused a moment. "Is this place usually so quiet?"

The man laughed. "As I told your captain, you'll need to be cast off before noon. It'll be packed with fishing boats when they all come in."

"Cool," Luna responded.

"Who are you people?" the man asked, respectfully looking over her braided hair and bangle-covered wrists, but avoiding eye contact with her loose, frilly blouse.

"We're a music group," she replied, "and that's our recording studio," she added, pointing to *Soundwave*.

The man scratched his head. "Really? The yacht? Should I have heard of you?"

Luna laughed. "Rollo would say yes, but I'm blown away anytime anyone knows who I am, even at a concert." Turning, she looked back over her shoulder. "My name's Luna, and thank you for letting us park our boat here."

He chuckled, and she jogged to catch up with the others.

A Cuban lady who barely spoke English seated the four of them at a table outside overlooking the harbour. She handed them handwritten menus.

"Café? Cortadito?" she asked.

"Tea, love," Panda said. "You got any tea?"

The woman shook her head. "Café. Coffee."

"Bloody hell," Panda muttered. "Okay then. Coffee."

"Coffee," Rollo said as he studied the menu.

"What was the other one?" Luna asked. "Corta... something?"

"Cortadito," the woman said, moving to Trina, who laughed.

"In for a penny, in for a pound, eh? I'll have a corta-whatsit too, please."

The woman nodded and left them to study the menu.

"I don't see sausage, egg, and beans on here," Panda moaned.

"Live a little, Panda," Luna ribbed him. "Try something local. Maybe it'll be what Hemingway had for brekkie."

"I thought we were still in America," he replied, holding up the menu. "All this is in Spanish."

"Cuba's not far that way," Rollo said, pointing approximately south. "Your man Hemingway hung out there as well, didn't he?"

Panda nodded. "Yeah. That was long before the missile crisis palaver. Probably turned in his grave when all that codswallop was happening."

The woman returned with two coffees and two smaller cups with what also appeared to be coffee.

Trina looked at Luna. "Like an espresso, I reckon."

Luna took a sip. "It's bloody hot," she said, and blew on the rich coffee. "But tasty, I must say."

"*¿Qué quieres comer?*" the waitress asked.

"I've no idea what to order," Panda mumbled.

"You decide," Luna said, pointing to the woman. "What should we try, love?"

She held her menu up and the woman seemed to understand. She tapped on one of the items, so Luna gave her a thumbs-up.

The others followed suit and once the woman had left, they laughed over what they might have coming.

"How's the coffee?" Luna asked Rollo.

He nodded, looking more relaxed than she'd expected. "Best coffee I've ever tasted."

"Good," she said, and he squeezed her hand. "This was a good idea."

Luna smiled. It felt like it had been a long time since she'd seen a glimpse of the man who had swept her off her feet. The realisation that he'd also taken on a huge amount of risk and stress hit home, and she felt a twinge of guilt. Rollo had sunk a fortune into *Soundwave*, with their new album being the big test. He'd told them all to keep the studio a secret, as he wanted the record company to hear the results before they knew where the album had been recorded, mixed, and produced. Everything hung on the unpredictable ears of a few fickle executives. Rollo smiled in return, and Luna leaned over and kissed him.

6

AJ left her parents at the cottage and trudged back to Cemetery Beach with a fresh air tank. Once they'd made it to shore and carried Bob and Beryl's gear home, AJ had called the police and left Bob to hose down their dive kits with fresh water. Beryl had gone inside for a stiff drink.

"Detective is on his way," Jacob Tibbetts said as he and Nora strung yellow police caution tape from the fence to a stake at the waterline.

"How is the body?" Nora asked.

"The body might be fine," AJ replied, trying to hide a grin.

She couldn't resist kidding with her friend, whose first language wasn't English. Nora frowned in return.

"It's just a head," AJ clarified.

"What condition are the remains in?" Nora asked, choosing her words more carefully.

"I don't think the skull is fresh," AJ replied, unsure of the correct terminology herself. "But it's intact, so probably not super old."

"Where is it?" Jacob asked as they began work on a second tape farther along the beach.

"Quarter of a mile out, I'd guess," AJ replied, looking to the road when she heard vehicles stop at the cemetery. "Thought it best not to move it."

"Probably right ting to do," Jacob verified.

A tall, slender local man in a suit and tie walked down the path alongside the cemetery and arrived at the beach. AJ had known Detective Whittaker for many years and had helped on several police cases in the past. She was one of the first the RCIPS called if they needed diver support. He nodded and brushed a hand across his neatly trimmed salt-and-pepper goatee.

"Good afternoon, AJ," he greeted her in a light Caymanian accent. "Can you tell me a little about what you found?"

"It's definitely a human skull. Couldn't see any other bones. Looks like it's been uncovered when the sands shifted from the past few storms. I didn't touch it, but I'd guess it's either been grown over by old coral or at least nestled tightly into it."

"So not a body recently deposited in the water," Whittaker commented.

AJ shook her head. "Been down there a while. Skull looked to be complete, but no algae or coral growth on it."

"Morning," came a cheery English voice and AJ looked past the detective to where a woman with a wetsuit pulled down to her waist walked their way.

"Hey, Rasha," she greeted the RCIPS's head of crime scene investigation.

She was also a friend and fellow diver.

"Just a skull, if I heard correctly," Rasha said.

"Yup," AJ acknowledged.

"You got here quickly," Whittaker said with a smile.

"Heard there was a dive involved and I've been lifting partial fingerprints from cups and plates all day. I needed a break. Can you take me to it?" Rasha asked.

"Sure," AJ replied. "Grab your gear and I'll switch my tank."

As Rasha began walking back towards the van she'd arrived in, several more vehicles parked by the cemetery. AJ didn't pay much attention as she buckled her BCD to the new tank. After a few minutes, she heard a man's voice calling to her. She looked up and groaned. Sean Carlson was a thin young man with spectacles and beady eyes. He called himself a journalist and wrote for the Cayman News Blog, an online-only publication. For which he was owner, editor, writer, and photographer. If there was a controversial angle to look at a story, that's the one he wrote. Facts were merely talking points to be used and ignored as he saw fit.

"AJ! What did you find?" he called out from behind the yellow tape which he was stretching to move closer.

"Hey, *drittsekk*," Nora barked at him. "Stay back."

"Constable Sommer," Whittaker scolded.

AJ laughed. They all knew Nora's Norwegian swear words by now, and as far as AJ was concerned, Carlson deserved them all.

"Mr *Drittsekk*," Nora said on her second attempt. "Stop bending the tape."

Whittaker shook his head. Carlson finally moved back a few feet under Nora's persuasive glare.

"C'mon, just tell me what you found," the internet reporter persisted. "A body, right?"

"Yeah," AJ replied. "It's Jimmy Hoffa."

AJ didn't really know who Jimmy Hoffa was, but she'd heard the name enough to know he'd gone missing decades ago, supposedly courtesy of the mafia.

Carlson shook his head.

"Actually, it's the lost treasure of the Spanish fleet," AJ added. "I'm going back in to get the rest of it."

She turned away and finished preparing her equipment while she heard Rasha chuckling, lugging her dive gear along and dropping it next to AJ.

"See any lionfish out there?" Rasha asked.

"Not one," AJ replied.

The invasive species were the only fish divers were permitted to spear in the marine park waters which surrounded Grand Cayman.

"That's okay," Rasha replied quietly. "Probably bad form to hunt lionfish while we're inspecting human remains."

"I don't think whoever it is will mind at this point," AJ chuckled, then nodded towards the police tape over her shoulder, "but The Weasel would have a field day with a picture of us walking out with a skull in one hand and dinner in the other."

Rasha laughed. "That's perfect. He reminds me of a weasel too. Those creepy little eyes and he's always wriggling into places he shouldn't be."

AJ lifted her rig to her shoulder and slipped her arms through the harness straps. "Mind you, bit unfair to weasels."

They both tried to keep their amusement under control as they strode into the water with a gathering crowd watching.

AJ led as she swam the reciprocal heading out to the coral head, choosing to stay on the surface most of the way for simplicity. Dipping her masked face in the water, she spotted the darker tone of the reef ahead, and scanned in both directions for the coral head. It was to the south of them as the gentle swells rolling to shore had pushed them slightly north. The two women nodded to each other, indicating they were ready, then wordlessly slipped below the surface.

Finning over to the coral head, AJ pointed to the skull, and Rasha moved closer to take a look. AJ hung off to the side to let her friend work. Getting a second and longer look, she noticed the skull appeared to be wedged more than embedded in the old limestone. After taking a series of photographs with an underwater camera, Rasha gently took hold of the skull to see if it would come free. From what AJ saw, it seemed to be clutched tightly by the reef.

Taking a chisel and hammer from a large pocket in her BCD, Rasha began chipping away at the limestone. The water soon clouded with tiny debris and curious fish showed up to see if there was a free meal to be had. AJ laughed behind her mask as a spotted trunkfish, a cute little clothes iron-shaped reef dweller, repeatedly sucked in a morsel, only to spit it back out and choose another. The fish seemed convinced the next bite would be tasty despite a dozen failed attempts.

After ten minutes, Rasha took a break to let the murky water clear out so they'd get a better look at what she'd accomplished. As the visibility around the coral head returned, she pointed out a small part of the limestone which held the jaw. Before this layer of coral had died, it had grown around the bone. From Rasha's chisel marks, AJ could see she'd been working on freeing the skull from the limestone's grasp. For coral to have grown around any part of the remains indicated it had been down there for some time. The slow growth rate of coral meant decades at least.

Rasha could now wiggle the skull a little, but the jaw remained in the clutches of the microorganisms, so she went back to work. After another ten minutes, she paused again, and once the clarity returned, she was able to pry the jawbone free, along with the skull. Holding the two together, Rasha nodded to her pocket and AJ took out a large evidence bag. Prying the opening apart, AJ held the bag while Rasha carefully placed the skull inside.

For some strange reason, for the first time since spotting the remains, it hit AJ that they were handling what was left of a human being. The skull wasn't just a curious, surprising, and rather creepy discovery; it had once been a person. Somebody's life had ended, and instead of their remains being respectfully interred, they'd been lost to the sea. Which could well have been where they perished. Or dumped. Or a hundred other scenarios which now raced around her mind.

She felt a nudge and looked at Rasha. The crime scene investigator was waiting for AJ to pass her the evidence bag. "Sorry," AJ grunted into her regulator and handed over the bag. Rasha carefully closed the top and dropped it in a mesh dive bag she'd carry back. After putting her tools away in her zippered pocket, Rasha tapped two fingers to her mask, then pointed all around them. AJ returned an okay sign. She was being asked to look around for further evidence. While AJ carefully inspected the rest of the coral head, Rasha swept back more sand from the base, searching for anything hidden beneath.

They spent another thirty minutes carefully looking until Rasha tapped her tank to get AJ's attention and indicated they should head in. Disappointed they hadn't found anything more, AJ reluctantly took her compass heading and led them towards shore. She wondered if they'd return for a full-scale grid search, but figured it was unlikely. Whoever the skull had belonged to had perished many years ago, so unless an examination found actual evidence of wrongdoing, there probably wasn't much to be done.

Surfacing in four feet of water, AJ was surprised to see quite a crowd gathered on the beach. Nora and Jacob had successfully kept everyone behind their yellow tape, but the scene looked a bit like the exit from a triathlon swim. The two divers had a clear path up the sand between the restrained crowd to a RCIPS pop-up tent. A few people began shouting questions and AJ picked out The Weasel's voice as the loudest. She refused to look his way.

Under the tent, Detective Whittaker waited patiently while the two women slipped out of their gear. Rasha placed the mesh bag on a folding table, hidden from onlookers by the three closed sides of the tent, which rustled in the wind.

"What can you tell so far?" Whittaker asked.

Rasha didn't answer right away, but extracted the evidence bag, and then carefully drained the water and took out the skull.

"As you can see, I had to chip away limestone to release the bones, which is quite interesting."

"Because the reef had grown over part of it at some time?" Whittaker asked.

"Because the reef had *only* grown over part of it at some point," Rasha emphasised. "As you know, the limestone is old, dead coral, which all the reef is built upon. New coral grows and suffocates the old like building blocks. Except in this case, no new coral continued to grow, and no coral grew on the skull itself, except for where it held the jaw."

"It must have been buried in the sand. By an event like a

storm," AJ said, following her friend's meaning. "It was exposed for a period of time, enough for the coral to grow around a piece of the jaw, but then covered, so the growth died."

Rasha nodded. "And now the sands have shifted and revealed the skull again."

"Ewwww," AJ muttered.

"What?" Whittaker asked.

"I just figured out why there's no coral growth on the skull itself."

"Yeah, that's the fascinating part of the timing," Rasha said. "Coral growth had to wait until the flesh and tissue decomposed from the skull. Looks like that must have been complete before the skull was hidden once more."

"Then how did the coral attach to the jaw?" Whittaker asked.

Rasha pointed to the jawbone. A small section was encrusted with broken limestone where it had been freed from the encrustation.

"It's hard to see because of the limestone, but notice the crack through the jaw?"

Whittaker and AJ both leaned in to get a better look.

"I think so," the detective said.

"Is it chipped or did your chisel slip?" AJ added.

Rasha laughed. "No, I managed to avoid causing further injury to our victim. That is a chip."

"Bloody hell," AJ muttered.

"Yup," Rasha agreed. "Obviously, these are just field observations and I'll need to do a proper study, but first impression is that this person was hit in the lower jaw hard enough to reveal the bone. That's how the coral began growing there."

All three of them spun around upon hearing a man yelp from the beach. Nora had Sean Carlson pinned to the sand with a knee in his back and handcuffs already on one of his wrists.

"Constable?" Whittaker called out.

Nora turned and looked up. She appeared completely unfazed by whatever altercation had taken place.

"Are the handcuffs really necessary?" Whittaker asked with a tone which suggested they weren't. "Perhaps best to just escort Mr Carlson behind the tape."

Nora looked disappointed as she hauled the man to his feet.

"I'm surprised she didn't taser him," AJ joked.

Whittaker shook his head. "We must call that progress, I suppose."

7

On the open ocean with Key West and the Dry Tortugas off their stern, the seas began rolling more, but Luna barely noticed. They'd rehearsed the reconfigured version of 'Wanted' and now played their parts while Rollo recorded them from the control room. Many bands were still recording songs by the old method where everyone played and sang live in the studio, then used the best recording of the entire song for the record. But Luna had never known that way of doing things. *Time and Light* had been multi-track recorded, then spliced together using the best sections, which had become the increasingly popular method.

"No, no, no, Trina," Rollo's voice boomed through the studio talkback speaker, and also her headphones. "The fill you did on the last run-through."

"I don't remember what I did," Trina replied, shrugging her shoulders. "I was kinda bored, so I just busked it."

"Come in here. I'll play it for you."

Luna hadn't realised Rollo had been recording their earlier session, so she got off the couch and joined Trina in the control room. Rollo hit play, and they all listened. The recording was from a single mic in the room, so he couldn't isolate the drum track, but their keenly tuned musical ears isolated the rhythm.

"Oh, yeah. That was pretty far out, wasn't it?" Trina laughed. "I can do that, I think. Play it one more time."

Rollo rewound the tape, and they listened again.

"My voice sounds weak," Luna commented, having thought she was singing well.

"It's the room mic," Rollo assured her. "You're fine."

Luna stayed in the control room while Trina went back to her drum kit, nestled behind the acoustic sound panel partition. Rollo's hands moved around the mixing board and various tape machines within his reach before he held down the button for the talkback microphone.

"Recording whenever you're ready."

Through the glass, Luna could partially see Trina. With her eyes closed, the drummer's hands twitched as she assembled her previous performance in her mind. After a few moments, her eyes blinked open, and she began playing. It sounded great to Luna, but at the end, Rollo opened the mic.

"One more time."

Trina played the segment again, which sounded exactly the same to Luna. She wasn't a drummer, but had played guitar since a young age. Everyone had always complimented her on her playing until Rollo had suggested, then finally insisted, that she focus on being the front woman singing and leave the lead guitar to him. At first, she'd felt elated and special, but after a while, she'd begun to wonder if the decision had been based on her guitar playing.

"Okay, that's good," Rollo said over the mic. "I can make that work from those two takes."

"Cool," Trina replied. "Hey, I was thinking, we're on a boat making rock music, yeah?"

Rollo ignored her, so Luna pressed the talkback button. "We're certainly rocking and rolling," she said, grinning through the glass at her friend.

"Right! So, we should call it Yacht Rock," Trina declared. "Got a ring to it, doesn't it?"

Luna laughed and was about to reply, but Rollo beat her to the button.

"Wake Panda up."

"I feel you," she chuckled. "Gotta live with the yacht rock thing for a day or two. Let it percolate and sink in. It's gonna be big."

"It's awful and will never catch on," Rollo said flatly. "Wake Panda up."

Luna heard Trina laugh as she slipped off her headphones and walked over to the couch where Panda had stretched his lean frame out and was fast asleep.

"What was the difference between those two takes?" Luna asked as Rollo switched reels on a tape machine and labelled the one he'd removed.

"Trina can be hesitant, so the first take always starts softer and her timing isn't great," he said. "After a bit, she settles in, so I need the second take for the intro."

"Wow," Luna murmured. "I've never noticed."

Rollo just raised an eyebrow.

"I think she's a great drummer," Luna added.

"Good, yes. Great…" Rollo looked up at Luna. "No. She's not great." He turned and looked through the glass at Panda, who yawned and rubbed his face before slipping his guitar strap around his neck. "But she's better than him."

Luna wanted to rush to defend her friend, but knew she'd be wasting her breath. If that's what Rollo thought, then nothing she could say would change his mind. Besides, he could be right. If she couldn't tell the difference between Trina's drum takes, then surely her ears weren't well tuned enough to determine whether Panda was a competent bassist. But that shouldn't matter, she thought angrily. They'd been friends for too long to get caught up in games over who played better than who. They were the Lanterns. That wasn't about to change.

Billy Hastings and Louise had grown up together, living two

streets apart and going to the same school. They'd met Catrina three years ago in a pub when she was playing for another local band who were playing their last show before their singer left for university. Billy, who'd been nicknamed Panda since his first day of middle school when the short and chubby kid had been teased wearing the black-and-white school uniform, suggested they start their own band. Louise, who'd insisted everyone call her Luna after a planetarium trip when she was ten, knew his suggestion had been motivated by his desires for the drummer. Which weren't reflected, but it didn't matter. The trio became inseparable.

"Then help him be better," Luna said, pausing by the door to the studio. "Panda's a Lantern, Rollo. He's not going anywhere."

Rollo frowned and was about to say something, but thought better of it. He returned his attention to the console.

"I'll make us all a cuppa," Luna said, and slipped out the door.

Panda's bass track didn't take as long as Luna was worried it might, based on Rollo's comments, so it was now time for Rollo to play the lead guitar part. He set the control room up, started recording, then rushed into the main part of the little studio to play. He had to make it in time for the count-off so he'd keep time. The other three hung out on the couches and stayed quiet so they wouldn't make a noise that could end up ruining the recording. After four takes, Rollo announced he was happy and finally ready for Luna to sing. She was ready to have something to do. But Rollo decided it was time for lunch first.

The crew knew to keep noise to a minimum and never enter the studio when the red recording light was on outside the door, but a few moments after Rollo called Stu to let him know they were ready to eat, the yacht's horn made everyone startle. Seven short blasts, followed by a longer one for the general emergency signal, let everyone know it was a muster drill. They all groaned, but made their way to the open upper deck behind the second set of helm controls, where two lifeboats hung from davits.

"It's lunchtime, man," Panda complained good-naturedly, slapping Sammy on the shoulder. "Couldn't we do this after grub?"

Sammy smiled. "Better than doing it in the middle of the night, eh?" he said in his broad Scottish accent. "Has to be within 24 hours of leaving port, you see. Captain's been waiting for that red light of yours to go off."

The yacht steadily slowed as the drive had been placed in neutral, and they all helped uncover the lifeboats and swing the davits out. It was a beautiful day, and apart from being blinded by the sun after the dim lighting of the studio, Luna didn't mind getting a few minutes of exercise and fresh air.

"Can't we use the switch to lower these things?" Panda asked, pointing to the electronic controls for the davits. "Bloody hard work winding these buggers by hand."

"No," Rollo replied before Sammy had a chance to. "We could be doing this when the yacht has no power. Or, the generator is all that's keeping power on and the studio needs most of that to keep the systems cool."

Trina nudged Luna. "We drown while the yacht sinks, but at least the bloody console fans were still running while it went down," she whispered.

Luna chuckled. "I know the captain has to, but does the record producer go down with his ship?"

"I bloody hope so," Trina giggled. "Sorry, love. I shouldn't say that."

Luna shrugged her shoulders and thought about Rollo's earlier criticism of her friends and bandmates. "That's okay. Sod him."

Trina cranked the handle, grunting with the effort. "We all know, you know," she whispered under her breath.

"Here, let me have a go," Luna said, then lowered her voice. "Know what?"

Trina put her hands on her hips and looked around to make sure no one was within earshot. Rollo was on the port side showing Panda how to work the davits and not paying them any attention.

"You only own two long-sleeved tops, love. When you wear them back to back for a week, it's a bit obvious."

If Luna hadn't already been beet red from the effort, then her embarrassment and shame would have shown in her cheeks. Her first reaction was to deny everything, but her best friend knew her too well, and wasn't above rolling Luna's sleeves up to prove the point. They'd always been honest with each other about everything. Until this. Luna had thought she'd been hiding it well, but apparently not.

The lifeboat touched the water, so Luna stopped cranking and looked over at Sammy.

"This good enough?"

Sammy came over and looked. "Yeah, that'll do. If it was for real, you'd need to drop it a bit farther, yeah? Just till the lines are slack enough to release. Gets tricky in rough seas, mind you."

Across the deck, Rollo was now using the electric winch to haul the port side lifeboat back up, so Luna did the same. She'd hoped Sammy would stay with them so she didn't have to respond to her friend, but he wandered back to check on the guys.

"He doesn't mean it," Luna whispered, and already hated the way she sounded. "He takes all the stress on his shoulders. The record company stuff, and he's put all his money into *Soundwave*, which I'm sure he won't see back until the album comes out."

Trina frowned in return. "So punch a bloody wall. Not you."

"He's never punched me, Trina," Luna quickly replied, louder than intended.

She quickly checked, but no one had heard her over the whirring motors and wind blowing across the Straits of Florida.

She softened her voice once more. "It's not like that, I promise. He's grabbed me a couple of times, that's all. I bruise easy too, which makes it worse. It only started later on the tour when the yacht build got delayed."

Trina shook her head. "I get that he's a big-time producer and probably a genius when it comes to the music, but that doesn't give him the right to treat us all like bloody losers. I'd rather go back to playing pubs than see him shove you about."

"It's not that bad, honestly, Tee. I wouldn't put up with it if it was."

"What do you think he'd do if you tossed him out on his ear?" Trina asked.

Luna thought for a moment. "I really don't know," she said, thinking it over.

Rollo was possessive and wanted to know where she was all the time, but he didn't strike her as jealous as much as controlling.

"I think he'd go back to shagging everything in a skirt."

Trina burst out laughing, which did get the three men looking their way.

"Gotta be lunchtime now," Luna said loudly, elbowing her friend as they walked across the deck.

"'Bout bloody time," Panda grinned.

8

"You know, once upon a time it wasn't unheard of for bodies to float out of the beachside cemeteries," Reg Moore said in his gruff London voice. "Over the years, they've figured out to use concrete crypts and cover stones to stop it from happening."

"Well, you need to get all this talk of dead bodies out of your systems before we sit down for dinner," his wife Pearl said with a shiver. "I'm losing my appetite hearing all about it."

"Sorry, Pearl," AJ said, standing beside her in the kitchen while Reg, Bob, and Beryl sat on bar stools along the kitchen counter.

Pearl reached an arm around AJ and gave her a squeeze. Reg's wife was a shapely middle-aged woman who never appeared to age in the many years AJ had known her. With blonde hair, a warm smile, and a generous bust, Pearl stood out from the crowd, but AJ had come to rely on her generous heart and mothering instincts. Traits her own mother lacked. Pearl and Reg had never been able to have children, so AJ had become their surrogate kid, encouraged by Bob and Beryl to keep an eye on their daughter while so many miles from home. If either of AJ's parents had become jealous of their girl's bond with her island family, neither of them had ever shown it.

The couples had originally met when AJ's parents had brought her to Grand Cayman for her first dive trip. They'd stayed in touch and Reg had been a mentor to AJ when she'd chosen to make her living in the business. He'd also given her a job as a divemaster on his boats after she'd gained a few years' experience working in the Florida Keys. After that, he and Bob had helped her set-up her own dive op, which still shared Reg's dock in West Bay alongside his three boats.

"How did the head become detached from the rest of the poor sod?" Bob asked. "Could your CSI expert tell?"

"Bob!" his wife scalded.

"We're not at the table yet," he said, and winked at Pearl.

She waved a hand in the air. "Go ahead, but I'm pouring myself another drink."

"Took a big ol' whack to the head with something, so could have happened then, or later when the body decomposed," AJ replied. "The crabs will do a number on a body."

The doorbell rang before anyone could respond and Reg's Cayman brown hound mutt, Coop, sprinted to the door, barked once, then stood excitedly waiting for a human to do something.

"That must be Nora and Jazzy," Pearl said, following the dog.

"She actually showed up," AJ said in surprise.

Pearl paused for a second. "You said she was coming."

"Yeah, but she didn't technically agree to it," AJ confessed.

Pearl rolled her eyes and continued. Nora, who wasn't the hugging type, had learned to succumb to Pearl's greeting, and after being embraced, walked into the large living area of the house.

"Hallo," she said, managing a smile for Bob and Beryl as she satisfied Coop with an ear scratch.

"Very nice to meet you, Nora," Bob said, slipping from his bar stool and offering her his hand.

AJ had prepared her parents to avoid her friendly natured father being tasered if he moved in for a hug. Nora firmly shook his hand.

"Nora Sommer. This is Jasmine Holder," she added, indicating the petite dark-skinned teenager, who appeared perfectly content in Pearl's arms as they walked towards the kitchen.

"Hey Jazzy," AJ said with a wave. "This is my mum and dad."

Jazzy smiled from beneath a wild mop of curly hair, which made her seem six inches taller than she really was.

"Hello," she greeted them in her Caymanian accent, which had softened since she'd been living with Nora.

They had a temporary foster situation as the Norwegian wasn't old enough to officially foster Jazzy, but along with the help of their social worker, they'd found a way to work around the system. Jazzy had been living on the streets for several years before befriending Nora. They'd somewhat rescued each other.

"Nora," Reg said, his deep voice booming across the room without him trying. "We were talking about this skull Indiana AJ found today. Can they take DNA from old bones?"

"Ja," Nora replied, leaning on the counter as Bob took his seat. "And we'll know the sex for sure."

"Nora's passed her requirements for detective, so she had to study all about forensics," AJ directed to her parents. "She's just waiting for a spot to open up."

"I thought you could tell sex from the shape of a skull," Bob said. "Although I'd be getting that theory from a novel or a TV show."

"Sometimes, but it's not always accurate," Nora replied. "The male forehead is usually more pronounced and the bone structure can be denser. But a smaller-framed male would be hard to identify."

"Your oversized melon would definitely be male, Reg," AJ laughed.

"My big brain needed more room," he replied with a grin.

"Size of the brain doesn't directly correlate to intelligence," Nora said drily. "Otherwise, men would all be smarter than women. Which is obviously not the case."

They all burst out laughing. Except for Reg. And Nora, who seemed confused that what she'd said had caused amusement.

"You could end up in encyclopaedias, love," Pearl said to her husband. "A fine example of a big-brained being of questionable intelligence."

Reg grinned at his wife. "I was smart enough to marry you, gorgeous."

"Get a room," AJ quipped, then turned to Nora. "So we have to wait for DNA tests to even know if our errant head was male or female?"

"*Ja*, to know for certain. But it's simple. Apart from a few very rare cases, the lab doesn't even have to look at the DNA sequence. If it has X and Y chromosomes, it's male. Pair of X chromosomes and it's female."

"That'll still take ages, won't it?" AJ asked. "Isn't there a massive backlog for running DNA testing?"

"*Ja*," Nora replied. "Months. Unless there's a rush put on it."

"Maybe they will, as the victim might have been murdered," Beryl suggested. "Depending on how old it is, a cold case sometimes gets higher priority if it's a homicide."

"They were murdered?" Jazzy asked.

"The victim had been bashed in the face," Nora replied. "But doesn't mean they were murdered. Could have been hit by a boat or something."

"Or floated from the cemetery, as bird brain... I mean big brain over there said," AJ chuckled.

Reg looked at Bob. "We've done our best, mate, but I feel we've failed you with this one. Got any other offspring we could try?"

Bob laughed. "No, we gave up after the first attempt didn't come out as expected."

"Bloody hell, Dad!" AJ complained. "I expect the abuse from his nibs, but not from my own flesh and blood."

"We big brains have to stick together, my dear," Bob rebutted.

"How about you bring those big brains over here and help carry some of this food to the table," Pearl said, and began handing out plates to everyone.

Conversation over dinner shifted, with AJ's parents attempting to ask Nora more about her life on the island. When they discovered she was less than keen to discuss herself, they wisely moved onto Jazzy, who was happy to chat about anything. Nora pointed out how well her foster kid was doing in 100-metre and 200-metre sprints races for her school in track and field events, which sprang an extended conversation. A perfect ploy by Nora to divert everyone's attention, and AJ felt very pleased with herself as her scheme had worked like a charm.

After they'd consumed the main dishes of fresh snapper from the market on the beach in Georgetown, Pearl produced a selection of desserts, including an English trifle, which contained an abundant helping of sherry. Jazzy was unimpressed when Nora cut her off after her first helping.

"I'm told we'll get to see you play on Friday night," Beryl said, referring to Pearl's gig at the Fox and Hare pub, where she entertained twice a month.

"That'll be lovely to have you there," Pearl replied as she began clearing plates. "Let me know if there's anything in particular you'd like to hear."

"Here," Reg said, peering through his reading glasses at his mobile. "I have a list somewhere I can show you of her current repertoire."

AJ, Nora, and Jazzy helped clear the table while Reg hunted for the list on his phone.

"I'm sure we'll love whatever you play," Beryl said, as Reg struggled to find what he was looking for.

"Need a hand there..." AJ began, but Reg quickly cut her off.

"Found it! Here it is," he announced, holding his screen for Bob and Beryl to read. "These are all the songs she's currently choosing her set list from for each show."

"I like everything on here, Pearl," Bob said. "At least all the songs I recognise. There's a few I don't know."

"She does an amazing job taking songs you might not think you know," AJ said, moving to the living room and dropping onto one of the soft pillowy sofas. "But you'll recognise the tunes when you hear them."

Drinks were poured and everyone followed suit, finding a comfortable seat in the lounge. Reg and Pearl had placed two large, matching sofas opposing each other across a coffee table, and a pair of recliners on a third side, which they used for watching their television. Like the rest of the house, the place had a welcoming and comfortable feel, arranged perfectly for entertaining friends. Jazzy chose the floor where she could fuss Coop.

"You still haven't retired yet," Reg said, looking at Bob. "When are you going to sell up and spend at least half the year down here?"

Bob smiled. "Sometime in the next year..."

He'd barely got the words out before Beryl and AJ both pounced.

"I call BS!" AJ announced. "You've said exactly the same thing for at least ten years now."

Bob laughed. "Maybe a year or two, but not ten."

"Annabelle Jayne is right about this, Bob," Beryl said. "It's been about ten years."

AJ used to cringe when people used her full name, which she'd been teased about as a little girl in school, but she'd grown to appreciate the classic tone as she'd grown older. Although it still annoyed her that her mother would only use her full name.

Bob held up his hands in surrender. "Okay, okay. I must say, being down here makes me think about it a lot more." He turned to his wife. "But I'm not the only one locked into a job."

"I can work remotely if we did, say, a month here and two or three months home," Beryl replied.

AJ was as shocked as her father looked. The idea of spending more time with her parents was both appealing and terrifying. She already felt under her mother's microscope having them here for a week, but months at a time might be stifling. Or, it might be more relaxed and less like everyone had to catch up on every detail in such a hurry.

"Hey," Jazzy announced, and AJ was glad to change the subject. She needed time to think about the possibility of her parents living close by even if it would be part time. But once she heard why Jazzy had grabbed their attention, she was less keen on changing the topic.

"There's an article online about the skull," Jazzy announced, holding her mobile in her hand. "There's even a picture of you, AJ."

"What?" AJ reacted. She and Nora both leaned over her shoulder from the sofa to look.

Jazzy laughed. "Nora, you get a mention too. This guy says you aggressively assaulted him to the ground. He's considering pressing charges."

"*Faen*," Nora muttered. "The *drittsekk* ran under our police tape."

"You should have tasered him," AJ said, only half kidding.

"Best you didn't," Reg pointed out. "Imagine what he'd say then."

Nora didn't comment as she read the rest of the article.

"Yeah, you need to be careful," AJ added quietly, knowing her friend had come under scrutiny before for her no-nonsense approach to apprehending suspects. "You'll be a detective soon if you keep your nose clean."

Nora's hand shot to her face. "I have something coming out of my nose?"

Jazzy laughed. "Even I know what that means."

"Your nose is fine," AJ chuckled. "Keeping your nose clean means you follow the rules, or don't do anything wrong."

Nora frowned even more. "That's why I didn't taser him. He deserved it."

"Maybe you should have after all," AJ groaned. "That wan… weasel, Carlson, got a picture with his phone before you grabbed him," she added, quickly adjusting her word choice in front of Jazzy.

AJ stared at the grainy shot of Whittaker, Rasha, and herself under the tent. Carlson had run under the tape to get a picture through the only open side of the tent. Rasha was pointing to the skull on the table. It was a lousy photograph, but clear enough to support the article's title: "Skull pulled from waters off Cemetery Beach."

9

Luna reread the piece of paper in her hand and pondered the changes Rollo had made to the lyrics for the track 'Wanted'. A song she'd written six months ago. Musically, the new wording flowed more smoothly, but the sentiment had been lost. The lyrics had reflected her revelation at how her own hopes and expectations had constantly changed as the band achieved success. When she'd been singing three nights a week in pubs and working as a typist in an office to make a living, simply making a record had been the dream of a lifetime. Once she'd made a record, then hearing it on the radio was the ultimate goal. Pretty soon, that achievement wasn't enough, and unless their song made the charts, she'd feel like they'd failed.

For someone who'd never considered herself to be wildly ambitious, the idea of her self-esteem being tied to record sales was shocking. And disappointing. Even as a newcomer to the music business, Luna understood that commercial success had far more to do with factors out of her control than talent or events she could influence. Record companies had any number of bands and artists they were promoting at one time. All it took was one executive or promoter to lean their support and budget in a different direction, and you could lose all momentum and slip into obscurity. But if everyone rowed in the same heading, which happened to be your band, then amazing things could happen. Money and sex were often the biggest influencers.

The first week when Luna and the Lanterns reached the top 100 in the UK had been a magical moment for the three original members. When their progress stalled at number 76, they'd been devastated. Luna had sat in her tiny flat and written 'Wanted'. The lyrics meant something to her, and reading the new version once again, she realised it wasn't hers anymore.

"Rollo," she tentatively said into the mic. "Can we see about…"

Luna stopped, unsure how to phrase her desire without making her producer, co-writer, and boyfriend mad.

"See about what?" he questioned, and she could see he was busy preparing the tape on the cabinet-sized Ampex MM-1000 eight-track tape machine. His pride and joy. Along with the mixing console, fancy tape storage box he'd fretted over before they'd left, and all the other studio equipment he now seemed to value more than the other humans in the band.

"It's just the words have changed quite a bit," Luna ventured.

"Some," Rollo responded, reaching for the talkback button without looking up.

She could see him through the glass, engrossed in getting the recording process as he wanted.

"Yes," she said. "It doesn't really say what I intended it to say any more, babe."

Rollo now stopped and stared through the window from the control room.

"What were you trying to say?" he asked.

"You know what it was about," Luna said, beginning to feel embarrassed.

She'd learned that baring her soul in a song was a delicate process. The words often flowed when she was alone, and occasionally she'd found a drink or a joint would loosen her inhibitions enough to allow an outpouring of creativity. But having someone else examine the words and analyse their meaning felt like she was being poked and prodded by a room full of scientists in lab coats. One benefit of Rollo taking most of the credit for the songs was her not having to explain her lyrics.

"Well, I had to change them to fit the melody," Rollo said over her headphones. "Because it sounded amateurish."

Luna closed her eyes tightly and drew in a sharp breath. Angry men wearing stark white lab coats closed in all around, yelling at her, and she quickly opened her eyes again. She looked to Trina, who was on the couch reading a copy of *Fabulous 208*. Luna and the Lanterns were on the cover of the teen music magazine. Rollo had spoken over the headphones, not the studio speakers, so Trina had no idea what he'd just said.

"I'm ready when you are, Luna," Rollo's voice echoed in her ears. "We've already lost too much time today."

Tears welled, but she kept them in check. Luna would have given anything to be somewhere else at that moment. Preferably unconscious. She needed the universe to stop playing tennis with her soul. Ten feet away, her picture graced the cover of the most popular magazine with kids in the UK, yet over her headphones, she was being told that her words were worthless. By the person who'd made her fame possible. Luna pictured a merry-go-round with flame throwers on one side and ice cream on the other while she swirled in circles. A marvellous visual she could turn into the lyrics of a song… to be hacked apart and discarded like rubbish.

"Louise?"

Luna hated when he called her by her real name. It was another method he used to strip her of her protective layers and reveal the tender flesh below. But what choice did she have?

Nodding, the music soon played in her ears, and Luna began singing the words on the page.

Lying on a padded bench on the open upper deck, Luna shared a cigarette with Trina. They both stared in awe at more stars than they'd ever seen before in their lives. With nothing but open ocean in every direction, the yacht's navigation lights were the only illumination beyond the sky's twinkly display.

"You were on fire today," Trina said, handing Luna the cigarette.

"Just another day in the Rollo factory of fun," Luna replied.

Trina laughed. "No, seriously, babe. There was something different in your voice today. More passion, or something. I don't know. It was bloody brilliant, whatever you did."

"Thanks," Luna whispered.

She'd noticed it too, and embraced the melancholy tone her voice had taken at the beginning of the session. Rollo hadn't commented either way and seemed happy to move quickly through the recording.

"What would you do if all this went away?" Luna asked.

Trina turned her head. "What do you mean?"

"You know. If we woke up one morning and the record company had dumped us and all these incredible gigs and records and charts and everything went away."

Trina took a few moments to reply. "Go back to playing pubs in town, I suppose. Why? Are we getting the sack?"

"No, nothing like that. At least I don't think so."

"Shooting star!" Trina yelped, pointing.

They'd seen about a dozen in the half an hour or so they'd been lying there.

"So, why are you asking about things ending?" Trina asked after a few moments of silence. "Something happen with Rollo?"

"Nothing we haven't seen before," Luna replied. "Just feeling a bit trapped, you know?"

"By him?"

"By all of it."

Trina sat up. "Say the word and we're off this yacht, babe."

Luna laughed. "Right. We'll step off into the deep blue sea and catch a ride on a yellow submarine."

Trina laughed with her. "I didn't mean right now, but next time we stop somewhere. I mean it, love. If you want out, I'm right behind you. And Panda. You know he'll do anything we tell him to."

"Thanks, babe, but I don't want to bugger it all up for everyone."

Trina laid down again. "No way. It's been a groovy ride, but nothing lasts forever. If you need away from him, then we're out. It's not worth it."

Luna knew her friend was being truthful. Trina would give it all up in the blink of an eye if Luna asked her to. But the thought of it made her stomach twist into a knot.

"We need to get the album finished," Luna said, trying to sound resolute.

Trina sat up again. "Do we?"

"We can't let Polydor down."

"We can if the price is too high," Trina countered. "It's not like we really know any of them. Rollo won't let us near anyone important."

They hadn't spoken of that before and Luna had wondered if the other two had noticed. She'd begun to think it was her own paranoia. Or the way things usually were with a record company. How would she know any different?

"I want to finish our album," Luna said more firmly.

"*Our* album?" Trina questioned. "*Time and Light* was our album. This one is his album with us singing and playing on it. So far, there's only two of your songs that he hasn't changed so much I don't recognise them. I mean, what's with the new lyrics on 'Wanted'?"

Luna sat up and held her friend's hand. "You noticed?"

Trina scoffed. "Of course I bloody noticed. He's torn the heart out of that song. He's also made it a catchy tune that'll get radio play, but without a message."

"Does it have to have a message?" Luna wondered aloud.

"'Give Peace a Chance' is as big a hit as 'Sugar, Sugar', so I don't think it matters," Trina replied. "Except your lyrics always say something and his just fill a line in the song. Our fans want more of what they heard on *Time and Light*, not a whole new sound."

"A sophomore slump," Luna said.

"Yeah," Trina agreed. "Which it shouldn't be."

"Anyway, no one is comparing me to John Lennon," Luna said, embarrassed she was being mentioned in the same conversation. "And what if what Rollo's doing is better?"

"Better how?" Trina replied. "Different isn't always better. Don't get me wrong, he took our little stage in the corner of the pub sound and turned it into radio hits, but at the core, it's still our vibe with your lyrics. This is going in a different direction. We're like a cross between Janis Joplin and Fleetwood Mac, but he's trying to turn you into Bobbie Gentry or Cilla Black. Catchy bubble-bloody-gum stuff our mums will like." Trina groaned. "The last thing I want to do is make music my mum likes."

Luna laughed, and Trina joined in. Tired, frustrated, and needing a release, it took several minutes for the two of them to stop rolling around and giggling.

"But seriously, Luna," Trina said, lowering her voice, although they were the only ones on the top deck. "What if we kicked him out?"

"Kicked Rollo out of the band?"

"Yeah. Sod him. We'll tell the geezer at Polydor that we want a new producer," Trina said, as though they could wave a magic wand.

Luna was about to tell her friend how ridiculous that was, but she paused and thought it over. While Rollo had made the deal with Polydor, they'd all signed the contract and met several of the people at the label. She knew David, the executive who'd Rollo had mainly dealt with, and she had his business card somewhere. *What would he say if they called him and said they'd be happy to finish the album, but not with Rollo? Would their fans care if the guitarist had changed?* Or that she, Luna, played lead on the songs.

A surge of renewed excitement shot through her. "Do you really think they'd listen?"

"How could they not?" Trina responded. "There's no Luna and the Lanterns without Luna, baby. The worst that could happen is they tell us to bugger off and we go back to playing at the Rose and Crown."

Trina had a point. If Polydor wanted a second album, they needed the Luna part, even if a Lantern changed. And she was also correct; they could tell them the deal's off and their new-found stardom would be a fleeting moment in the rear-view mirror.

"Christmas," Luna exclaimed. "Polydor want the album released for Christmas. We'd never be able to do that if we started over."

"Christmas release really means mid-November for the first single, right?" Trina questioned.

"Yeah. And they need six to eight weeks to get the album mastered and do the first run of pressings, including the single."

They both sat quietly as they did the maths on the timing.

"Oh," Trina muttered.

"Yeah," Luna agreed. "I think I need a drink."

Walking across the deck, Trina looped her arm through Luna's. "We can still do this. Don't forget that. Screw them all. I'll go back to playing pubs, and besides, labels will knock down our door if they hear we're free of Polydor."

Luna wasn't so sure and didn't say anything more as they walked down the steps to the bridge.

"Ladies," the captain greeted them. "I have a telegram. Would you mind giving it to Mr Fletcher for me? The recording light was on when it arrived a few minutes ago."

"No problem," Luna said, taking the slip of paper.

The two women continued to the galley, and Luna read the telegram while Trina poured them gin and tonics.

"What the bloody hell is this about?" Luna muttered, rereading the message.

"What does it say?" Trina asked, handing her friend her drink.

"Impatiently waiting. Don't disappoint me," Luna read aloud. "And it's signed LMT."

"Just the initials?"

"LMT. That's it," Luna clarified.

"You think it's another bird?" Trina asked with anger in her eyes.

"If it is, we're going to meet her."

"We are?"

Luna nodded. "I expect so. This telegram was sent from Grand Cayman."

10

AJ hung neutrally buoyant in the water column at 20 feet down. Her group of divers she'd just guided around the shallow reef known as Mitch Miller's – named after the famous conductor who'd owned a house on the nearby beach – patiently watched from either side of her. Right below AJ's Mermaid Divers Newton dive boat, *Hazel's Odyssey*, and above the reef, a school of reef squid danced back and forth, putting on a spectacular show.

Through a series of colour changes and movements, the six molluscs moved in unison like a well-choreographed dance troupe. Their translucent fins along either side of their bodies fluttered in a mesmerising pattern with occasional waves of their sleek tentacles, gathered together as though one appendage.

Several of the divers filmed the display with underwater cameras, and when the school finally flitted away across the reef, everyone exchanged excited okay signs and applause. With a thumb pointed to the surface, AJ directed the group to the stern ladder, which her employee and friend, Thomas, had dropped into the water.

Back aboard, the divers chatted and raved about everything they'd seen while they slipped out of their wetsuits and prepared for the short run back to the dock. AJ secured the aluminium ladder while Thomas fired up the diesel engines, then she moved to the bow and released them from the DOE dive site buoy.

As Thomas eased into the throttles, AJ peeled off her Mermaid Divers rashguard and hung it over a tank in the racks behind the bench seats lining the deck. She tied one sleeve around the frame so it couldn't fly away when the wind began rushing by as they picked up speed.

"Back by 12:30 please, for those who are coming out this afternoon," AJ told her eight customers. "It'll be Thomas and Carlos again. We'll take care of your gear if you're with us this afternoon or tomorrow. Which I think is everyone," she added.

"How are you enjoying your parents' visit?" a customer asked.

A vision of the skull flashed through AJ's mind, followed by her mother's words about spending more time on the island.

"It's been lovely," she replied, choosing the expected response over the more complicated truth.

Although, it had been lovely to see them, and she felt a pang of guilt for her trepidation over them spending more time on Grand Cayman. Which she knew was far more about her mother than seeing more of her dad. Grabbing a towel, AJ began drying her hair, and out of habit, checked her mobile, which was tucked in a pocket of her rucksack. She had a text.

"Anything you can tell me about your discovery yesterday?"

It was from Lahaina Jones, a journalist with the local paper, the *Cayman Compass*. Despite her Hawaiian-sounding name, Lahaina was Irish, a real journalist, diver, and friend. AJ stood poised with thumbs hovering over the phone's keyboard, but couldn't think of what to reply. It was a police matter on which, as a consultant and diver to the RCIPS, she shouldn't comment. But she'd discovered the skull on her own time, so her role wasn't in any official capacity. Although taking Rasha out to retrieve the remains could be construed as such. Undecided, she tucked her mobile away to deal with the message later.

"Short ride home," AJ announced to the group, and scrambled up the ladder to the helm on the fly-bridge.

She put on a Mermaid Divers long-sleeved sun-shirt to protect her skin and her tattoos from the rays.

"Sounds like a good dive," Thomas said in his sing-song Caymanian accent.

"Yeah. They're happy campers," AJ replied, her eyes on the ocean ahead.

She picked out the buoy for the *Doc Polson* and the larger moorings on the *Kittiwake* wreck, then looked towards the beach, where she could see the cemetery.

"Must have bin quite da surprise," Thomas said.

"Surprise?" she asked, forcing her stare from the landmarks she'd been using the day before.

Thomas raised his eyebrows and grinned.

"Right, the skull," she replied, realising what her perceptive first mate was referring to. "Yeah, it was. But quite honestly, I was more fascinated and curious. Until Rasha held this poor bugger's head in her hands. Then it felt really creepy and weird."

Thomas shivered despite the blazing sun. "Woulda made me suck down a tank of air."

He slowed the Newton as they crossed the shallower water over the sandy bottom, as it was common to encounter snorkellers who could be hard to see sometimes in the light afternoon chop. Up ahead, several dive boats were unloading their customers at West Bay Public Dock. Reg's smaller pier was just beyond, extending from a small waterfront lot he owned. Two of his boats were already tied up.

With well-practised efficiency, Thomas pulled *Hazel's Odyssey* alongside the dock and AJ leapt ashore and secured the lines. They helped their customers off the boat and AJ took care of a couple of T-shirt sales while Thomas dragged the air line and manifold to the boat and began refilling the tanks. AJ joined him as soon as she was done.

"I'll finish this if you want to grab lunch," she said, shutting off the valves on the first six tanks and moving the manifold over to the next set.

"Brought my lunch today, so I'll eat when we're done," Thomas replied. "Go spend time wit your family, boss. Carlos'll be here in a minute, and we got dis handled."

AJ always felt guilty about leaving when her crew was still working, but her parents were only here for a week. And she'd chosen to still work the mornings as the boat was full every day. She finished securing the lines to the six tanks and put a fist on top of her head, using the diver's surface signal for okay. Outside the little hut, Reg returned the signal and opened the valve from the compressor. Air hissed through the lines.

"Alright, I'll go," she sighed. "But call me if anything happens or Carlos doesn't show up."

Thomas laughed. "Already texted me, boss. He was on one of Big Boss's boats dis mornin'. He gettin' sandwiches for da crew, den he be here."

AJ grabbed her rucksack and hopped to the dock. "At least tell me you'll miss me," she said, looking back at her friend.

Thomas laughed again in his infectious way. "It won't be da same witout you, boss, but we'll get by best we can. Now get along."

AJ grinned. "Alright, alright, I'm going."

She gave Thomas a wave and began walking up the pier towards Reg. Coop came bounding down to meet her, furiously wagging his tail, which caused his whole body to sway so he couldn't run in a straight line.

"Hey, boy. You keeping that grumpy dad of yours in line?" AJ said as the mutt rolled over to get his belly scratched.

"Come on, let's go sort him out," she said, and he leapt to his feet as she walked away.

Looking up, AJ was about to tell Reg about the reef squid encounter when she spotted a man walking down their little sloped car park.

"Oh great," she muttered, and lifted her chin in the visitor's direction.

Reg took the hint and turned. His expression tightened when he saw Sean Carlson approaching.

"We're all booked up this week, but if you call the office, I'm sure we can accommodate you at some point," Reg said without sounding the least bit inviting.

"I'll keep that in mind," Carlson replied. "But I'm actually here to speak with Miss Bailey."

"Oh, thank you," AJ said brightly. "I have a few spots open next week."

Carlson laughed and AJ did her best not to cringe. She found the guy incredibly creepy. Nicknaming him The Weasel was being kind. To him, not weasels. Even Coop sat down next to her instead of going over to greet the man.

"I'd actually like to get your comments on finding a dead body off Seven Mile Beach yesterday."

"Oh, okay," AJ replied. "Do you have a notebook or a recorder? I don't want you to miss a detail or get a fact wrong."

Carlson looked at her suspiciously, but took out his mobile and started a recording.

"I'm speaking with AJ Bailey of Mermaid Divers who discovered the human remains in the water off Seven Mile Beach yesterday. AJ, where exactly did you find the skull you brought ashore with the Royal Cayman Islands Police Service crime scene investigator, Rasha Howard?"

"Hi, Sean. Thanks for stopping by, but I'm afraid I can't discuss an ongoing police case."

Carlson rolled his eyes and stopped his recording.

"You're not a police officer, AJ."

"I'm a contractor with the police department," AJ replied. "I fall under the same restrictions."

"Not when you first found the skull," Carlson challenged. "Let's talk from that perspective."

AJ thought for a moment and glanced at Reg. He shrugged his

shoulders, which gave her no help. On one hand, if she said nothing, The Weasel would print whatever rubbish he concocted from speculation. On the other hand, if she said anything, he'd probably twist it anyway. But she didn't need Sean Carlson as an enemy. Between his online newspaper and its associated social media site, he had an unfathomable reach, and she didn't need any bad press for the business.

"We found an intact skull, nothing else."

His eyes lit up. "Okay. Obviously I know that as I published a picture of it."

"Which was illegally obtained," AJ couldn't help herself from pointing out.

"Creatively obtained," he countered. "Which exposed the police brutality which I'm planning a future story about. Your Swedish friend, Miss Sommer, will feature heavily in that piece."

"Norwegian," AJ corrected.

"Whatever. All the same," Carlson said with a dismissive wave of the hand.

AJ subtly shook her head at Reg, who was listening in while he worked the compressor valves for Thomas's tank fills.

"Could you determine the cause of death?" Carlson asked.

"I couldn't, no," AJ replied, "because I'm not a forensic pathologist."

The Weasel sighed.

"Was there any obvious trauma to the skull?"

"Yes," AJ replied, and Carlson took the bait again, hanging on her next words. "The body had been detached. Again, not my field of expertise, but I'd call that traumatic."

"C'mon, AJ, give me something I can print here," he complained. "The people deserve to know what's happened when bodies show up on their beaches."

There was plenty she could react to in his statement, beginning with his use of '*the people*' as though he represented the citizens' best interests. But she resisted and reminded herself of the not-needing-bad-press angle.

"My best guess is that these are remains which have been uncovered by recent storms, and date back a while."

"What's a while?" he asked. "A year? Three hundred years?"

"Between the two."

"Narrow it down for me."

"Decades, but not centuries," AJ reluctantly replied. "But that's a guess."

The Weasel paused in thought for a moment.

"I have to go," AJ said, pouncing on the break. "You really need to contact the RCIPS for official information."

Carlson scoffed. "Like they're any help. You know they won't say anything for days."

"Well, I have to go. I'm late to meet someone," AJ urged, and walked closer to Reg.

Carlson appeared to weigh up his chances of gleaning anything more for a few moments.

"Thank you," he said, and AJ was relieved that he figured out he'd extracted all he could from her.

Still, she dreaded what drivel would appear on his site attributed to her.

"I think I'll ban him from the property," Reg said once Carlson was out of earshot.

"You'll be the feature of a worst dive operation in the Cayman Islands article," AJ warned.

Reg grunted.

With press on her mind, AJ remembered the message, and retrieved her mobile.

"Lahaina called me while we were out this morning. She was asking about the skull."

"At least you know she'll print what you say instead of what that wanker dreams you said," Reg grumbled, while signalling to Thomas and opening the valve. "Hey, wait a minute. How old do you think that skull is?"

"I really don't know. Rasha didn't want to guess," AJ replied.

"More than ten years, less than a hundred would be a tighter range, which I think would be accurate."

"The *Cayman Compass* doesn't go back that far, but it started in the early seventies I believe, and soon after merged with another publication which had been around at least a decade. They might have records going back 60 years."

"You thinking we do a little horse trading with Lahaina?" AJ grinned.

"The idea crossed my mind," Reg replied. "We could see if they have any articles about floating bodies from a graveyard. Maybe they never found some poor sod."

"Until now," AJ said, as she called Lahaina Jones.

11

The curtain swayed and the bright sunlight caught Luna's eyelids, luring her awake. Once again, she was alone in the berth. She wondered what she'd face in the studio today. Rollo had been dismissive as usual about the telegram and laughed cynically when she'd asked if LMT was a woman. She'd gone to bed and left him stewing in the control room. When he'd made it to bed, she pretended to be asleep.

Trina's words from their conversation on the upper deck still hung in Luna's mind. In fact, they resonated even more in the morning light. She wasn't ready to completely abandon ship, but she left the bed in determined fashion and quickly used the bathroom and cleaned her teeth. Selecting a colourful sleeveless sundress, Luna looked at the blue bruise which had begun to fade on her arm. She wasn't going to hide the evidence today.

Knocking on Trina's door didn't wake her, so Luna opened the door and roused her friend.

"What's going on?"

"I need you with me, babe," Luna said, without explaining anything more. "Get dressed while I wake Panda."

"Are you staging a coup?" Trina asked as she rubbed her eyes.

Luna paused at the door. "Maybe a small revolution."

"Che bloody Guevara," Trina replied, punching a fist in the air. "*Viva la revolución*, sister!"

"Shush!" Luna laughed, closing the door and banging on Panda's. "Are you up?"

When she heard no response, Luna opened his door and found the lanky Londoner face down on his berth, still clothed.

"Panda? Are you alive?" she asked, only half kidding.

To her relief, he stirred.

"What? Is the boat sinking?"

"If that'll get you up, yes," Luna replied, tugging on his skinny arm.

"Nah, man. I'll go down with the ship. That lifeboat shit was too much hassle."

"Get up, Panda. I need you upstairs."

He rolled over. "We recording?"

"Hopefully," Luna told him and dragged him upright. "The original Lanterns are circling the wagons."

"I've no idea what that means, man. But give me a minute and I'll be there."

Luna waited at the base of the stairs. With only a handful of steps between her and facing Rollo, self-doubt began seeping in and she felt nauseous with nerves. She often got this way before performing live, especially to a larger audience, and knew to take a few breaths. If she let her fears escalate, then nothing would change.

"Victory or death!" Trina hissed, coming out of her berth.

Luna looked up and burst out laughing. Her friend had used lipstick to apply war paint across the top of her cheeks. Two bold stripes ran from one side of her face, across her nose, to the other side. She grinned at Luna.

"Nothing like announcing the conflict, babe," Luna said, shaking her head.

"Remember the Alamo!" Trina responded, holding her fists up like a boxer.

Luna laughed again. "Pretty sure the Indians didn't give a toss about the Alamo, love."

Panda's door opened, and he took one step out of his berth before stopping in his tracks and staring at Trina.

"Are you attacking the wagons we're circling?"

"History isn't one of Trina's strengths, but she's ready for battle."

Panda just nodded. "Cool, man. What are we doing?"

"We're taking back the Lanterns!" Trina announced with more fist raising.

"Not exactly," Luna said. "We're going to talk to Rollo about keeping the new album more about our sound."

"Yeah, okay," Panda replied thoughtfully. "Sort of feels like we've become the means for Rollo to make his own project. It's like The Velvet Rollo Lanterns."

Trina tapped a finger on Panda's chest. "Exactly. And the lunatics are taking back the asylum, brother."

Luna stood. "Okay," she said with a deep sigh. "Let's go talk to our producer and pray he's in a good mood this morning."

"He won't be in a minute," Trina whispered, following Luna up the stairs.

Rollo looked up from the console as the three entered the studio. His expression didn't change before he returned to whatever he was doing. Luna walked over and opened the control room door.

"Hey."

"Hey," Rollo replied, still focused on the console.

"Can we talk for a minute?"

"Sure," he replied without looking up.

"Out here. All four of us," Luna urged.

That got his attention. "What for? We need to get to work. Can this wait?"

"No, we think it's important to have a discussion now."

Rollo's eyes narrowed, and he stole a glance out the control room window. His brow furrowed and Luna guessed he'd seen

Trina's war paint. Which was funny at the bottom of the stairs, but Luna now realised it was probably not going to help their cause.

"What are you doing?" Rollo asked in an eerily quiet tone, turning back to look at Luna. His eyes fell on her sleeveless arm and she swore she detected the slightest of flinches.

"We want to have a discussion. As a band."

Rollo slowly shook his head, looking her in the eyes. "Those two would jump off a cliff if you told them to follow you, but no chance they'd come up with whatever this is on their own. So, Louise, what do you think you're doing?"

Every fibre in Luna's petite body tensed. Her plan had instantly derailed before leaving the station and, as usual, Rollo had her questioning herself.

"We're having a discussion about the band," she replied, trying her best to keep her voice steady.

"About what, exactly?"

Luna's feet felt frozen in place, but she willed her legs to drag them away from the control room.

"About what we're doing with this album," she forced from her lips as she unsteadily walked to the couch and sat next to Trina.

Her friend squeezed her hand. "Good on ya," she whispered, and then they waited.

Through the control room window, Luna watched Rollo grit his teeth and fidget in his chair. If she'd attempted this alone with him, she'd likely have another bruise coming her way, and that knowledge gave her the determination to remain strong. After what felt like an hour but was probably half a minute, Rollo rose from his chair and slowly meandered into the studio. He stopped by the drum kit partition and looked from one couch to the other. Panda sat across from Luna and Trina and didn't look away when Rollo stared him down.

"Okay. I'm here."

"Could you sit down with us?" Luna asked.

"I'm fine. Get on with it," he responded.

His tone wasn't angry. More disarming and cold. Which was worse to Luna. At least he was predictable when he yelled.

"We're concerned this album is getting too far away from our first album and the way the band has always sounded," Luna said, realising there was no point waiting for the man to lower himself to their level.

"We promised Polydor something new, not a revamp of *Time and Light*," Rollo responded flatly.

"Sure, and we want to evolve, yeah?" Luna said, looking at the other two, who both nodded. "But this is starting to sound like a different band altogether."

"You're not using Luna's songs anymore," Trina said, squeezing her friend's hand again. "How come you're rewriting it all now or using stuff you wrote?"

"Because we used the best of yours on *Time and Light*, and even then I had to rework them." Rollo said, throwing his hands up. "There's only so much I can do. If you had better songs, I wouldn't have to use mine."

"That's BS, man," Panda weighed in. "Luna's written plenty of great songs."

"No. Luna has written a bunch of lyrics with maybe a hint of what the melody could be. Those are not songs."

And there they were again. Those men in lab coats pulling Luna's soul apart as her songwriting was torn to shreds before her eyes.

"That's how we've always written our songs, man," Panda said, sounding more passionate than Luna could ever recall. "She comes up with cool lyrics and a basic tune, then we work out the rest."

"Except you don't work out the rest," Rollo snapped back. "You put basic guitar chords and a beat to the words so you could play them in a pub. None of the songs were even close to being in any kind of shape to put on an album."

"That's a load of bollocks," Trina said, standing up from the couch. "You barely give them a chance before turning them into something we can't even recognise. Not once have you asked us to work with you on pulling them into shape. You either toss them away or butcher them yourself."

Rollo took a step towards Trina. Luna and Panda both leapt to their feet.

"What?" Trina shouted. "You gonna shove me around too? Try it, I dare you."

Rollo threw his hands up. "You lot have no idea what you're doing."

"We know we don't have your experience," Luna said, feeling the situation spiralling desperately out of control. "But we're asking you to work with us, not around us."

Rollo growled and shook his head. "That's not what I meant."

"Then what did you mean?" Luna asked.

Their producer and her boyfriend looked down and rubbed his head with both hands. "We don't have time for this bullshit."

"It's not bullshit, Rollo," Trina said, and Luna was glad her friend had softened her tone. "All our names are on this bloody record."

"We know they want it out by Christmas," Luna added. "We get that it needs to be done in a month to give them time for all the mastering and pressings."

Rollo looked up and scoffed. "That's not the problem," he muttered. *"They're* not the problem."

The other three all looked at Rollo.

"Then what is?" Luna asked.

"Not what," Rollo replied. "Who."

"Okay," Luna persisted. "Who's the problem?"

He shook his head again. "Look, that's my problem to sort out. What you need to know is that we need to deliver the album to Polydor well *before* their deadline."

"I don't get it," Trina admitted. "I mean, I get why they'd be happy if we did, but why it's such a big deal?"

"Because we need the bloody money," Rollo fumed. "That thing that you lot know nothing about because I handle it all."

"Yeah, only because you won't include us," Panda said. "Not because we don't care."

"Because it's bloody complicated," Rollo rebutted, losing some of the sting in his voice. He took a moment to compose himself. "The album needs to be finished sooner. That's what you need to know."

"How much sooner?" Trina asked. "We figured we had another month or longer."

"We don't," Rollo replied, but offered nothing more.

"But the problem isn't finishing the album, right? It's the money," Luna asked.

"Yes, but the record company pays me for delivering them the album, and that's how I get the money."

"What happened to all the money from *Time and Light*?" Trina asked.

"You're standing in it," Rollo replied.

Trina looked around them at all the equipment in the studio. "So, what do you need money for now?"

"Same thing," he replied. "Have you any idea how much all this cost?"

Trina shrugged her shoulders. "No. But I bet it's a lot more than if we'd gone back to the studio in London."

Rollo bristled at her response. "Why do you think we don't have a studio tech with us?" he shouted. "Because we can't afford one so I'm doing it all!"

It hadn't occurred to Luna that the guy who'd appear and fix things in the London studio was missing from theirs. Rollo was covering that job too.

"None of that matters now," she quickly interjected, seeing Rollo steaming again. "What matters is getting the best album recorded we can, and making whatever deadline we have."

"Which is what?" Panda asked.

"Yeah," Trina chimed in. "You still haven't said when we have to be done."

Rollo took a deep breath. "In theory, tomorrow."

"What?" Luna gasped, which melted into a chorus of complaints from the other two.

Rollo held up his hands. "Obviously, that's not going to happen. But that's the original date that was set. The delays getting *Soundwave* up and running ate into our recording time, so I'll try and buy us a week, maybe two."

"What happens if you don't get this money in time?" Luna asked.

"Don't worry about that," Rollo replied. "But now you understand why we can't screw around. The album must get finished."

"At any cost?" Trina asked.

Rollo frowned at her, clearly unsure of her meaning.

"Our vibe and sound is getting tossed out in the name of meeting *your* deadline," she clarified. "For the rest of us, we would have another month or more to make the album we want to put out."

Their producer opened his mouth but thought better of what he was about to say. He took a moment before responding.

"What do you want to do? We can't start from scratch."

"How about we rerecord the vocals on 'Wanted', and let Luna take a shot at adjusting her own lyrics?" Trina said.

Luna looked at her boyfriend, who met her gaze. "Okay. We'll start there. What else?"

"'Empty Head' should be on the album," Luna blurted.

"Bloody right it should," Trina added.

"Gotta be, man," Panda joined in. "So should 'Blue Face'."

Rollo nodded. "Okay, but we have six tracks recorded. If we rework 'Wanted' and add those two, that's only eight and we planned twelve."

"Let me work on 'Loving Like Last Time'," Luna suggested. "And we'll record another one of yours and make it ten."

"So the album will only be ten tracks?" Rollo questioned. "You were the one who said you wanted to give the fans more songs than most bands do."

"And now I'm saying I'd rather give them ten Luna and the Lanterns tunes than twelve songs we don't all believe in."

"That isn't to say your songs aren't good, man," Panda said. "They're just not us like Luna's songs are."

"Exactly," Luna and Trina both agreed.

"Fine with me," Rollo replied. "Polydor only pay us for ten anyway."

"What?" the other three all responded.

"Standard record company contract," Rollo said. "But that doesn't matter now." He bit his lip. "The important thing is we need to get on with it. When we arrive in Grand Cayman, I'll have a meeting which might take a while, so we'll lose half a day."

"Then we'll work half the night to make it up," Trina countered. "How about we get started?"

There was no group hug or handshakes to recognise the end of their disagreement, but Luna still felt optimistic about what they'd accomplished. Maybe they'd make the album they all wanted after all. But one thing lingered in her mind as she tried to shift her brain from squabbling to making her original lyrics fit into Rollo's arrangement of 'Wanted'. She followed him to the control room.

"This money thing has something to do with LMT, doesn't it?" Luna asked softly, so no one else would hear.

Rollo nodded. "Yes, it does."

He sat down in the console chair and handed her a sheet of paper from a stack. It was her original lyrics to 'Wanted' with his rewrite scribbled over the words he'd struck out. "Hopefully you can still read this. Let me know when you're ready."

12

"Hello, Roy," AJ said, using the hands-free system in her van as she drove into George Town. "I was wondering if anyone had come forward with an idea about who our mysterious skull belonged to?"

"Hello, AJ," the detective replied. "No, and I'll be honest, our resources are stretched a bit thin at the moment, so we probably won't make any progress until Rasha presents her report."

"That'll be a while, then," AJ said.

"I'm afraid so. Rasha seemed pretty sure the skull had been underwater for at least 20 years or more, so we'll get to it, but it won't be anytime soon. Unless, of course, someone comes forward with a suggestion of who it might be – then it's possible we could match DNA and identify the remains without too much trouble."

AJ glanced over at Reg in the passenger seat, who'd insisted she make this call. He raised his thick eyebrows. AJ frowned in return.

"Would it be stepping on toes, Roy, if we did a bit of research to see if we could find out if a body or two had gone missing from the cemetery on the beach?"

"We, as in who?" Whittaker asked.

"Just Reg and me."

"Hello, Roy," Reg grunted. "She's dragged me along on this escapade."

AJ's mouth dropped open, and she smacked Reg on his burly arm. He just grinned in return.

"Hi, Reg," Whittaker replied. "No, I suppose that would be fine." He paused a few moments. "I do have someone looking up our missing persons in the system, so a body from the cemetery might slip through the cracks there. Not sure how we'd file a missing dead body."

"We're starting at the *Compass*," AJ said. "Going through their records. We'll let you know if we find anything useful."

"Great. Thank you," Whittaker said. "And if you haven't heard from him already, prepare yourself to dodge that Carlson fellow. He's calling everyone."

"He already came by earlier," AJ admitted. "I didn't tell him anything new, but I'm sure he'll make up stuff I said for his next article."

"Anyone with an ounce of common sense doesn't take his stories seriously," Whittaker said. "Thanks for the heads up and keep me posted. See you Friday night."

"Yup," AJ replied.

"See you Friday, mate," Reg added, knowing the detective was referring to Pearl's gig at the pub.

AJ ended the call. "The Weasel must have direct access to an amazing number of people with no common sense," she said, shaking her head. "His followers and subscribers, or whatever they're called, are in the tens of thousands."

"Sounds about right," Reg grumbled.

Lahaina Jones met them at the front entrance. "You two weren't kidding when you said you'd be right over."

"I'm supposed to be having lunch with my parents, so we don't have much time," AJ confessed.

"I'm supposed to be having lunch with Pearl," Reg said. "Who's having lunch with her parents."

"Well, unless you're planning lunch for dinnertime," Lahaina laughed, "you'll be making them wait a long time. Our system isn't exactly streamlined when you go back a while."

"I feel an emergency coming on," AJ said, cringing and looking at Reg.

"She'll have both our guts for garters if we stand 'em up," Reg responded.

"Best we come clean, then."

Lahaina shook her head and held the front door open. "While you two figure out how you're going to explain yourselves to Mummy and Daddy, you want to come inside so at least I can get back to work?"

As she led them through the *Cayman Compass* offices, AJ texted Bob and Beryl while Reg texted Pearl. By the time they'd arrived at the journalist's office, they'd agreed on the excuse message and hit send.

"How about we start with what you can tell me about this skull or whatever you found?" Lahaina said, offering them seats on the other side of her desk.

"Yeah, so I can't say much as it's a police matter now," AJ began. "But Whittaker won't mind you hearing the basics."

Before AJ could continue, her and Reg's mobiles both buzzed at the same time. They looked at their screens. AJ laughed and held hers up for Lahaina to see. It was a selfie of Pearl, Bob, and Beryl outside Heritage Kitchen, AJ's favourite food shack by the water in West Bay.

"Guess we're off the hook," AJ said with a chuckle.

"We should probably feel insulted they went ahead without us," Reg grumbled.

"Apparently, you're both predictable," Lahaina pointed out. "Now what were you about to tell me, AJ?"

"Right," AJ said, putting her mobile away. "So I can tell you we found a human skull on a freshly exposed section of limestone just short of Cemetery Reef in about 20 feet of water. It appears to be an adult but we couldn't determine sex as yet."

"So, a smaller-sized skull?" Lahaina asked. "But larger than a child?"

"That was the impression I got from Rasha, but she was pretty tight lipped. You know she likes to be sure before she says anything."

The reporter nodded. "I have a call in to her. She texted that she'd get back to me when she could."

"Her examination should be soon, but the DNA testing will take ages," AJ pointed out.

Lahaina nodded. "What else can you say?"

AJ thought for a moment, trying to figure out how to word more information without saying something Whittaker wouldn't want out there.

"Rasha needs to confirm all this, okay?"

Lahaina nodded again.

"There's nothing initially suspicious about the decapitation," AJ said carefully. "Meaning, it appeared consistent with the natural decomposition of a body in the ocean with sea critters assisting. But there were signs of a blunt force type of trauma to the face. But again, this could easily have been post mortem. Current theory is this might be a body floated from the cemetery during a storm. Which is why we want to sniff around your database."

"That sounded almost professional," Reg said. "Until the last bit. Can't really see Rasha using the term 'sniff around'."

"I was impressed for a while there," Lahaina agreed.

"I was basically repeating what Rasha told Whittaker before we left the beach," AJ admitted.

"We know," Reg and Lahaina said together.

Staring at the screen on the computer in a spare office where Lahaina had set them up to work, AJ and Reg both sat back in their chairs.

"There has to be a better way to do this," AJ complained.

"I hope so, or we'll be here for a month of Sundays," Reg groaned.

They'd already spent over an hour trying to search the newspaper's database by every word they could think of that might trigger an article about a missing body or person. Plenty of hits came back from the past 20 years or so, but nothing much older, and none talked of a body going missing near Cemetery Beach.

"Wait a second," AJ exclaimed. "We're a pair of plonkers."

"It's beginning to feel that way," Reg agreed.

"The internet," she continued, and began looking for a way to search by date in the database.

"I believe we're using it to access their servers," Reg said, trying to follow her point.

"Exactly. Which you couldn't do until sometime in the nineties."

Reg thought for a moment. "So unless someone took all the articles before that and either rewrote or scanned the text, then the database would only return whatever title or tags were associated with the edition. I bet they scanned the physical pages and stored them by date and edition."

Picking a date in 1980, AJ clicked on the daily issue and sure enough, the whole paper for that day had been scanned and stored under nothing more than its date.

"We're up the creek," she muttered.

"Not a paddle in sight," Reg agreed.

They both sat back again.

"No way we can go through day by day and page by page," AJ grumbled.

"Hang on," Reg said, perking up. "Doesn't have to be that bad. A body didn't get up and walk out of a grave."

"You hope," AJ interjected with a laugh.

"They floated out after flooding," Reg continued. "And what caused the flooding?"

"Big storms and hurricanes," AJ replied. "So we search the days following big storms."

"Exactly."

"Nice going, big brain," AJ chuckled. "So let's search the web for a list of hurricanes and tropical storms affecting Grand Cayman."

After a few clicks of the keyboard, she brought up the results in a window on the right side of the screen and kept the database on the left.

"Good old Wikipedia," she said. "Blimey, that's a lot of storms."

"Right, but scroll down," Reg urged. "The paper didn't exist until sometime in the sixties, and that was in its original form and title."

AJ slid the page until she reached the section for the 1960s. There were six major storms reported.

"Start here, or work backwards?" AJ asked.

"Try one of these and let's see what they have from back then. We still don't even know they scanned any copies that old. You can skip Hurricane Hattie as it was before the *Tradewinds* paper started publishing. Let's try the unnamed storm on June 28, 1966."

AJ searched the date and returned a hit. She opened the file, revealing a scan of the pages of an old, yellowed newspaper.

"It was weekly back then," AJ observed.

"Makes it easier again," Reg said, reading the headlines. "This issue hardly gives the storm much mention. Looks like it formed close by and moved away."

AJ went back to the Wikipedia page for the next storm from the list. "Looks like 1969 was a busy year. Four major storms. May, June, August, and again in August."

"Two tropical depressions, and two hurricanes," Reg read from the screen. "Those two hurricanes in August would have saturated the ground. I bet the second one will be our best bet."

"Slow down, Lewis Hamilton, let's do this methodically," she said, and worked her way through the dates, finding the corresponding newspaper editions from the weeks following the two tropical depressions. No missing bodies.

"Okay," she said, coming to the first of the hurricanes. "Here's Camille."

"This one was a whopper," Reg said. "Worst hurricane to hit the US since 1935. A cat 5."

"Yeah, but initiated near Cayman, so didn't cause much damage on the island," AJ countered. "Here's the paper, and it talks more about Cuba and then America getting hit."

Reg tapped on the computer screen with his big finger. "Check the next one, Hurricane Francelia. Talks about heavy rainfall."

AJ moved to the next edition, just to make sure nothing strange happened in between, and quickly scanned the headlines. It talked more about a pop band visiting the island than anything else.

"Come on, get to the next one," Reg nagged.

"Alright, keep your hair on," AJ chided and clicked the next edition, which was more of the same, so she clicked again. The next publication had reports on Hurricane Francelia.

"This is more interesting," AJ said.

"Told you to go there in the first place," Reg groaned. "See, look," he added, tapping the screen again. "Heavy rain and extensive flooding causing damage."

"Get your fat paw out of the way so I can read it," AJ said, and swatted his hand aside. "Still nothing about bodies being carried away on the front page."

"Probably wouldn't be too keen to announce they had grave sites coming unglued," Reg replied, but she could hear the disappointment in his voice. "Pretty upsetting for the families."

AJ clicked to the scan of the second and third pages, which made up the majority of the rest of the publication.

"Stone the bloody crows," she blurted. "Look at that!"

It was her turn to point at the screen, and Reg leaned in to read the article.

"Extensive flooding caused issues at the cemetery by the beach on West Bay Road," he read aloud, "where several cap stones shifted, and one was reported to have been completely removed by the water. The Merren family are distraught over the missing remains of their recently interred beloved father of four, Ormond

Merren, which are believed to have been carried out to sea with the retreating tide."

AJ and Reg sat back once again.

"What are the chances of a Merren family member still being on the island?" AJ wondered.

"Pretty good, I'd say," Reg responded. "Nathaniel Merren owns the petrol station at the four-way stop sign in West Bay."

13

Nervous and unsure whether she could pull it all together quickly enough, Luna sat down and began adjusting her original lyrics for 'Wanted'. Rollo had cut and changed the words to shorten each line, and she realised he was right – the song flowed more smoothly and the lyrics less rushed. But he'd focused just on making them fit instead of making them fit while keeping the point of the song intact.

Luna began by fixing the chorus, as she hoped it would be the easiest part. By sliding through a couple of the conjunctions, she figured she could make her original lyrics fit.

"Okay, can we try the chorus, please?"

"Just the chorus?" Rollo asked through her headphones.

"Yeah. You don't have to record. I just need to see if what I have works. Then I'll try the verses."

He nodded to Luna through the glass, and the song began playing through her headphones. The previous vocal track was either erased from this tape or muted, so she had to drop in at the right moments. She half hummed, half sang her way through the first two verses, then gave it everything for the first chorus.

At the end, she held up a hand, and the playback stopped in her ears.

"I can make that work," she said and looked up towards the window. "What do you think?"

"It's close," Rollo replied, using the studio speakers instead of her headphones.

From the couch, Trina and Panda both gave a thumbs-up. It felt like a weight off Luna's shoulders. She'd expected nothing but resistance while Rollo battled to get back to his original plan. But *close* was a promising start, and his tone sounded amiable. Not to mention he'd used the speakers to include the others. Or hit the wrong button. But Luna didn't believe that. Rollo knew the console like the back of his hand. He could find most of the buttons and faders with his eyes closed, and there were hundreds of them.

"I think I need to hang on the second line a little more," she said, jotting a note on the page in her hand. "It's like it's *too* short now. I can lengthen the word 'wanted'."

"Give it a Nashville twang," Rollo suggested. "Like Linda Ronstadt."

Luna laughed. "I'll try."

"Ronstadt the hell out of it," Trina said from the couch. "You sound great, babe."

Luna smiled at her friend.

"You can try the verses using the same thing you just did with the chorus," Rollo suggested. "I'm not sure you'll need to change a thing if you contract some of the conjunctions."

Luna stared at the lyric sheet, which now looked like a small child had scribbled and drawn all over it. But that was okay. She didn't need it to sing her original words. She sat on the stool and turned away from the mic for a few minutes, working out the cadence and rhythm in her mind as she softly sang through the verses.

"Okay. Let's give it a try," she announced, hoping she'd embedded the new timing in her brain.

The guitar intro began in her headphones, and she noticed the red recording light came on above the control room door. He'll be wiping this track, Luna thought, right before she sang perfectly through the whole song.

When the red light went off, Trina and Panda both applauded.

"Was that alright?" Luna asked, truly unsure. She'd been lost in the song and had ultimately let her natural musical talent guide her voice.

"Bloody brilliant," Trina assured her.

"That'll probably be the one we'll use," Rollo said over the speakers. "Give me one more take for backup, please."

And just like that, the atmosphere felt like the vibe they'd had making *Time and Light* in the London studio. The fun was creeping back into the recording. Luna sung 'Wanted' again. Her voice had a little grit she could conjure sometimes, and she found it the second time through. Not Janis Joplin level, but enough to add a great rock edge to a line.

"Okay, I was wrong. That's our version," Rollo announced. "Now you need to give me one more like that as backup."

Luna smiled and felt a warm glow inside. Only twelve hours earlier, their circumstances had seemed hopeless, yet now her optimism and joy filled her heart with glee. She sang through 'Wanted' once more, enjoying every word and every note.

"I think I liked the verses better that time," Luna said once she was done.

"Me too," Rollo agreed over the speakers. "I'll piece the three takes together and pull the best of each one."

"What next?" Luna asked, ready to press on.

"I'd like Trina to sing the choruses," Rollo said, stepping from the control room.

"You what?" Trina responded in surprise.

"I want you to sing the choruses and we'll double the vocal track."

"I can't sing like she does," Trina pointed out, aiming her thumb at Luna.

"Few can," Rollo said. "That's the point. Your deeper tone will give her vocal more depth. Don't worry, it's not a duet, you'll be background. Humour me, and if we don't like it in the mix, we'll leave it out."

"I love the idea," Luna said, so Trina shrugged her shoulders and walked over to the stool by the vocals mic.

It took five attempts, but Trina finally matched the new cadence Luna had put on the chorus, and Rollo told her he had what he needed.

"What's next, then?" Trina asked, still sitting on the stool.

"Why don't we lay down the drums for 'Empty Head'?" Rollo asked, joining them again in the studio.

"Thank goodness," Trina laughed. "I was worried you wanted me to sing again."

They spent the rest of the morning piecing the new song together. Trina set the tempo on the drums, then Panda filled in with his bass. When it came time for the lead guitar, Luna picked up her acoustic, ready to show Rollo the chords she'd written the lyric to.

"I have a better idea," Rollo suggested. "You play the lead. If we come up with a solo or fill section later, either you or I can play that and I'll splice it in."

Luna was stunned. "Are you sure?" she asked, although the question she wanted to ask was more along the lines of what had changed his mind.

"We're rolling along pretty well today, and I don't want to disrupt that," he replied. "It makes more sense for you to play it right now. I can learn it from listening later."

The door had still been left open for Rollo to change his mind, but it sounded like her guitar playing might make the song, and Luna was overcome with a mixture of nerves and excitement. Strumming out the basic tune was not the same as laying down a perfect track for the recording. She'd also only played it on her acoustic and would need to record on electric. And this song was important to her.

Their first single from *Time and Light* had just moved up inside the top 20 in the UK charts and Luna and the Lanterns had appeared on *Top of the Pops* for the first time. Luna was on cloud nine. Walking down the street near her parents' home in Finchley, chatting away with Trina as they weaved through the other pedestrians, a man had stepped in front of them. He was probably in his 50s, with a neatly trimmed moustache, and wore a business suit and a bowler hat.

"You should be ashamed of yourselves," he barked, shaking his furled umbrella at the two girls.

They had both been stunned.

"For what?" Trina asked, knocking the tip of his umbrella aside.

"Look at the way you're dressed!" he exclaimed. "Pair of hussies!"

Luna had looked down at her miniskirt, thigh boots, and a flowery high-neck tank top, which she loved.

"It's 1969, mate," Trina snapped back. "Get over it."

"Empty heads!" he shouted, and stomped around them, continuing down the pavement. "Empty heads," Luna heard him say again.

Trina burst out laughing, but the incident had bothered Luna. People stared, some shook their heads, and others laughed. Luna felt incredibly embarrassed on a day that she'd spent feeling on top of the world. Arriving home, she'd hurriedly written the words to her new song, 'Empty Head', while the awful feeling had been fresh in her mind.

"That tempo, Luna," came Rollo's voice over her headphones.

She'd been lost in trying to remember the chord progression and his voice brought her back to the moment.

"There's something missing," she said into the mic. "This sounded fine on my acoustic, but something's not right now."

Rollo came out of the control room and walked over, picking up his guitar on the way. He strummed the chords she'd just been playing.

"Go again," Luna told him, and this time sang the words to the first verse as he played.

"Try this," he said, and played the tune again. He'd changed a chord.

"Again," Luna urged, and sang along this time. "That's better."

"One more time," Trina called out, slipping behind her drum kit.

She began playing a beat and Rollo dropped in with the guitar. Luna sang through the first verse.

"Keep going, Trina," Rollo said as he put his guitar aside and rushed to the control room.

The red record light came on, and Trina continued playing the beat she'd been keeping.

"A little faster," Rollo said over the speakers, and Trina picked up the tempo.

After another few minutes, the red light went off.

"Okay, Luna, I'll punch the drums through your headset. Are you ready?" Rollo asked.

Luna nodded and waited for Trina's drums to play in her ears. Trina and Panda both had headphones on to listen in, and Luna could tell from the way Panda's fingers moved along the frets of his bass that he was planning out his parts.

Resisting the urge to sing aloud, Luna heard her lines in her head as she played the guitar. Although she winced after a couple of small mistakes, it felt like the song was coming together.

"Okay," Rollo said over the studio speakers. "That'll work for now. I'll have you play it again later, but do you feel like singing first? You'll have drums and the guitar you just cut as a guide."

Luna nodded. They'd never recorded this way before, but it felt looser and more fluid, building the song by improving each part in layers.

"I gotta redo some of the drums," Trina urged. "I've got fills in my head now."

"Lyrics, drums, bass, then lead guitar again, and finally backup vocals," Rollo said over the speakers.

Trina and Luna glanced at each other and grinned. This was new territory. Even when recording went well on *Time and Light*, Rollo had never been this open and communicative. Deadlines had evaporated from everyone's minds, and the studio was brimming over with creativity and the joy of making music.

'Empty Head', despite its title and message about judging young people, was an upbeat tune. Luna knew many listeners to the record wouldn't register the meaning and simply hum along to the catchy tune, but she didn't mind. If the point reached one person who thought twice before instantly writing off a young woman because of the way she looked or dressed, then it would be worth it to her.

They worked a long day, which didn't end until well into the evening. The girls took several longer breaks to grab food while Rollo pressed on, listening to every note played and word sung, choosing the best, and splicing the performances together. The studio in London had supplied a tech assistant who'd helped a lot with everything from moving mics, instruments, and cables, to troubleshooting equipment problems. Panda couldn't do much about technical issues, but he stepped up and helped Rollo with everything else.

"We need to confront Rollo more often," Trina kidded as she and Luna ate dinner at the table by the galley. "He's been a star today."

Luna laughed. "I'm hoping the one time did the trick. I really don't want to go through all that turmoil again."

"How's supper, ladies?" Captain Garrison asked, leaning into the room.

"Stu outdid himself once again," Luna replied. "Would you like to join us?"

"Thank you for the offer, but no," the captain replied. "Mr Dumfries has just taken over the helm, so I'll catch forty winks before my next shift."

"Where are we?" Trina asked.

"South of Cuba. East of the Mexican Yucatan Peninsula," Garrison replied. "We'll reach Grand Cayman in the morning."

As the captain bid them a good night, Luna couldn't help but wonder what awaited them tomorrow. Completely absorbed in their music, she hadn't thought about LMT and the Cayman Islands all day.

14

"Aren't you supposed to join your mum and dad?" Reg said from the passenger seat as AJ drove north on Esterly Tibbetts Bypass.

She looked at her watch. It was nearly three o'clock. "Think they're done with lunch?"

Reg laughed. "About an hour or two ago, I reckon."

"Has Pearl texted you?" AJ asked.

Reg shook his head. "Surprisingly quiet on that front."

"What do you think that means?"

Reg grunted and thought a moment, scratching his unruly salt-and-pepper beard, which matched his equally unruly hair.

"Usually, if she's home or at the dock working on bookings or accounting, she'd be asking me stuff or explaining how I'd bollocksed things up."

"I'm guessing it's more the latter," AJ commented.

"Mostly," he admitted. "Which means she's not doing either of those things."

"So you think she's still with my mum and dad?"

Reg shrugged his shoulders. "Pretty good chance, I'd say."

"Should you text and find out?"

Reg laughed again. "And say what? We're still running around chasing clues to a mystery which basically has nothing to do with us, instead of spending time with you lot?"

AJ's jaw dropped open. "Why on earth would you say that?"

"Because that's what we're doing."

"I know, which is why you never want to say that!"

"Let me get this straight," Reg responded. "You advocate telling porky pies to a spouse and parents?"

AJ nodded and grinned. "When required for their own good."

"Whenever I wonder why you're still single, I need to remind myself of this moment."

AJ gasped and put a hand to her chest in mocked shock. "I'm single because I have very selective taste and few men live up to my high standards."

"The standards which include lying to loved ones you mean?" Reg laughed. "You're single because you never go anywhere to meet a bloke."

"That's not true," she replied defensively. "I'm in the Fox and Hare at least twice a week."

"That doesn't count," Reg replied.

"How does a pub full of people not count?"

"Because you've already turned down every eligible and non-eligible bachelor whoever frequents the gaff."

"You never know what fresh stock may show up," AJ grinned.

Reg frowned. "Like tourists?"

"Of course not, I'm looking for love for a lifetime, not a week on hols."

"My delicate sensibilities are glad to hear it. So you're waiting on the next divemaster to get hired and show up?"

AJ shook her head. "No way. They're working here for great diving, parties, and tourists looking for love on their hols."

Reg threw his hands up. "I think you just made my point for me."

"You had a point?"

"Yeah! You're single because you never bloody well go anywhere to meet anyone."

"Alright, alright," AJ fussed. "What do you suggest? Go bar crawling every Friday and Saturday night?"

"No. You could try that internet dating thing. Isn't that how people meet these days?"

AJ scoffed. "Guys tell enough lies when they try chatting you up at a bar. Imagine the bullshit they come up with when they have time to sit down and write a profile on the computer."

"I suppose," Reg grunted.

"Too bloody right. It's not like when you dated, old man. Didn't they call it courting back then?"

"I'm not that bloody old."

"Did she have to ride side-saddle when you led her horse to the barn dance?"

"We were dating in the nineteen eighties, not the eighteen bloody eighties. It was all sex, drugs, and rock 'n' roll in our era."

AJ laughed. "Right, 'cos the Royal Navy were big on you getting stoned and cranking Pink Floyd."

"And see, there's the main reason you're single," Reg said, shaking his head some more.

"What do you mean?"

"You're a pain in the bloody arse."

"No way," she rebutted, pulling into the petrol station by the junction known to everyone on the west side of the island as the four-way stop. "I'm loveable, like a cuddly bunny."

Reg opened the passenger door. "More like a cross between a hedgehog and a slow loris."

AJ got out and met Reg around the front of the van. "A slow loris? Is that one of those venomous monkeys?"

"Yup," he replied, holding open the door to the building.

"So a hedge loris," AJ said, going inside. "Or a slow hog. Ooooh, that's even better. I could use that on a dating profile."

"You may have missed the point," Reg grumbled as they walked to the counter.

"You had a point?" AJ replied with a grin.

Reg shook his head once more, then addressed the young woman at the checkout. "Hello, we're looking for Mr Merren."

"Which one?" the woman asked in a heavy local accent, looking the visitors over with a hint of suspicion.

"Nathaniel, please," Reg clarified.

"He don't come by so much anymore," the woman replied. "Can I help you wit someting?"

"Hey, how old would he be?" AJ asked Reg.

"My age, I suppose," Reg whispered back, although his deep voice didn't have a low volume available, so the young woman undoubtedly heard him.

"Oh bollocks," AJ muttered, turning aside. "Lucky he hasn't kicked his clogs then."

Reg frowned at her. "Thank you, Hedge Loris."

"I prefer Slow Hog."

"I know, that's why I'm using the other one," Reg replied.

The young woman gave up on them and started a video on her phone. Hip-hop music played and voices shouted unintelligibly. The woman giggled.

"Can you tell us where we might find Nathaniel?" Reg persisted.

The woman paused her video with a deep sigh. "Will he want you to know where he at?"

AJ laughed, and Reg frowned at her. Again.

"What? You gotta admit that's a fair question. Some bloke who looks like he just stepped off the *Pequod* with Captain Ahab strolls in and asks about the boss. I know I'd be hesitant."

"Thanks for the help," Reg groaned under his breath.

AJ turned to the woman. "Are you a member of the Merren family?"

The woman nodded. "Granddaughter."

AJ thought for a moment. She was about to be completely honest with the young woman, but she noticed the smartphone clutched in her long, painted fingernails and quickly decided against it. She hated to be untrusting, but one post on social media and they could kick off a storm in a teacup when they still had no idea whether the skull belonged to the woman's great-grandfather or not.

"Who manages this place these days?" AJ asked instead.

"My father," she replied. "But he ain't here right now. Who are you two?"

"Sorry, we've been very rude," AJ replied, and took a business card from her pocket. "Here. I'm AJ and the bear with me is Reg. If you wouldn't mind asking your dad or your grandad to call us, we'd be very grateful. It's about a family matter."

The young woman eyed the card and then the two strangers on the other side of the counter. "Okay," she finally said, and tossed the card aside, sat back on her stool and returned to scrolling her phone.

Reg was about to say something more, but AJ grabbed his arm and nodded towards the door.

"I was just about to butter her up and find out where he lives," Reg complained as they got back in the van.

"No, you were about to annoy her a bit more and waste another five minutes," AJ replied, taking out her mobile. "I have a better idea."

She started the van and dialled a number on her phone. It rang three times before being answered.

"Hey," came Nora's voice.

"You busy?" AJ asked.

"*Nei*. Just driving two drunk *drittsekk* back to their hotel."

Two American male accents could be heard cheering after she spoke. "Cayman Uber, baby!"

"Shut up, or it'll be the station," Nora snapped at them and they quietened down. "What do you need?"

"If I give you a name, you can look up an address, right?" AJ asked.

"Try Google," Nora replied.

"I did, now I'm trying you."

It was partly true. Reg had searched the internet for Nathaniel

Merren on their drive to the petrol station, but AJ didn't fully trust his fat fingers searching.

"We not supposed to do dat sorta ting for serial speeding offenders," came Jacob's voice.

AJ laughed. "I can get my hands on a helping of Pearl's trifle, if that helps?"

"Look it up for da lady, Nora," Jacob said and laughed.

"Name?" Nora asked.

"Nathaniel Merren."

AJ spelt out the name, then she and Reg waited while they could hear Nora tapping away on the keyboard.

"Which one?" Nora asked after a few moments.

"In his sixties," Reg replied.

"Ready?" Nora asked.

"Shoot," AJ said, opening the maps app on her mobile.

She typed in the address Nora gave her.

"When you gonna pay up?" Jacob asked.

"Tonight," AJ replied, using a weird attempt at a secret agent's voice. "Come by Reg and Pearl's after six. Make sure no one follows you, and the code word is tasty."

Jacob laughed again, and the line went dead. Which meant Nora had hung up.

"That's over by Hell," Reg commented, referring to the black limestone tourist attraction in West Bay.

"In that case," AJ said, now using a deep, menacing tone. "We're going to Hell."

"Strewth," Reg muttered. "Let's go, Hedge Loris."

Chuckling to herself, AJ drove them to Miss Daisy Lane, a narrow, paved single track off Hell Road, leading to a handful of homes. Merren's place was a typical single-storey block home, which had been economical for locals to build for decades. The blue-grey exterior showed signs of ageing, but the grounds were tidy and a shiny white SUV sat in the driveway. AJ parked next to the vehicle so she didn't block the road, and they walked to the front door.

After a few moments, their knock was answered and a dark-skinned man in his early sixties grinned at them.

"Hi, Nathaniel," Reg said. "Don't know if you remember me. We've met a few times over the years. I'm Reg Moore, and this is AJ Bailey."

The man nodded, and the wry smile didn't leave his face. "I remember you," he replied with a heavy local accent. "Granddaughter just called and told me two white folks were just asking around about me. Dis about someting we talk about out here, or should we go inside?"

AJ smiled to herself. She took his question as more of a subtle warning that he'd toss them out if they came inside to talk about anything he didn't care to discuss.

"Inside, I'd say," Reg replied.

Nathaniel was a broad-shouldered man, but not as tall or burly as Reg, who could handle himself in most situations despite his age. Not that she anticipated any kind of confrontation.

Nathaniel stepped aside, and the two walked into a clean and tidy, well-furnished living room.

"Get ya a drink of someting?" he offered as he closed the door.

"No, we're good, thank you," Reg replied for both of them. "We won't keep you long."

"What's dis about, den?" Nathaniel asked, gesticulating for them to sit on the sofa. He took a recliner, which he sank into like a familiar and comfortable throne.

"If we could ask you to keep what we have to say to yourself," Reg began. "We'd appreciate it."

"Got nuttin' to repeat so far, so dat shouldn't be too hard."

It wasn't exactly an agreement to confidentiality, but AJ took over when Reg gave her a nod.

"Not sure if you heard about it, but we found human remains in the water off Cemetery Beach yesterday."

Nathaniel nodded. "Didn't know what, but heard there were some fuss down that way. It weren't me you found if dat's why you come checkin'."

He broke into a wide grin, and AJ laughed.

"No, sir. We think who we found has been down there a while longer."

"I didn't put dem dere either," Nathaniel said, and grinned again.

"The reason we're coming to see you, Nathaniel," Reg said, "is about your grandfather. We looked up an article in the old newspaper which mentioned your granddad's grave was flooded back in the late sixties."

Nathaniel nodded knowingly, like he'd connected the dots on why they were talking to him.

"Dat were a crazy deal, for sure."

"Sorry to bring up what I'm sure is a difficult memory for your family," AJ offered.

Nathaniel laughed. "It's more of a funny story gets brought up most family gatherin's."

AJ wasn't sure what to say. Losing the body of a loved one after they'd been interred didn't seem like a story to be described as funny.

"Papa Merren never could sit still," Nathaniel added, and now AJ was fighting not to laugh.

"You read 'bout what happened?" the old man asked.

AJ nodded. "Yeah. The floods with Hurricane Francelia took your grandad's coffin out to sea. That's why we wondered if the remains we found could be him."

Nathaniel laughed again. "You didn't read all da articles den."

AJ and Reg looked at each other.

"Few days later, when water settled down," Nathaniel explained. "We found Papa's coffin down da beach some."

"You did?" AJ gasped. "I guess we should have checked the following week's edition," she added, rolling her eyes at Reg.

"Suspiciously close to a bar he spent more time in dan Grandma care to remember," Nathaniel said, and burst out laughing.

Reg and AJ couldn't help but join in.

"Well, we're sorry for wasting your time," AJ responded, still chuckling. "And I'm glad your grandad is where he's supposed to be. I presume you popped him back in his grave?"

"We did, and dey figured out a way to use concrete and such to keep him dere."

Reg rose to his feet. "Like she said, Nathaniel, we apologise for bothering you, but thanks for your time."

"It's no bother at all," the old man replied, seeing them to the door. "Nice seeing you again, Reg, and nice meetin' you, young lady."

"Cheers," AJ said, giving the man a wave as she walked to the van.

"Hey, you sure dis body you find from back dat far?" Nathaniel asked.

AJ paused at the driver's door. "Could be a few decades either side of when your grandad went for a ride."

"I just ask, 'cos I sure you saw from da paper around dat time. But a music band made da news den too."

"I saw something about them being on the island," AJ replied. "But I didn't read the article. Why?"

"Cos dey and dere boat all went missin' 'bout a week before."

15

Luna woke as she often did with a section of a new song playing in her head. Whatever lyrics she'd been hammering out lately and the melody she'd put with them. Occasionally, a slightly different version would be playing and she'd have to quickly make a note or find a guitar and play the chords to cement them to memory. On this morning it was yesterday's recording of 'Empty Head' replaying in her mind and she smiled.

Reaching out, she discovered Rollo wasn't next to her, which she'd become used to on this trip. The next thing she noticed was how incredibly calm the ocean felt. Pulling back the curtain from the porthole, Luna squinted against the bright morning sunshine, then gasped at the smooth turquoise water stretching away to a long sandy beach. Palm trees and shrubs beyond the sand were occasionally interrupted by a few buildings and a handful of people walked along the beach. Luna had never seen anything like the tropical island outside of a book or a cinema screen.

She hastily threw on a T-shirt and a pair of shorts, then scurried up the steps to the studio. Rollo waved to her from behind the glass of the control room, and she smiled and waved back, but turned the other way. Bursting through the doorway, she went straight to the bridge, where Captain Garrison greeted her.

"Good morning, Miss Luna. Welcome to Grand Cayman."

Ahead, Luna could see a town by the water with taller buildings, but the colour of the ocean took her breath away.

"It's gorgeous," she enthused. "Are we docking here?"

"We'll enter the little harbour in George Town where we'll check in with their immigration officials, then you'll be able to go ashore if you'd like."

"Oh yes! I can't wait."

"Once we've refuelled and bought supplies," the captain explained. "Mr Fletcher wants to moor along the beach."

"How close to the beach can we get?" Luna asked, recalling all the talk of shallow water and reefs along the Florida coast.

"We'll need to stay a few hundred yards out," he replied. "There's a reef running all along here but a stretch of sand between the shallow section and the deeper part, which is where it drops steeply away. We'll anchor in the sand between the two, but we can launch the tenders to ferry you to the beach."

There had been so many firsts over the past year for the nineteen-year-old from a terraced home in Finchley, but arriving at a tropical island in the Caribbean ranked as one of the most memorable for Luna.

"I'll be right back," she said, and ran down the steps and through the studio.

Rollo looked up from the console and she gave him another wave as she went down the steps to the berths and banged on Trina's door. Hearing a groan from inside, Luna burst in and strained her eyes to see her friend in the dark room.

"Come and see where we are, Trina. You have to get up right now."

"No. No, I don't," came a muffled voice from under the covers. "I already got up early for a revolution yesterday. I'm sleeping in today."

Luna switched on the light, jumped onto the bed, and pulled the covers back. Trina threw an arm over her face to hide her eyes from the brightness.

"Nooooo, babe. Turn the bloody light off."

Luna wasn't taking no for an answer and pulled her friend's arm until Trina slid like a dead weight across the bed.

"Don't make me drag you to the floor."

"Go ahead. I'll go back to sleep down there."

Luna laughed and tugged on Trina's arm again until her petite, naked body hung over the edge of the bed.

"Okay, okay," Trina moaned, swinging her legs out of bed before she fell. "But you should know your enthusiastic attempt at including me in your fun is no bloody fun at all."

"Put some clothes on," Luna ordered.

"Do I have to?"

"I think you'd test the captain's delicate sensibilities if you showed up on the bridge starkers."

"See, no fun. The most fun is always naked," Trina complained, but found a shirt and a skirt to put on.

As Luna herded Trina up the steps, it dawned on her how she'd been hell-bent on sharing their arrival on the island with her best friend… instead of the man she lay next to each night. As they crossed the studio, she looked back and again caught Rollo's eye. She smiled, and he briefly smiled back before returning his attention to whatever he was working on. Luna felt guilty for choosing the company of Trina over her boyfriend, but also because he was working his arse off while they were sleeping in. On *their* album.

The negative thoughts soon evaporated when Trina squealed in excitement as she looked out the windows of the bridge.

"He had a stick up his bum," Trina commented after the customs and immigration official departed *Soundwave,* leaving the band and the crew standing on the forward deck.

The captain thought for a moment, but Sally, the young stewardess, spoke before he'd sorted out his words.

"I think you'll find this is a more conservative island, miss."

"Exactly," Captain Garrison said, appearing relieved. "Thank you, Sally."

Luna and Trina looked at each other.

"Did we say something wrong?" Luna asked, trying to recall how she may have offended the man. She'd barely said more than a few words.

"No, I don't believe so," the captain replied, and then glanced at the stewardess again.

Sally now hesitated, and First Mate Sammy laughed.

"I think what they're trying to say, lassies, is you ought to put on a bra before you go ashore."

Trina burst out laughing.

"Oh, bloody hell," Luna muttered. "I'll have to find one. I haven't worn a bra for ages."

"I don't know that I even have one with me," Trina giggled.

"You have swimsuits, don't you?" Rollo asked.

"Right, yeah," Luna replied. "We can wear them underneath."

Trina laughed even more. "There's not much to mine. Hope they don't kick us off the beach."

Luna turned to Rollo. "So, what's the schedule today? Are we recording? We would like to explore a bit while we're here, but I know we have to get on with things."

Rollo had been quiet throughout the process of docking and waiting for the official to come aboard, and Luna hadn't been able to tell what was troubling him. After such a productive day yesterday, she couldn't believe things could regress again, so she tried to remain cheery.

"I have a meeting, so take the morning to look around or go to the beach. We'll meet back here for lunch and make a plan from there. I hope we can work this afternoon."

"Is this your LMT character?" Luna whispered.

Rollo frowned, but nodded. "I'm meeting *him* shortly," he replied.

Luna noticed the emphasis on *him*, which was Rollo's unsubtle way of reassuring her that the meeting wasn't romantic. It was about money. She'd already established that, although Rollo hadn't expanded on his comment and she hadn't pushed him. Having come from barely scraping by to having money in her bank account and all her expenses paid, Luna hadn't thought much about finances. She had no idea if she was receiving her fair share or not. None of the three original members did. They were simply elated now they didn't have to worry about saving up to buy a pair of jeans.

"Here, or on the island?" she asked.

"Here," Rollo replied. "And it would be better if I met with him alone, so why don't you put underwear on and then go find a beach?"

"I don't really do the beach thing, man," Panda said, looking at the town across the water. "But I'm sure they have a pub somewhere."

"Don't you want to get a bit of colour?" Sally asked the tall, pasty-white bassist.

He laughed. "I only do two colours, man. Ghost white and lobster red. The sun ain't for me, man."

As curious as Luna was to stick around to see who the mysterious LMT man was, she was more eager to hit the pale-yellow sand beach stretching endlessly into the distance. The locals were a mixture of dark skin tones like she'd never seen before, and men and women alike seemed curious of the visitors. They were also friendly, and while neither of the girls could understand everything they said with their heavy local accents, there was no mistaking the universal language of smiles and waves.

Captain Garrison had arranged for a young local man to guide them and he had an old four-door Humber Hawk in which to drive them around. He introduced himself as Sonny, and to Luna's relief, his accent was lighter than the other folks they'd talked to.

"How many people live here?" Luna asked once they'd explained that a beautiful beach was their first priority.

"'Bout 10,000 or so, I believe," Sonny replied as he drove along a two-lane road with the ocean on their left.

Luna hung her arm out the open window, trying to direct the breeze inside to combat the heat and humidity. Trina nudged her, nodded towards the driver, and gave her friend a wink. Luna frowned in reply and mouthed the words *'you go ahead'*. Trina grinned and mouthed, *'yes please'*.

It hadn't gone unnoticed to Luna that Sonny was a good-looking guy with a toned physique and a ready smile. She'd been around black men in London, but not many, and had been surprised by how many more came to see the band in America. She hadn't admitted it even to Trina, but she had fantasised about what it might be like to be with someone who outwardly appeared so different. But she had a boyfriend. Who was also in the band and managing them. It was starting to become clear how complicated things would be if their relationship fell apart.

"Congratulations on dat album of yours doin' so well," Sonny said from the front, glancing at the girls in the rear-view mirror.

"You know who we are?" Luna asked. "I guess I assumed pop and rock music wouldn't make it all the way to an island like this."

Sonny laughed. "We have electricity, you know, and we live in houses, not caves."

Luna blushed, but Trina laughed. "You even drive cars."

"Some of us do," Sonny replied in good humour. "Although I admit dis one is borrowed from my uncle."

"Have you always lived on the island?" Luna asked.

"Mostly. But I spent time in Florida too. My father works in construction over dere."

Sonny pulled the Humber off the road into a dirt parking area between two stands of trees. As soon as he turned off the engine,

Luna could hear the ocean gently lapping against the beach. The girls leapt from the back seat and ran between the palms to the long sandy beach, kicking off their flip-flops as they went.

"It's bloody hot!" Trina yelped as her bare feet hit the sun-scorched sand.

"Race ya," Luna shouted, and they both ran screaming towards the sea, each trying to be the first one with their toes in the water.

Sonny brought the towels they'd left on his back seat and spread them out on the beach. Trina jogged back to him, pulling her shirt over her head and then dropping her jeans shorts onto the towel.

"Coming for a swim?" she asked, putting on her most inviting smile.

"I'm a land-based creature," Sonny replied. "But I'll enjoy watching you two."

Luna noticed the young man's eyes had looked her way when he'd spoken, and she blushed again. Trina was gorgeous, fun, and most importantly, single. But of course Sonny was gravitating to the one he couldn't have. And Luna didn't want to make Trina feel bad. Although her friend was usually perfectly capable of landing men she really wanted, and moving on if she didn't care too much. She'd left a trail of broken hearts in her wake across the world since their whirlwind life had taken off.

Walking to the towel, Luna stripped down to her two-piece bathing suit, which was only slightly more conservative than Trina's.

"What do you do here, Sonny?" she asked. "Apart from driving visitors around in your uncle's car."

"I own a little bar by da beach," he replied.

"I told Panda he should've come with us," Trina laughed. "Where is your bar?"

"Back towards town," Sonny replied. "We passed it on da way here."

"You should have pointed it out," Trina admonished playfully. "Do you play music there?"

"We do."

"Live music?" Trina pressed.

"We do."

Trina wriggled with excitement. "Do you play?"

"I do."

Luna stayed quiet as Trina seemed to be winning Sonny's attention over, but visions of Elvis Presley movies with a bar full of young people dancing and singing in exotic settings played in her mind.

"And you weren't going to tell us?" Trina asked, putting her hands on her slender hips.

Sonny laughed. "I'm embarrassed to say I play music to you two. You're making records and playin' festivals and big concerts. I'm just havin' fun wit a few friends."

"Completely understandable," Trina said, forcing a serious voice.

She then stood there staring at Sonny and tapping her foot in the sand. Sonny looked over at Luna with a worried expression, clearly unsure what he was supposed to say or do.

"I would ask her to come play with you at your bar if I were you," Luna said.

Sonny's face lit up. "You would? You'd come play at my place?"

"I suppose we could," Trina replied as though she was thoroughly bored with nothing better to do. "Seeing as you asked nicely."

16

AJ pulled to the end of Miss Daisy Lane so they weren't sitting in front of Nathaniel's house, then came to a stop.

"What do we do now?" she thought aloud.

Reg was tapping on his mobile with his banana-sized thumbs.

"Could go back to the *Compass*," he said, still typing, most of which appeared to be followed by the delete key from what AJ could see.

"I think that would be asking a lot of Lahaina," AJ replied. "I noticed her boss was asking her what we were up to. Didn't look enthralled with us having free rein over one of their computers."

Reg swore a few times under his breath. "Here. Finally," he grumbled. "Found an article from a music magazine dated 2010. Says here a band called Luna and the Lanterns went missing in a hurricane near the island of Grand Cayman in the Caribbean."

"Luna and the Lanterns?" AJ questioned. "I don't think I've ever heard of them."

"Talks about them being the next big thing in 1969," Reg went on. "They were believed to have been nearly finished with their second album, which was being recorded in their studio on a yacht they'd converted. All lost without a trace, including the crew."

"Have you heard of them?"

Reg thought for a moment. "Name rings a bell. Pearl will know. I think she has an album of theirs, come to think of it."

"I wonder why that wouldn't have come up on Whittaker's missing persons search?" AJ said. "I'd say a boat full of people should have been a red flag."

"Might not be in the Cayman Islands' system," Reg replied. "This article is more about the band and how they slipped from everyone's minds. This geezer thinks they were destined for greatness. Doesn't say much about how they went missing."

"Must have been the storm before Hurricane Francelia," AJ pointed out. "Hurricane Camille was the one which formed near Cayman, then hammered Cuba and the US."

"We need a computer to search properly instead of my bloody mobile," Reg complained. "And maybe we ask Lahaina if she can send us a copy of the newspaper scans from the weeks we skipped."

AJ pulled away, turning on Hell Road. "I have my laptop. Let's go to the dock, where we have Wi-Fi."

"What about calling Lahaina?" Reg asked.

AJ bit her lip, thinking it over. "I don't know. I don't want to take advantage of our friendship."

"We could be uncovering a big story here if you stumbled across poor old Luna," Reg said. "There's a picture of her in the article. She was a gorgeous girl."

"Didn't look so hot when I saw her," AJ replied, without humour. "Besides, talk about long shots. If they were lost at sea with no wreckage ever found, I doubt they were close enough to the island for a body to wash up here. We don't have a story for the *Compass*. All we have is a wild notion. And look how the first one went. Grandad Merren is tucked up snugly in his concrete sarcophagus."

"Good name for a band," Reg chuckled through his beard.

"Not as good as Luna and the Lanterns," AJ pondered. "That's a pretty cool name. I wish my parents had named me Luna."

Reg laughed. "Don't really see them as the hippie types." He started his lengthy type, delete, and repeat process of texting again. "I'll message Pearl and see if she knows of them."

"Luna Bailey," AJ mused to herself as she drove to the little car park at their dock.

Where she groaned, "Not that wanker again."

Reg looked up. "And he's got Pearl cornered," he growled. "No wonder she didn't reply. That little weasel might have to go in the water today."

"Easy there, big fellow," AJ urged, parking the van and switching off the engine. "I'll get rid of him."

"Fine," Reg muttered, getting out of the van. "But if he's bothering Pearl, then he's going for a swim."

"I was just explaining to Mr Carlson that I didn't think you had anything new you could share about your find yesterday," Pearl said with a roll of her eyes as AJ and Reg approached.

"No harm in checking," The Weasel added. "If you don't have anything new for me, then I'll be off."

To AJ's surprise, the man hurried away to his car he'd parked across the road.

"What the bloody hell was that all about?" Reg asked, watching Carlson leave.

"I pulled in and he was already here," Pearl replied. "I figured he was waiting for you two, but I told him I didn't know where you were."

"Good job, love," Reg said and put an arm around his wife.

"Well, it was easy, seeing as I haven't known where you were all afternoon."

"We've been investigating," AJ said with a grin. "Hot on the trail of the case of the mysterious missing head. Which is actually the case of the missing body, I suppose."

"Good for you, Miss Marple," Pearl replied. "But your mum and dad didn't come all this way to sit around your cottage all day. Best you give them a call."

AJ's shoulders sagged. "I'm sorry, Pearl, but thank you for taking them to lunch."

"Actually, we had a lovely time, and I only just dropped them off at your place," Pearl admitted. "So, where exactly have you been?"

"Tell you what," AJ decided. "Pull out another chair and a few drinks, and I'll be back with the 'rents in two shakes of a lamb's tail. Then we'll tell you all about it."

"I'm starving," Reg complained. "We missed lunch."

AJ's stomach rumbled in sympathy. "We did, didn't we?"

"Fine," Pearl huffed. "You get the chairs sorted. I'll go with AJ and we'll grab something at Fosters market."

"So, I'm staying here on my tod, and getting the drinks out?" Reg verified.

"If you can manage that," AJ said.

"Get on ya way, Hedge Loris."

"Hedge who?" Pearl asked, as she followed AJ to the van.

"Have you had him checked lately?" AJ replied, opening the driver's door and giving Reg a two-finger salute. "I think he's going a bit doolally."

"Tell me about it," Pearl whispered, giving her husband a wave and a big smile as she climbed into the passenger side. "But what's a girl to do?"

They laughed as AJ pulled out onto North West Point Road and turned right towards the T-junction with West Bay Road. She glanced to her left where the triangular corner lot was used as a car park for their customers and the public dock. She noticed The Weasel was still sitting in his car and made a note to make sure he'd left when they came back.

It took twenty minutes to drop Pearl, round up Bob and Beryl, who wanted to know where they were going and where they'd be after that so they'd know what to bring, pick Pearl and her snacks up, and drive back. During which, AJ devoured half a bag of crisps while explaining to her parents that flip-flops, shorts, a T-shirt, and a thin rain jacket covered them for almost any eventuality 24/7 on the island.

Reg had a cooler by the five chairs he'd arranged in a semicircle looking over the water where their dive boats were returning to the dock from their afternoon trips. They sat, opened cold bottles of Strongbow cider, and relaxed under the shade of the umbrella with Reg and AJ enthusiastically snacking to make up for the missed lunch.

"Out with it, then," Pearl urged. "What's had you two tied up all afternoon?"

"We went to the *Cayman Compass* to search their database for missing persons on the island," AJ replied. "See if we could figure out who the skull belonged to."

"Surely the police are doing that," Beryl said. "Do they have a cold case unit here?"

AJ shook her head as she wiped her fingers on her shorts before pulling her laptop from her bag. "No, not a dedicated department, and they're swamped, so Detective Whittaker was keen on us doing some digging."

Her wording was deliberate. She didn't want to outright lie to her parents, but saying they'd taken it completely upon themselves to investigate also suggested that she'd preferred to do that than spend time with her mum and dad. Which was sort of true, if she was completely honest with them. And herself. But more than covering up her motives, AJ didn't want to offend her parents, so she hoped by hinting that she and Reg had been asked to search would avoid any ill-feeling. She noticed Reg raised an eyebrow.

"What did you find?" Bob asked, and relieved, AJ moved on.

"We found a story about a coffin floating out of the cemetery in the flooding from a hurricane in the late 60s, which seemed to match our best theory, so we visited a family member."

"The thought of bodies coming out of graves sounds like a horror movie," Beryl said, wrinkling her nose.

"It's okay," Reg assured her. "This geezer just dropped by his old watering hole. They rounded him up and popped him back in his grave a few days later."

"So he's not the skull you found?" Bob asked.

"Nope, but just so happens," AJ took over again, "two weeks earlier, a rock band was here on a boat, and they were all lost in a hurricane."

"There were two storms that close together?" Pearl asked.

"August 14th, then August 29th," AJ confirmed, reading from her screen. "First one was called Camille, and it was a tropical storm on the island, as it formed here. Went on to knock the stuffing out of Cuba and Mississippi. We're trying to find more details about what happened to the band and their yacht."

"Who was the band?" Bob asked. "Anyone we would have heard of?"

"Luna and the Lanterns," AJ replied, and turned her screen around to show everyone a photograph of the band members.

The shot was onstage at a festival, which, according to the article, was the band's last event.

"Why couldn't you name me Luna?" AJ said, grinning at her parents. "Coolest name ever."

"Luna Skye," Pearl said. "Skye spelt with a Y-E. I have their record at home. Haven't listened to it for a while but it's a great album. Had it for donkey's years. I used to play a couple of their songs. I had no idea they had ties to the island or were lost here."

"Luna Skye!" AJ exclaimed. "Beyond cool."

"You know that'll be a stage name, right?" Beryl replied.

"So what? You could have given me a mega cool name like that."

"We weren't really the tie dye and weed sort of folks, Annabelle Jayne," Beryl replied. "Besides, you have a lovely name."

"It's okay, but it's no Luna Skye I can tell you that," AJ muttered.

"I remember them," Bob said, leaning in to see the photograph. "They had a couple of big hits, then disappeared. I forgot about the boat part. I thought it was another rock band in a tragic plane crash story."

"I can't say I've ever heard of them," Beryl admitted, turning to AJ. "But I'm a few years younger than your father."

"And didn't mix with the tie dye and weed sort of folks," AJ laughed.

She searched on her mobile to see if Luna and the Lanterns' music was available to download, but couldn't find it.

"We'll have to give it a listen on Pearl's vinyl. Whoever has the rights to their music hasn't made it available."

"So what's next?" Bob asked, looking at his daughter.

AJ hesitated and Reg jumped in.

"Your girl needs to call our friend at the newspaper and get us another look at their records."

"Notice how it's *our* friend, but *I* have to call," AJ pointed out as she picked up her mobile and dialled the number, putting the call on speaker.

Reg just grinned.

"Am I gonna regret answering this call?" Lahaina said after enough rings that AJ expected to get voicemail.

"I'm just calling to thank you," AJ said, cringing and waving at Reg, who began to laugh.

"You can pay me back in tank fills," Lahaina said, and now AJ laughed.

She already filled her friend's tanks for free and let her on the boat if there was space.

"There was one little thing I'd like to ask while I have you on the phone," AJ said.

"You're as subtle as a bear in a honey shop," Lahaina replied.

"Everyone's calling her the Hedge Loris these days, love," Reg volunteered.

"What on earth is a Hedge Loris?" the Irish woman asked.

"Prickly as a hedgehog and venomous like a slow loris," Reg explained. "She'll get you one way or another."

Lahaina laughed. "That's a very endearing name, I must say, but for the sake of my tank fills, I'll refrain from using it. Although Slow Hog has a better ring to it."

AJ threw her hands up. "That's what I said! But I think I'll be adopting the name Luna from now on."

"Looney, more like," Reg chuckled.

"So what is this one little favour you still needed, Luna Loris?" Lahaina asked.

"Could we nip back in and have another quick peek at your archives?" AJ asked.

"That'll be a hard no, I'm afraid," Lahaina replied. "I got in trouble for letting you on our computers today. No chance I can get you back in."

"Well… fiddlesticks," AJ said, holding back the word she wanted to use. "Wait, they're all PDF files, aren't they?"

"I think so."

"Could you send us the files?" AJ asked. "All we need are the articles from those old publications, so if the problem was us being on the company computer, just send us the files."

The line went quiet.

"Or would screenshots work?" Pearl offered.

There was a sigh over the speaker. "Which editions?"

"A week before and three weeks after August 14th 1969," AJ replied.

"That's a lot of bloody screenshots," Lahaina groaned.

"Start with the first two," Reg offered, and looked at AJ. She nodded in return.

"Yeah. Start with the week before and after Hurricane Camille."

"I've left the office, so it'll be tomorrow at the earliest. No promises, but I'll see what I can do."

"You're a star, thank you," AJ said.

"I'll be a star with my boss if you get me a decent story after all this malarkey," Lahaina said. "Talk to you later."

She hung up, and AJ sat back in her chair and took a swig of cider.

"I think we'd all like to see her break a good, honest and accurate story before The Weasel spouts more rubbish," Reg said.

"Oh, bugger," AJ blurted, jumping up. "I completely forgot."

"Forgot what?" Reg asked as AJ jogged up the sloping car park.

"The Weasel was still hanging around when I left," AJ called back.

Stopping at the road, AJ scanned the dirt parking area opposite. A scruffy little white car was pulling out and joining North West Point Road.

There was no mistaking The Weasel's beady little eyes glancing back at her as AJ watched the man leave.

17

Panda stood and watched Luna and Trina come aboard, grinning from ear to ear.

"Have a nice time?" Luna asked, grinning back at him.

He just nodded, and by the state of his eyes, she guessed he'd found a bar which served alcohol all morning. Any bass recordings might have to wait until later in the day.

"Has Rollo's guest left?" Luna asked Sammy, who was helping Sally polish the safety railing.

"I don't think so, but I can't say I've been paying much attention. Stu came up and told me a few minutes back that he has lunch ready to serve on a fifteen-minute warning. Want me to tell him you're ready, miss?"

Luna was hungry after swimming and lying in the sun all morning, but she was unsure without hearing from Rollo. His meeting was important, so she didn't want everyone taking over the galley if his guest was still here.

"Let me check with Rollo," she said, and entered the bridge.

Descending the steps a half-level down, she knocked on the door to the studio, before realising it was pointless. With the sound proofing, there was no way to hear anyone's response unless they screamed, and she wasn't even sure Rollo would hear her knocking. She opened the door and was taken aback when a large man she didn't recognise stepped forward and blocked her path.

"No one's allowed in," he said in a Cockney accent.

His working-class voice didn't match the suit he was wearing, and she wondered who on earth wears a business suit in the Caribbean heat.

Luna stared around his bulky form to see Rollo sitting on one of the sofas. He was leaning forward with his elbows on his knees, but now looked her way. On the other sofa, opposite her boyfriend, was a portly man much older than Rollo in a cream-coloured linen suit and a straw boater.

"Let the young lady in, Kayo," the stranger in the hat ordered, and his bodyguard stepped aside. "Don't you know who that is?"

The man, who spoke with an upper-class English accent, beckoned Luna into the room. As she walked forward, Kayo closed the door behind her. Rollo looked... well, she wasn't sure what the expression on his face meant. She'd never seen it before. Concerned, perhaps?

"This is the talented Miss Luna Skye," the man continued. "A precious commodity and more beautiful than her pictures convey."

He struggled off the sofa to stand, using a cane for support. He looked at Rollo, who seemed to take the hint.

"Luna, this is Lord Thorburn."

She stepped forward and shook the man's clammy hand, although she figured her own grip was probably still salty from the beach.

"This is an absolute pleasure, my dear. I've been following your success with great enthusiasm."

"Nice to meet you, sir," Luna replied, surprised this man was a fan of their music.

Lord Thorburn, she thought, which might explain the LMT initials.

"Please, call me Malcolm," he said, and now she understood. At least where the initials came from, but little else.

"How do you like our studio?" Luna asked, sitting down next to Rollo.

Lord Thorburn dropped awkwardly back down as well and placed his cane aside.

"It's quite remarkable, I must say," he replied, looking around the compact but efficient room. "But Rollo and I were just discussing the delays with the new album. That's of some concern to me."

Rollo reached over and placed a hand on Luna's knee, giving her a light squeeze. They were in uncharted territory, but she assumed he was giving her a warning of some sort. He liked to be the one doing most of the talking with the press, and a firm grip usually meant she was saying too much, or something he didn't approve of. His reasoning had always been that they needed to control the message from the band, and be careful not to be taken out of context in print. She figured this might be a similar situation, although she doubted Thorburn had anything to do with a newspaper, unless he owned it.

"We've made great progress on the trip from Miami," Luna replied. "Things are really moving along now."

"That's what Rollo has been telling me," Lord Thorburn said with a smile she didn't believe. "But the fact still remains that the album was supposed to be delivered to Polydor by now, so we find ourselves in a bit of a quandary."

This delivery date was news to Luna, but she tried her best to hide her surprise.

"We're making art, you know, so sometimes it has to happen when it happens."

Rollo softly patted her leg, which she took as meaning she hadn't screwed up too badly.

Thorburn lifted himself from the sofa once more and gathered up his cane. "Unfortunately, business doesn't operate on the same flighty schedule, my dear. So there are consequences." He smiled again. "I'm so glad I was able to meet you, Luna. I shall take my leave so you can all get back to work." He nodded to Rollo. "I'll be in touch."

Rollo nodded in return but didn't say anything. Thorburn ambled to the door, which Kayo opened for him. When he closed it behind them, Luna turned to her boyfriend.

"What the bloody hell was all that about? We missed our deadline?"

Rollo's face began turning red, and he gritted his teeth. "Not with the label. With him."

"How does he have a deadline? Who the hell is he?"

Picking up his empty glass, Rollo's hand shook as he clenched it tightly.

"He funded this," he growled, gesticulating at the studio around them.

"He paid for the studio?" Luna asked.

This was all bewildering to her. She had no idea how much any of it cost and had presumed Rollo had paid for everything from what he'd earned in the past.

He shook his head. "No. I paid for the studio."

"Then what's Thorburn's part in all this?"

He turned and faced her. "The yacht, Louise. He loaned me the money to buy the damn yacht."

Luna wanted to ask more, but Rollo flung the glass at the wall where it shattered into a million pieces. He swore loudly and stomped towards the control room, so she bolted the opposite way. The best thing she could do was leave him alone until he calmed down, but any hope of returning to yesterday's work environment seemed to have left *Soundwave* along with Lord Malcolm Thorburn.

Lunch was a sombre meal with Panda trying to sober up, Rollo exuding rage, and Luna and Trina feeling like their fun-filled morning was forever ago. The afternoon in the studio wasn't much better. Trina played bongos, tambourine, and several shakers to each track they'd recorded so far, and finally Rollo told them to leave him alone for the evening while he started the mixes.

Luna thought about trying to talk to him, but Trina talked her out of it. And she was right, Luna decided. There was no discussing anything with the man while he was still so angry. So they tried on a dozen outfits each before finally settling on their look for their night on the town. They even talked Panda into coming along after he'd slept most of the afternoon on the couch in the studio.

Sonny was waiting with the Humber at eight o'clock as they'd arranged. The sun had long set, but the air was still very warm and humid, tempered only by the steady breeze off the water. If Luna hadn't spent much of the summer in America, where everywhere she went seemed to be sweltering hot, then the Cayman Islands' climate would have been stifling. Now acclimatised away from the chill English weather, she found the evening pleasant.

It was not surprising they'd missed Sonny's Soggy Wreck Bar on the drive to the beach earlier in the day. Blending in with the local flora, the place was little more than a long shack, open on both sides. Stools lined the front and rear facing bars, and the small stage sat under a palapa off to one side. The place was already busy and buzzing with chatter and laughter as offbeat rhythmic music played over the speakers.

"That's reggae!" Trina enthused as they walked towards the makeshift building. "Crazy percussion sounds. It's the latest thing out of Jamaica."

"I'm surprised you've heard it before," Sonny shouted to be heard. The barman came straight over and the two men greeted each other. Luna noticed Sonny's accent was much stronger when he spoke with other locals.

"What you want to drink?" he asked, turning back to the girls.

"Something local," Luna said, and Trina gave him a thumbs-up.

"Whatever you drink, man," Panda said, more interested in the local women looking at the newcomers.

Sonny nodded, smiled, then relayed their order to the bartender.

"Run a tab and I'll settle with you at the end of the evening," Luna told him when he'd finished ordering.

"Not a chance," Sonny replied. "My bar, my rules. If you play, you don't pay." He nodded towards the stage.

"We didn't bring any instruments," Luna said.

Trina pointed to the little stage where there wasn't a drum kit, but a variety of percussion instruments, including congas, bongos, and a kettledrum.

"I'm in heaven," she grinned.

"We got guitars for you," Sonny assured Luna. "We'll start jamming soon. Once Clement get here."

"Who's Clement?" Trina asked.

Sonny grinned again. "He's da black music on dis island. You want to groove, den he da man."

Panda leaned in closer to Sonny. "Hey man, are we alright here? It's just everybody's looking at us a bit weird, you know what I mean?"

Sonny laughed again. "You fine, brudda. Don't worry bout a ting. Some lookin' 'cos we don't get too many white folks comin' by. Some lookin' 'cos dey recognise you guys. Word been goin' round da island. And some just lookin' 'cos dese two ladies are fine to be lookin' at."

"Cool," Panda said. "Mind if I smoke?"

"Course not," Sonny replied.

Panda pulled a joint from his pocket and held it up.

Sonny beamed. "Even better, man. You gonna be friends wit everyone in no time. Just smoke on da ocean side so da breeze give everyone at da bar a hit."

Panda grinned and walked around the wooden building to the sand, and Luna turned at the sound of a few live beats of a drum. The house music died away, and she noticed a man who had to be at least seventy, standing behind the tall congas. He was skinny, very dark-skinned, with grey-and-black dreadlocks down to his waist. The old man began tapping out an amazing rhythm with his hands.

"Clement?" Luna asked.

"Dat's Clement," Sonny confirmed. "I'll be right back."

Luna watched the old man, transfixed by his playing, and by Trina standing beside her, trying to follow the beat with her hands on her thighs.

"He's bloody incredible," Trina enthused.

"Here," Sonny said, returning behind them and handing Luna an acoustic guitar. "See the low mic stand on the right of the stage? Use that for the guitar and I'll get you one for vocals."

Luna grabbed his arm. "I've never played this kind of music before! I've no idea what to do."

"It don't matter," Sonny replied. "Just play. You'll feel it. Everybody feel it."

Before Luna could think any more about it, Trina grabbed her hand and dragged her to the stage, where Clement briefly looked up. He grinned and nodded. Luna tried to gather up her courage and fiddled with the mic stand to buy herself time. Trina wasn't waiting. She sat on what looked like a wooden box stood on its end and began playing by slapping her hands against the face. Luna watched her friend begin with a few taps until she picked up the rhythm, and within a minute Trina was playing along as though she'd grown up on ska and reggae.

Luna stepped away from the mic to find a few chords which fell in step with the percussion, and once she had a progression figured out, she played to the mic and the crowd cheered. Sonny soon joined them, bringing with him another mic stand, which to Luna's relief he kept, and he began singing.

Sonny's voice was rich and smooth, and he'd been right. The music began flowing through Luna, and pretty soon she was simply playing with the chords coming naturally. By the end of the song, which seemed like it could have continued all night, she was singing backup to Sonny and thoroughly enjoying herself. Although she was taking a guess at the lyrics.

Once the cheers and applause died down, Clement looked over at Trina.

"What you wanna play now, girl?"

Trina grinned and shouted to Luna. "'Wanted'!"

She began tapping out a rhythm which was the right tempo for their track and Luna joined with her guitar. It took Clement only a few bars to pick up the song and add in a reggae beat. Luna hummed the first few lines until she found a new cadence for the lyrics with Clement's offbeat rhythm. The crowd began clapping along, so Luna stepped up to the mic, and sang a more fun version of her new song than she'd ever dreamed possible.

18

AJ held the album cover in her hand. Despite its age, Pearl had kept the cover in remarkably good condition with only a few scuffs along the tiny spine, but the front and back were still glossy and clean. Spending the majority of its life between other albums on a shelf away from the sunlight had preserved the colour. The front image was a painting of a clock dial behind a brilliant teal and silver moon with three antique lanterns hanging before it. Wispy clouds filled the background to complete a surreal, hippie vibe. The name Luna and the Lanterns stood out in bold pinkish purple letters along the top, and the album name, *Time and Light,* lived in smaller white lettering at the bottom. She couldn't quite read a faint signature from the original painting in the lower right corner.

"This cover is so cool," AJ enthused. "I wonder who they had do the painting?"

Pearl carefully lowered the needle down onto the LP and a faint, scratchy, rustling sound came through the large speakers on stands in the corners of the room.

"Probably says in the credits on the back," Pearl pointed out.

An acoustic guitar intro began as AJ flipped the album cover over and studied the smaller print at the bottom.

"Cover artwork by Trina," AJ read aloud.

"The drummer," Pearl said, and AJ scanned the other credits.

"You're right. She plays drums, percussion, and sings backup vocals."

A female voice began singing the first verse, so AJ put the cover down and dropped into the pillowy sofa to listen. She pulled her bare feet up and wrapped her arms around her knees. Coop sat on the floor, leaning against the sofa, and nuzzled her toes.

"She's really good," AJ said, reaching down and petting the dog's head.

"Great tone," Pearl agreed, sitting next to AJ.

"Got a touch of that smoky quality. A bit like your voice," AJ pointed out.

"Hasn't got the same power though," Reg said, and winked at his wife.

She smiled in return, but shook her head. "Give her a chance, love. She's only on the first verse, and I don't think this one's a belting song."

The next 35 minutes passed by in what AJ thought was an instant, only briefly interrupted by a brief delay while Pearl flipped from the A side to B.

"You've gotta sing some of those songs," AJ raved, sitting forward, much to Coop's delight. "I love this album."

"Brought back a few memories," her father said from the other sofa. "I recognised several of the songs, but it's been a while since I've heard them."

Reg picked up the album cover and looked at the song titles on the back.

"You did used to play a couple of these, didn't you, Pearl?"

Pearl nodded. "I did. I was only a youngster when the album came out, but I remember finding it amongst my parents' records and falling in love with it when I was a teenager. Glad I'd hung on to this copy, too, or it'd be at the bottom of the sea with so much more of my mum's stuff."

Pearl held back a tear and AJ knew her friend was referring to the container full of her late mother's possessions, which slipped from a cargo ship in a terrible storm. They'd discovered the container's precarious location offshore and dived to recover everything they could, including several pieces of furniture now in the house. But an album cover certainly wouldn't have survived, even if the vinyl had.

AJ fell back into the cushions of the couch and put her hands to her face. "Do you realise what we're looking at here?" she groaned.

"A great album I'd forgotten about," Bob replied.

"Yeah, but I think I know what she means," Reg said, and stared at the back cover, which included a picture of the band.

"Oh," Pearl muttered. "Right. What you found could be all that's left of this poor girl."

"Or anyone from the band," AJ said, dropping her hands to her lap.

"Still unlikely though, isn't it?" Reg responded. "I mean, nothing we've seen suggests their yacht went down near the island, and we know it's not sitting on the seabed anywhere close. Every inch of Cayman waters has been scoured for wrecks, even the deep stuff."

"That's true," Beryl added. "Seems like this particular possibility only came up because you happened to find the floating coffin article."

"Which turned out to be a dead end," Reg said. "Pardon the pun."

AJ rolled her eyes at him. "I hope so. I mean, maybe her family would like closure, if any of them are still around. But I think it'll be even more traumatic hearing about your daughter's or sister's skull showing up after fifty or sixty years."

"That would be a bit gruesome to deal with," Pearl said. "I'm sure the families have processed the loss a long time ago."

"We should have kept looking," Reg said thoughtfully, placing the album cover down on the coffee table. "You know, while we were there."

"On the reef?" Pearl asked.

"No, he means at the *Cayman Compass* offices," AJ replied. "We got excited when we came across the first article that matched what we thought we were looking for. We should have kept going. Who knows, we may have found another three articles talking about bodies floating away from the cemetery."

Reg nodded. "It was my fault."

"I think everyone already assumed that would be the case," AJ replied. "But how exactly was it your fault in this case?"

Reg tried to hide a grin. "It was me who insisted on leaving 'cos I was worried about being gone so long, what with your family here and all that. If I'd listened to you when you said 'screw them, we should keep looking' then we might have found something more."

Everyone laughed. Except AJ, who looked around for something to throw at Reg. He effortlessly caught the soft pillow in one big hand without flinching.

"Anything from Lahaina?" he asked.

"She said tomorrow," AJ replied, but picked up her mobile to check her email anyway.

"I thought the newspaper made their old articles available online," Pearl said, refilling glasses with wine as she walked around the living room.

"Only more recent stories," Reg replied. "Last ten or fifteen years, I think."

"And there's no chance the skull is that recent?" Bob asked.

"We searched the website for any cemetery mishaps," Reg replied. "Nothing came up."

"But the cemetery angle is just a theory, right?" Beryl asked. "You don't have any evidence to suggest the body was once interred."

"That's true," Reg replied. "Although the forensic tests could show trace elements of chemicals used in embalming and what have you. But I doubt they'll have those results for months."

"Hey," AJ said, reading from her phone. "Lahaina sent us something. The email says she's having internet issues at her house, but she managed to download one of the PDFs from the newspaper's server. Looks like it's from the week before the first hurricane."

"That was Hurricane Camille, then," Reg said. "But the week before doesn't do us much good."

"I presume she started there as we asked for the date range covering the events of the two storms," AJ replied. "We need to look at this on a bigger screen."

AJ got up, and Coop followed her to whatever exciting new adventure she was about to lead him on. Which was picking up her rucksack she'd left in the kitchen and returning to the couch. Coop seemed to think that counted as something as he wagged his tail and looked on expectantly when she unzipped the bag.

"As hard as it is to understand, mutt," she told him as she pulled her laptop out, "this doesn't concern you."

"Everything concerns his lordship," Reg said. "Doesn't it, mate?" he added as the dog turned to look at Reg as though he knew he was being discussed.

AJ put her rucksack aside and opened up the computer, petting Coop while waiting impatiently for the machine to boot up. Opening her email, she clicked on the attachment from Lahaina, and looked at the scan of the newspaper from August 1969. Luna and the Lanterns were front-page news that week. An article talked about their arrival on the island with a grainy black-and-white photograph of their motor yacht.

"*Soundwave*," AJ announced. "That was the name of their recording studio boat."

"Clever name," Bob commented.

"I thought so," AJ replied as she scanned the article. "Most of this talks about who they were and how well their first album did in the UK and in America. Apparently, they'd just come from playing a festival in New Jersey."

"Hey, this was August 1969, right?" Reg said. "Wasn't Woodstock around that time?"

AJ opened an internet browser and typed in a search. "August 15th to 18th on a dairy farm in New York state," she read aloud.

"Hurricane was the 14th," Reg responded. "So I guess they didn't go to Woodstock."

Pearl sighed. "Bet they wish they had, as things turned out."

AJ tapped the screen with her finger. "Says here they declined an invitation to Woodstock as they were eager to work on their second album."

"Why did they come to Cayman?" Beryl asked. "Does it say anything about that?"

"Hmmm," AJ mumbled, reading on. "Not really. A few quotes from Luna and this fellow Rollo Fletcher, formerly of the chart-topping Velvet Rollo Band. They both say nice things about Grand Cayman, as you'd expect."

Clicking to the inside pages, AJ found where the article continued. "Hey," she blurted. "Says here the two girls from the band and their bassist played a jam session at a local bar with owner and musician Sonny Watler. He had a place on Seven Mile Beach called Sonny's Soggy Wreck Bar."

"Another good name," Bob said with a laugh.

"I've heard of that bar before," AJ said, trying to recall from where she may have run across it.

"It closed donkey's years ago, before we even came to the island," Reg said. "Used to be where a condo complex went up. Can't recall which one."

"Yeah, but…" Pearl began, but Reg interrupted.

"Hold up, I wasn't done yet, love," he said with a big grin.

"Well, one of you spit it out," AJ urged. "What's the *'but'* bit?"

"Sonny must be 80 years old by now, but he's still alive, last I knew," Reg explained. "And when he was run off Seven Mile Beach, he moved Sonny's Soggy Wreck Bar to the back of George Town."

"That's where I'd heard of it!" AJ yelped, startling Coop, who looked around for whatever threat he needed to ward off.

"Yup," Pearl smiled. "It's still there."

AJ jumped to her feet, which sent the dog into further defensive mode. "Let's go see Sonny Watler!"

Reg laughed, and Pearl shook her head.

"What? Doesn't he own it anymore?" AJ asked.

"Best I know, he does," Reg replied. "But it's not a place most people drop in for their evening tipple."

"What do you mean?" AJ asked. "It's a bit dodgy or something?"

Pearl waved a hand. "I think he had a bit of bother there years ago, but I'm sure it's fine."

"Put it this way," Reg said. "I wouldn't let Pearl play there when she was asked."

"So you actually know this Sonny fellow?" AJ asked.

Pearl nodded. "Not well, but we've met. He seemed like a lovely bloke. And he's a great musician too. I think he's fine with the place having a reputation just to keep the tourists away."

"Then what are we waiting for?" AJ urged. "Let's go see him. If nothing else, he should have a good story about the band visiting."

Everyone turned to Reg. Coop did too, as it seemed like the action was around his owner.

"I could see if Nora could come with us if we need a bobby in tow," AJ offered.

Reg laughed. "That'll have the regulars running for the car park. I'm sure Sonny would appreciate that."

Pearl looked at her watch. "It's gone seven and I've not started anything for dinner yet. You two go see if you can learn anything useful, and I'll throw something together."

"I have a better idea," Beryl said, getting to her feet. "You two run off and play amateur sleuths, and we'll take Pearl to Ragazzi's for dinner. If you hurry, you might make dessert."

AJ groaned. "You'd go to my favourite posh restaurant without me?"

Beryl smiled. "Shit happens when you have better things to do than spend time with your parents, my dear."

Reg laughed, and AJ shot him another glare.

19

Stepping aboard *Soundwave* felt like crossing a line, and Luna let out a long breath before opening the door to the bridge. Having just returned from one of the most enjoyable evenings of her life, she now prepared herself to walk into the black cloud which hung over the luxury yacht. She put a hand on the door before Trina could open it.

"We need to be quiet, okay?"

"Screw him," Trina muttered with a sly grin on her face.

Luna shook her head. "Come on, babe. We'll all pay for it if we piss him off even more."

"You mean you'll pay for it," Trina replied and her mirth was replaced with a scowl. "You can't put up with this anymore, love. We won't put up with it."

She turned to include Panda, but in her tipsy state she'd forgotten their bandmate had last been seen leaving the bar with a young woman.

Luna kept her hand on the door. "Even more so after today with Lord stick-up-his-arse we need to get this album finished as best as we can. And that means keeping Rollo from blowing up every five minutes."

"Alright, alright," Trina moaned, shifting from one foot to the other. "I'll be nice to the prick, but only until the album's done. Now let me in 'cos I'm gonna pee. Your choice if it's here on the floor or in the loo."

Luna swiftly moved her hand.

Quietly opening the door to the studio, Luna wasn't surprised to find Rollo in the control room. He looked up and didn't quite smile, but appeared to be calmer than when she'd left him. She noticed all trace of the glass-smashing incident had been cleaned up as she walked through the dimly lit studio.

"Hey," she said, hanging on the door frame to the control room.

"Hey," Rollo replied as he placed a one-inch reel in the tape storage cabinet and carefully closed and latched the door. "Have a fun evening?"

Luna took a moment to gauge the intent behind his question. She'd fallen for the calmly asked question trick before, only to have her head bitten on when she'd enthused about having a good time. Without him.

"It was nice," she said, playing it safe.

"Where did you go?"

"A bar along the beach," Luna replied, still wary of offering too much. "What's the plan for tomorrow?" she asked, moving the subject away from her evening.

Rollo rubbed his eyes. He looked tired. He sighed before speaking. "Sit down, Luna." He pointed to one of the chairs.

She hesitated, still weighing the situation. The fruity rum drinks Sonny had been feeding her weren't helping her judgement.

"Please," Rollo urged in a soft tone. "Sit down for a minute."

Luna did so. The vibe in the room felt like the day her father had told her that her grandmother had passed away. The air was thick with a strange sense of sorrow. Thoughts of everything they'd built over the past year crumbling raced through her mind.

"I've kept the finances from all of you for several reasons," he began hesitantly, searching for the words. "The first being simply because they're complicated and I've seen too many bands tear themselves apart over money. Especially when they have plenty of dough flowing in after growing up without it. As the band's manager, as well as producer and guitarist, I felt it best to sit down with everyone once we were done travelling all over the place, while we're living from an expense account, anyway."

Luna wasn't sure what to say. It seemed like a perfectly reasonable explanation, but also one a manager fiddling the finances would use. She stayed silent and waited for him to continue.

"As I told you back when we first talked about it, I've had the idea in my head for a studio aboard a ship for years, and adding my royalties from *Time and Light* to my savings, I figured I could finally make it happen. A friend of mine in Florida had already discovered this yacht and negotiated a deal for me, so I began ordering the equipment."

Rollo took a moment to sip from a glass of what looked to Luna like Scotch. He wiped his lips, then continued.

"That's where problems first began to arise. Almost all of this equipment I'd sourced in the UK," he said, pointing to the mixing board and tape machine, then resting a hand on the tape cabinet. "Like the tape storage. I had to have this custom made with a seal to withstand the salt air, humidity, and water in case we dropped it while carrying it on or off the yacht. Ended up being twice the original quote. Then shipping everything to Florida turned out to be a fortune. And on top of that, customs held it, insisting I had to pay import duty despite the fact it was going in a vessel registered overseas."

"You couldn't buy all this gear in America?" Luna asked.

"Probably, or something like it," he replied. "But this was the gear I knew, and I'd already done deals with people on most of it. Anyway, every step of the process took twenty-five to fifty percent more than I'd budgeted, so I wasn't going to be able to cover it all. My bank in England didn't want to know about a loan for a boat in Florida, and the American banks wouldn't touch me, as I wasn't a resident. I'd already shelled out a big wedge, and I was up the creek without a paddle. That's when someone I knew in London suggested I talk to Lord Thorburn. He's a finance guy who'd loaned money for creative projects in the past."

"But he lives here on the island?" Luna asked.

"He has a place here. And another in London, and the family estate in the countryside somewhere. Surrey, I think. Anyway, I met with him and arranged terms for a short-term loan to get us to the point I'd get paid by Polydor for the production."

"But why a date so much earlier than we needed to submit the album?"

Rollo looked at the floor and shook his head. "His Lordship's terms are, let's say, one sided. The interest rate is stout and every week it compounds, so I picked a date I thought we could make. And then Polydor added gigs to the summer tour, then the festival, and of course the yacht upgrade wasn't ready on time either."

Luna thought for a moment. "So, why is Thorburn pressuring you to finish and pay him? Surely he makes more money off you the longer it takes to pay him."

Rollo sat back in his chair and looked at the ceiling. "When I say the terms are one sided, I'm not joking. The initial deadline was actually two weeks ago. The interest rate has gone up each week since. Today was the second deadline which has a penalty, and the interest rate goes up again. And you're right, that just means more money for him. But after this, I have two weeks, with the interest going higher each week, before he forecloses. Which means he takes *Soundwave*."

"Bloody hell."

"Exactly. Which also means we can't finish and get paid."

"He'd really take the yacht?" Luna asked in disbelief. "That doesn't seem like the best solution for him. I bet people aren't lining up to buy a floating recording studio on a luxury yacht."

"They're not, and he'd never get back what's been spent on the yacht and the fit-out," Rollo explained. "But he doesn't care. He'll offload it to a dealer, double the money he lent me, and I'd get pennies on the dollar back from what's left. And no studio. I'll be finished. We'll all be finished." He groaned loudly. "He comes out like a king either way."

Luna stood, but her knees felt weak, so she sat down again. There had to be a solution. "What about our royalties?" she blurted. "I'll talk to the other two. I'm sure they'll agree. Use our shares to pay this wanker."

Rollo visibly tensed.

"Oh no," Luna muttered. "You already did, didn't you?"

He wouldn't look at her. "That's how I've made the payments so far and the penalty today."

"Damn, Rollo. That's not cool, man."

As unsurprised as she was to hear he'd used their money, it still felt unbelievable. An inevitability that she couldn't quite wrap her head around.

"Shit, we're on a boat," she said, standing once more and looking down at Rollo. "What's he going to do if we sail off into the distance? We'll finish the record, dock somewhere, and get Polydor the album. We can sort Lord Swindler out afterwards. At least we'd get the album made."

Rollo sighed, then glanced up. "Did you see that bloke he brought with him?"

"The Kayo guy?"

"Yeah, that guy. What do you think he has him around for?"

"He's his heavy, right? But what's he gonna do? Swim after us?"

"He doesn't have to," Rollo replied. "Thorburn insisted Kayo now stays with us. He's in one of the crew berths."

Luna paced around the control room. "That's ridiculous. How are we supposed to work with that Neanderthal hanging around?"

Rollo just shrugged his shoulders.

"Who the hell calls their kid Kayo, anyway?"

Rollo scoffed. "K-O, Luna. As in, he knocks people out. I doubt that's on his bloody birth certificate."

"Oh," Luna huffed, and dropped back into the chair. "Rollo. What the hell are we going to do?"

"Work as hard as we can and try to finish the album."

"We can do that in two weeks."

"I need ten days to complete the overdubs and mixes, Luna. I've tried to do as much as I could as we went along, but I still need a day per track."

"So we only have four days," Luna groaned.

"Now you see why I was pushing us along," Rollo said.

"At the expense of our music," Luna surprised herself by saying.

Usually, she'd never be so bold. For fear of sounding disrespectful and ungrateful, but recently, also a more physical fear of making him angry. Somehow, that wide canyon between them had narrowed. Despite their age and experience difference, it was Rollo who'd now screwed up, which forced them to stand next to each other instead of her trailing in the wake of whatever he desired.

"Let's call it a night," he said softly, and began powering down the equipment in the control room.

"Okay," she replied. "I need to clean up. I'll see you down there in a minute."

As she turned to leave, he took hold of her arm, and she reflexively flinched. But his touch was gentle, and he eased her to him.

"I wish I could wind back the clock and change all this," he whispered.

"We'll just have to make the best of it," she replied, unwilling to completely let him off the hook.

"I mean," he stammered. "I'm trying to say... there's a lot I wish I could take back."

He gently rubbed her arm where the bruise was finally fading.

"I've not been myself with all this craziness going on."

Luna swallowed and desperately searched for a reply. He hadn't been the same man she thought she'd fallen in love with. In retrospect, she realised he'd never hurt her until near the end of the summer tour for *Time and Light*. Panda had talked her and Trina into dropping acid with him. Things didn't go well. Panda swore they just needed to do it a few times and learn how to steer the trip, but for Luna it had been the worst night of her life. She remembered the paranoia and weird faces with melting flesh far more than a euphoric high.

Rollo was livid with them all. He'd usually drink with them after the shows and occasionally share a joint to relax, but the early-morning phone calls had started, and his mood had changed. After they'd come around in the tour bus, he'd yelled at the three of them, and out of sight of the others, he'd grabbed and shaken Luna for the first time.

It all made sense now. The shift in Rollo had coincided with the studio and yacht plans coming apart. In a brief break between gigs, he'd flown to London for two days while they'd all stayed in Nashville. When he'd returned, his mood had lightened, but only for a week or so. Which was when Polydor added the tour dates. But making sense of the events didn't justify his actions.

"I'm trying to say I'm sorry," Rollo said, filling the void left empty by Luna's inability to find a response.

"Okay," she managed to utter, and he leaned closer to kiss her.

Their lips met, and he squeezed her tightly to him. He was desperate for her to let him know that it would be alright. That they, as a couple, would survive this. That he was forgiven. She sensed the urgency in his body and his heart, wanting her to respond with passion. Needing her to return his feelings. But she couldn't.

He slowly pulled away, and she quivered in anticipation, expecting his anger to consume him once more. But he stood there, with tears forming in his eyes.

"Don't give up on me, Luna," he uttered and the plea floated between them on his exhalation.

She reached up and touched his cheek. He leaned his head into her hand, taking every ounce of physical connection she was willing to surrender. Luna felt a rush of emotions pour through her as though her soul was emitting her truths whether she consented or not. Feelings which came from somewhere hidden inside her and reached deep inside him. Revealing themselves. The feelings she'd been burying underneath a strange blend of excitement and fear.

Rollo gasped in a breath, and took a step back, severing the connection too painful to bear. Luna saw the realisation in his eyes that the chasm he'd created had become too broad to bridge. Whether it had been love, she couldn't be sure, but whatever passion and bond they had shared was now out of reach. Stripped away, one bruise at a time.

"You go ahead," he said, turning away. "I have things to finish up."

20

Following Reg's directions, AJ drove her van into George Town and recognised the building they were looking for at the corner of Eastern Avenue and Godfrey Nixon Way.

"I've driven past this place a million times and never knew the name," she commented, parking out front. "I just remember it being the yellow building."

"This side faces Eastern and a regular part of town," Reg said. "But behind here is Rock Hole Road."

Which AJ knew explained part of the bar's reputation if the patrons came from one of the lowest-income neighbourhoods in town. Grand Cayman was a very safe island, but it wasn't recommended for tourists to walk through places like Rock Hole Road. Just like any town in any country, there was always somewhere best to avoid.

The sign was small and painted on a large old piece of driftwood, mounted above the front door, and AJ wondered if it had come from the original location on Seven Mile Beach. She could tell the lettering for Sonny's Soggy Wreck Bar had certainly been repainted more than a few times.

Most of the cars lined up out front were older models in various states of disrepair, but as they'd easily found a spot to park, AJ figured the place was having a quiet night.

"Blimey," she muttered as Reg opened the front door and held it for her.

Inside, the bar was packed, and chatter and laughter mostly drowned out the reggae music playing from the speakers. Apparently the serious drinkers must walk to Sonny's, or there was a lot more parking out back she hadn't seen. Faces turned from the nearest high-top bar tables and it was immediately obvious that she and Reg were not the place's average clientele. The Cayman Islands were a wonderful melting pot of skin tones, but they were without question the palest in this neck of the woods. Still, AJ knew it was less about colour and more about territory. They were newcomers in a dive bar where fresh faces usually arrived with a regular.

Unperturbed, Reg nodded and smiled at everyone as he pushed through the crowd towards the bar. AJ dropped in line and followed. She didn't find the atmosphere intimidating, as most of the patrons were now nodding in return, but her introverted nature bristled at the focused attention.

"Sonny around?" Reg asked the woman behind the bar.

She was pretty, with long dreads and a ready smile. It was hard to tell in the shadowed and multi-coloured lighting of the bar, but AJ guessed she was in her forties but could easily have passed for thirties.

"I'm not sure he's here," the woman replied as she popped the top of a pair of Caybrew bottles she held in one hand. "Can I get you a drink?"

AJ noticed the bartender glance at the far end of the bar where an older woman served other customers. She had a slight build, grey hair, and a deep tan. With a barely perceptible nod, she communicated with her co-worker.

"Couple of Seven Fathoms over ice, love," Reg replied.

The bartender nodded in response. "I'll see if Sonny's here."

She turned away, but instead of going to look for the owner, the woman poured their drinks and slid them across the bar.

"He'll be out in a minute," she said, and AJ looked down at the other end of the bar, where the older woman was nowhere to be seen.

If the two had communicated again in some way, AJ had missed it, but a few moments later, a man with short, curly grey hair arrived from a back room behind the bar. He looked to be at least seventy, but moved with the ease of a younger man. He smiled when he saw Reg.

"Reg Moore, man. What brings you dis way, brudda?" Sonny greeted them.

"Hi Sonny, I'm impressed you remember me," Reg replied. "This is a good friend of mine, AJ Bailey."

Sonny reached over the bar and shook both their hands in turn.

"Truth be told, Reg, I remember you 'cos you're married to one of da best singers on da island, man. Dat stage in da corner is Pearl's anytime she'd grace us wit her talent." He pointed towards the far end of the bar. "Come down here where it a bit quieter."

Reg and AJ made their way through the crowd packed against the bar to a high-top table at the end, where a reserved sign sat permanently attached to a little stand. They took a seat on the stools once Sonny had joined them.

"You da young lady who found dat submarine a few years back, aren't you?" he asked, looking at AJ.

"Yeah, that was me. With plenty of help from Reg and my first mate, Thomas. I run a dive boat from Reg's dock in West Bay."

"Brave girl from what I read," Sonny said, then turned his attention to Reg. "So what bring you down to see dis ol' man?"

"Hoping to jog your memory from a few years back, Sonny," Reg explained. "Might help us with something we've been looking into."

Sonny laughed. "Good luck gettin' anyting useful outta dis ting," he replied, tapping on his head. "Best I'm good for dese days is keepin' a beat and a few chords."

"Well, it has a musical connection," Reg replied. "So maybe we'll stir the old grey matter."

Sonny smiled. "Okay, try me."

"A band called Luna and the Lanterns spent a few days here on Grand Cayman before they very sadly went missing at sea in their custom yacht. Do you recall anything about that time?"

The old man's expression turned serious for a moment, then slipped into a nostalgic smile. "I hope dat's one of da last memories I ever lose, Reg. Dey were only here a few days, but I got to spend a bit of time wit dem. Had my place at da beach back den." He got up and shuffled behind the bar, picked a framed picture off the wall and brought it back, setting it down facing his guests. "Dat's dem playin' wit me and ol' Clement. Some special guy dat man was, let me tell you."

"Bloody hell, is that you on stage with them?" AJ asked, staring at the faded black-and-white photograph.

"Yes, ma'am. Dat's Luna right dere, and da udder one is Trina, da drummer. Little bundle of fun, dat one." Sonny turned and pointed to a pair of T-shirts pinned to the wall. "She design dat logo for me. Never changed it all dese years. The original drawing she did is on da wall in my office."

"Trina painted their album cover design, too," AJ mentioned.

"Working on one for dat second album when I met her," Sonny said. "Dat little girl could sit down and sketch or paint anyting."

AJ looked at the cartoon-style design of a dreadlocked man playing tall drums with palm trees either side and an old galleon sinking in the ocean behind. Sonny's Soggy Wreck Bar was painted on a piece of driftwood across the bottom of the image, styled after the bar's sign out front.

"The other two band members didn't play with you?" Reg asked. "Weren't there two blokes as well?"

Sonny nodded. "If I remember right, da bassist Panda was dere dat night, and he played some. Mostly, he smoked weed and chased after da local girls. He were a super chill dude. Da udder guy, Rollo Fletcher, he didn't come by, but we met him on da *Soundwave*. Dat was da boat wit a recordin' studio inside."

"You saw the studio?" Reg asked.

"Yes, sir. Clement and me went by. Ended up staying all afternoon and we both played some for da new record."

"No way!" AJ enthused. "That must have been incredible. We were listening to their first album earlier today. They were so good."

"I bet Pearl got a copy of dat album," Sonny said, and winked at Reg. "Dat woman know her music."

"What happened to all the recordings?" Reg asked. "Everything go down with the yacht?"

"Yes, sir," Sonny replied. "Everyting. Damn shame too."

"Why were they out in the storm?" AJ asked. "We read in the archived newspaper about it. They were lost out at sea."

Sonny shook his head. "Can't say I rightly know. Surprise to everyone dey up and left just as dat hurricane start building." His expression saddened, and he looked over his shoulder for a moment before continuing. "Don't tell da missus, but I were mad in love wit dat girl, Luna. She were someting else, man. Knew first time I set on eyes on her dat she were different. She had so much soul when she sang. It was all from da heart. Luna was one gorgeous woman from da outside, but twice as beautiful on da inside, man."

The three sat in silence for a few moments and AJ could tell they'd taken Sonny back in time to a special memory. She wasn't sure whether that was a good thing or a bad thing. Maybe they'd given him a reason to savour a precious place in time, or perhaps they'd taken him somewhere painful he'd tried hard to put behind him.

"What's brought up dis sudden interest in da past?" Sonny asked, seemingly snapping out of his reminiscing.

AJ and Reg looked at each other. She certainly hadn't contemplated the dilemma of the man being so attached to the past, and guessed by the look on his face that Reg hadn't either.

"I take it you don't follow internet news too much, Sonny," Reg said.

The old man shrugged his shoulders. "My daughter handles social media for da bar, if dat's what you mean."

"Is that her we met?" AJ asked.

"Yes, ma'am. I just got da one. Smart girl, too. 'Bout runs dis place nowadays. I'm just here for show," he added with a laugh.

"There's a story that'll be in the *Compass* tomorrow," Reg said. "But was leaked on a cheesy internet news site first. AJ here came across human remains in the water off Cemetery Beach. Been down there sometime best we can tell. Forensics will confirm for sure, but we've been helping the authorities track down old incidents which might explain who it is."

Sonny frowned. "You tink it might be Luna Skye?"

"We have no way of knowing yet, and might never be able to tell for sure," Reg quickly replied.

"But dey female?"

Reg winced and looked at AJ, who frowned in return. She didn't want to explain how the remains which could be of someone Sonny cared for were in fact only a skull with no body.

"Can't tell for sure until they perform DNA tests," AJ said, hoping to move on.

"Dey can't tell from da skeleton?" Sonny pressed.

"They could," AJ replied hesitantly. "But the remains are... incomplete."

Sonny opened his mouth to ask another question, then appeared to check himself.

"Hmm," he muttered instead. "I always thought deir boat had gone down out at sea somewhere. Dey never find any sign of it, you know. Figured you divers woulda come across someting over da years if it anywhere near da island."

"That's a fair assumption," Reg said, and AJ gave him another glare for showing up again when the going got easy.

"How dey gonna figure out who it is?" Sonny asked. "Gotta have DNA to compare to, right? Doubt dey got anyting from anyone on dat boat from back den."

Reg nodded. "That's a very good point, but I think they're a long way off that stage. Once they figure out whether they're male or female, approximate age, and when they died, we'll have more to go on. There's more chance this has nothing to do with *Soundwave* or the band at all."

"And it'll likely be months before any of that comes back," AJ added. "We were looking into the last reports of bodies floating out of the cemetery during flooding, which is how we stumbled across Luna and the Lanterns. Then we saw the connection to you and wanted to talk to you about your experience with the band."

Sonny nodded. "I'm happy to chat wit you two about all dat, but I'd prefer it not become a big ting, you know? Was so long ago."

"Did it make international news at the time?" AJ asked, wondering whether they should check for archives in the US and UK.

"Not like you'd tink. Best I recall," Sonny replied. "Hurricane Camille went on and hit America someting awful. Hundreds of people died. We were still gettin' daily stories about da moon landin' in July and Woodstock was da weekend we had da storm, so lot of udder tings goin' on."

Reg rose from his stool and extended a hand to the older man. "We've taken up enough of your time, mate, but we really appreciate it."

AJ would have preferred to stick around and talk more about the band she was quickly becoming enthralled and fascinated by, but that wasn't an option now, so she stood and shook Sonny's hand as well.

"Yeah, brilliant talking to you, Mr Watler. Thank you."

Sonny laughed. "It's Sonny to my friends, and I'd like to say we are now."

"Then thank you, Sonny," AJ said, and glanced at the T-shirts on the wall. "I don't think my life will be complete without one of your shirts," she announced and took her mobile from her pocket to grab her cash.

"Drinks and a T-shirt are on da house tonight," Sonny replied, reaching to a shelf behind the bar and retrieving a shirt. "On two conditions."

Reg laughed. "Okay, let's hear 'em."

"First. Dis better not be da last time you drop by."

"That's an easy one, Sonny," AJ replied. "I can't wait to come back with my friends, especially to hear some music."

"Live music Friday and Saturday nights and lunchtime Sunday. All local musicians. We mix it up. Wife and I play sometimes too," he replied. "Which brings me to da second condition. Will you ask Pearl one more time if she'd be willin' to jam wit us one night?"

Reg rested a big paw on Sonny's shoulder. "I'll call you and let you know which days she's available."

21

Luna rocked from side to side as though the yacht was being thrust about by the seas. Slowly stirring awake in that dream-like phase which feels like reality, but the conscious brain hasn't quite taken control. A no-man's-land where the Sandman plays his final tricks for the night.

"Luna!" she heard Trina scream, but it wasn't Trina.

A giant greenish-blue beast rose from the roiling seas, shaking the yacht like a bathtub toy, while calling her name as it grinned through razor-sharp teeth.

"Luna. Wake up," Trina insisted, and Luna jolted fully awake.

The boat wasn't rocking. Trina's hand relaxed on her friend's shoulder from where she'd been shaking her out of a deep sleep.

"You're not green," Luna muttered, and sat up.

"I'm a bit red in spots from too much sun yesterday," Trina replied, touching a finger to her bare shoulder, causing her flesh to momentarily pale under the pressure. "Rollo asked me to wake you."

"What time is it?" Luna asked, rubbing her face.

"I don't know. Mid-morning, I think. Late for you."

Luna was always out of bed before Trina, who, in turn, was

always out of bed before Panda. Yet now she realised notes from a bass guitar were coming from the studio above.

"Sorry," Luna mumbled, and swung her legs out of bed. "I couldn't sleep last night."

"Hmmm," Trina replied, raising her eyebrows.

"Oh, no. Not that. Believe me," Luna quickly explained, wondering how much she should share with her best friend.

Who would understandably go bananas if she knew the extent of the situation. Which was probably exactly what Rollo had told himself when he chose not to share details with them over the past few months. But it was still a weak excuse.

"I'll get you a cuppa, babe," Trina said, and was gone before Luna could begin sharing anything.

Moving slowly, she forced herself to the sink, where she splashed water over her face and stared at her tired visage in the mirror. Sleep had indeed eluded her. It felt like hours before Rollo finally came downstairs and she'd pretended to be asleep when he quietly climbed into bed. She'd heard his soft snoring long before she herself had drifted off.

Waiting until Panda was done recording, Luna made her way up the steps and was taken aback to see Kayo sitting on one of the sofas. He acknowledged her with a brief nod. Trina came in from the galley carrying two cups of tea, and Luna gratefully took one. She'd kept herself from looking towards the control room, but when the door opened, she couldn't avoid facing Rollo any longer.

"Morning," he said, and his tone sounded pleasant, albeit a little dry and professional.

Which would be the best scenario Luna could imagine.

"Morning. Sorry I'm late."

"That's okay, but I'd like to record vocals now we're done with bass," Rollo said, then turned to Panda. "I think I still prefer the third version, but we've got plenty on tape to choose from. Thank you."

"Cool," Panda replied and put his bass on its stand. "I'm gonna grab a bite to eat if that's okay?"

Rollo nodded and smiled in return. "Sure."

Luna couldn't fathom what was going on. The situation was too bizarre. Kayo sat there, literally the size of an elephant in the room, yet everyone else seemed to be going about recording like it was business as usual. How had Rollo possibly explained this to Panda and Trina?

"Lord Thorburn asked if Kayo could hang out with us for a few days as he's interested in the recording process," Rollo said, as though he'd read her mind.

"Oh. Okay," Luna replied, playing along.

Kayo glanced up and forced a smile from the sofa.

"Your phone," Trina said, pointing at the control room window, where a light flashed on a telephone.

Rollo went back inside and picked up the receiver from the table beside the mixing board.

"Hello?" he answered, then listened for a moment to whoever on the bridge was calling him. He frowned and then his eyes flicked to Luna. "News to me, but I'll have the girls come out and see you. Thanks."

He hung up and stepped outside the control room once more. "Did you invite someone called Sonny to visit us?"

Luna and Trina looked at each, both sharing the same regretful expression.

"Yeah, I guess we did," Luna said. "He owns the bar we went to last night. Can we show him around for a minute? I promise this won't take long and he's a super nice bloke."

"Bloody good singer and guitar player," Trina added.

Rollo looked at his watch and sighed. "Quickly then," he urged and looked directly at Luna. "You know we need to press on."

She nodded. "I understand."

As she hurried from the studio, Luna made sure the door closed behind them, then pulled Trina aside before reaching the bridge.

"There's loads I need to tell you, but it'll have to be later."

"Is it about that Kayo bloke, and the weird vibe hanging over the studio where everyone's being too nice to each other?"

"Yup, and I'll tell you everything. But for now, what's important is that we need to finish recording this album in the next few days. So we can't afford distractions."

Trina looked forlorn. "Not even sexy local bar owner distractions?"

"Not even sexy local bar owners," Luna replied. "Well, not during recording time, at least. Nothing stopping you after that, as long as you show up ready the next morning."

"Says the bird who slept in," Trina giggled.

Luna rolled her eyes. "Don't remind me. Now come on, we'll give Sonny a quick tour, then tell him we have to get on."

Luna started for the stairs to the bridge, but Trina held her back.

"Define *ready the next morning*? 'Cos I think I'll be able to play drums, but I might not be able to walk straight."

"I mean sober and not hung over," Luna replied.

"That's not why I won't be able to walk straight, babe," Trina said and broke into a huge grin. "I'm betting he's got a huge…"

"Okay!" Luna quickly interrupted, shoving her friend forward. "Spare me the details! Let's go."

Trina laughed as the two of them bumped each other along the narrow passageway.

"Are you telling me you don't want to know?" Trina whispered.

Luna laughed. "No, I definitely want to know everything," she replied as she trotted up the steps to the bridge. "Thank you, Captain," she continued as he greeted them.

Sonny beamed at the girls. "Dis boat is incredible."

"Isn't it cool?" Luna replied. "Come with us and we'll give you a quick tour."

Sonny stepped aside, revealing another man. "I hope you don't mind, but Clement wanted to come see too."

The older man grinned as he waved hello to them.

"Magic, yeah," Trina enthused. "Let's check out the studio."

Luna smiled as she let them pass by and follow Trina, but already knew the tour had almost no hope of happening swiftly. A few days prior, that thought would have brought joy to her heart, as she enjoyed their company, but too much was now on the line.

Trina made introductions, and to Rollo's credit, he was gracious and polite. Prompted, no doubt, by Sonny raving about The Velvet Rollo Band. Kayo was introduced as a friend of the band, and Thorburn's heavy looked on with disdain. Although it seemed to be his default expression, so Luna wasn't certain if he further disapproved of the guests, or was simply observing as he had been all morning.

Luna followed Sonny to the control room as Rollo invited him over to see the equipment, and it didn't take long for Trina to start playing her drums. A few moments later, percussion joined in and Rollo immediately stopped mid-explanation of the mixing board.

They all moved back to the studio. The sound screen had been moved aside and Clement played bongos, complementing Trina's drumming, which sounded to Luna like their track 'Empty Head', but with a different rhythm.

"Dat's it girl," Clement grinned, his hands barely moving yet banging out a range of incredible sounds from the little drums.

"This is crazy," Rollo said.

"Mind if we join in?" Sonny asked, and Rollo smiled.

"Jam away, man."

Luna couldn't believe it. Their new friends had been there less than five minutes, and already the international language of music had thrown all the tension and stress out the window. Pretty soon, they were all playing some kind of instrument and grinning from ear to ear. Except for Kayo. But even the thug was tapping a foot.

When they wound down after ten minutes of non-stop jamming, Panda whooped with joy.

"So cool, man," he said, and pulled a joint from his pocket.

Luna started to panic and was about to say something, but Rollo didn't blink an eye. Instead, he turned to Clement.

"Would you be willing to lay down some percussion on a track or two for us?"

Clement turned to Trina behind the drum set. "Dat's up to my girl, Trina. I ain't here to step on no toes. She play fine, best I seen."

Trina stood up, which allowed her to barely see over her cymbals. "It would be an honour for me to appear on the same record as you, Clement."

The old man shook his head. "Honour's mine baby, honour's mine."

"But," Trina added, stepping out from behind the drums. "I have a condition."

"You do?" Rollo asked.

"Name it, girl," Clement replied.

"You gotta bring your drums in here, 'cos Rollo's gonna freak when he hears those congas."

Clement laughed. "I dare say we can make dat happen, li'l lady."

"I'll go right now," Sonny said, jumping to his feet.

"Make sure you bring that wooden box I was playing," Trina told him before he reached the door.

"Dat's a cajón," Clement said. "Picked dat up from dis guy from Peru."

"I gotta find me a man from Peru with a nice cajón then," Trina laughed and wiggled her eyebrows.

But Luna noticed her friend's attention was on Sonny, who smiled in return. Luna suddenly realised their little exchange irked her, and she couldn't believe she felt jealous. Her own situation was a complete mess with Rollo, so there was no way she was about to compound their woes by chasing a new man. And besides, Trina had already claimed her interest in the Caymanian.

"Okay," Rollo said. "Maybe we can do a few takes with what we have here, and please hurry back, Sonny. We're under a bit of a time element."

"I can help," Panda offered and followed Sonny out the door.

"If I give you a set of headphones and play the songs to you, could you work out that offbeat rhythm you've been playing to fit?"

"I expect so," Clement said. "I done some studio playin' back in Jamaica."

Trina brought her headphones around from behind the drums and handed them to Clement. He pulled his dreadlocks back and slipped them on. Rollo moved a mic in front of the bongos, then returned to the control room and patched cables into the correct slots to record. Trina picked up her sketch pad and continued drawing something she'd already started. Luna peeked over her shoulder at the cartoon-style illustration. It was of Clement playing congas.

Luna smiled and left Trina to her art, joining Rollo in the control room and taking a seat.

"Hear me okay?" Rollo asked into the talkback mic.

Through the window, Luna saw Clement nod.

"Okay, I'm gonna play you the song. Take your time figuring it out."

Clement nodded again, and Rollo flicked switches, pressed buttons, queued up a spot on the one-inch reel-to-reel tape and finally let it play for the old man. Luna slipped on a headset to listen. It didn't take long for Clement to begin tapping away to the recording of 'Empty Head'. He was soon adding a unique layer while being respectful not to overpower the music. Rollo set up a second reel and prepared to record. When the song finished, he rewound to the beginning of the song.

"What you had going at the end was perfect, Clement. I'll play it again and we're recording this time."

"Yes, sir," Clement replied. "Dat Luna girl sure sound good, man. She sung da hell outta herself last night, too."

"Yeah," Rollo replied over the mic. "There's a reason our album's on track to go gold by the end of the year, and it ain't because of me."

Luna looked over at Rollo, but he didn't turn to face her. She wasn't sure he even knew she had a headset on.

"Here we go," Rollo said and started the recording.

Luna slid the chair to the back of the control room, listening, but the music had become a backing track to her thoughts. A mixture of guilt and confusion had her head spinning. Tipping the chair backwards, she closed her eyes and let her hands fall on either side of the arms. Her fingers touched a notepad on top of the tape cabinet to her right. She opened her eyes, and for a moment wondered how one of her spiral notepads had ended up in the studio. She picked it up and quickly realised it wasn't hers. It was full of Rollo's handwriting. Budgets, lists, notes, and as she let the pages flick past her thumb, she soon came to the end of what he'd written. Luna paused on the last page, which had appeared different from the others.

It was. Rollo had written the lyrics to a song in pencil, erasing and rewriting until the page contained a complete song above a bed of faint ghost images of the ideas and smudges which had been the building blocks. It was titled 'Elastic Heart'. Luna read the first line, and her own heart skipped a beat. She swallowed hard and read on. By the end, tears tracked down her cheeks and she knew Rollo had written this song last night, after she'd gone to bed.

Luna slipped the headphones from her ears, not even noticing that the music was no longer playing.

"Rollo," she said, but her voice was hoarse and came out like a whisper. "Rollo," she said louder, and he turned.

"What are you doing?" he responded, taking off his headphones and staring at her holding his notebook.

"This is beautiful, Rollo."

"That wasn't for anyone to see," he said in a defeated tone. "Especially you."

"We *have* to record this," Luna insisted.

He shook his head. "No way. It's like you guys already pointed out. I don't write your style."

"This is different, Rollo," Luna said, leaning towards him. "This is the most beautiful and honest song you've ever written."

"It's not ready," Rollo protested, wiping the back of his hand across his face. "I'm not ready."

"Rollo. We have three more days to make the best music we can possibly put together. Ten tracks that will blow everyone away, and I'm telling you right now, this could be the first single."

He let out a long sigh. "I don't think I can, Luna. You have no idea what losing you means to me."

She held up the notebook. "I know exactly how you feel, babe. I don't know how I'll get these words out, and I don't know how you'll be able to hear them over and over, but I'm telling you, this song will touch the hearts of millions of people. You've written something beyond you and me. This isn't about having a hit record, it's not about fame, and it's not going to even be about us. This song will beat in the hearts of anyone who's ever gone through anything like this. You've done the hard part. You've finally bared your soul in a song. We're now obligated to make it into the best track we can. And we have three days to do it."

Rollo looked into her eyes as she felt the tears running down her face, his own eyes moist. They both rose and threw their arms around each other.

"I love you," he whispered, his voice breaking.

"I know," she replied in sobs.

22

AJ waited for Thomas to release *Hazel's Odyssey* from the mooring buoy, then eased into the throttles and aimed the Newton north. Both morning dives had gone well and, as she'd had two spots open on the boat, her parents had joined her. Thomas looked up from the bow, tapped his chest and then pointed to the fly-bridge. AJ shook her head. She was happy to drive them back to the dock. He flashed a smile and made his way alongside the cabin to the deck, where he'd help the customers dismantle their gear.

"Mind if I join you?" came her father's voice.

AJ turned as he finished climbing the steps.

"Of course not, Dad. We picked the right morning for you to come along, eh?"

"Too right," Bob agreed, gently squeezing her shoulder as he stood beside the helm seat. "I wouldn't mind getting to do a bit more of this."

"Finally pull the trigger on the 'R' word and you could," AJ said, grinning at him.

He smiled in return. "Careful what you wish for, AJ."

"I've been telling you to retire for donkey's years."

"True, but I saw the look on your face the other night when we talked about spending more time here."

AJ winced. She'd never been good at hiding what she was thinking. Her expression usually telegraphed her feelings clearly. Her Nordic friend Nora had the stone-face look down to a science, but AJ had never mastered control over her countenance.

"Sorry, Dad. It was a bit of a surprise, that's all. You know I'd love to see more of you," she said, leaving the key element of the statement unsaid.

Bob laughed. "You know she'd be glued to her computer even more than she is at home, love. I doubt either of us would see much of her. Come to think of it, I bet your mother wouldn't stay here for more than a few weeks at a time."

AJ waved to the crew of one of Reg's dive boats as she gave them a wide berth with their divers still underwater. The wind blew her hair dry as the Newton cut through the slowly building chop and the canopy shaded them from the midday heat.

"I feel terrible even having a conversation about this, Dad. I should be jumping for joy at the idea of you both being around more, and part of me is. But it would also be a big change in my little world." AJ stopped and groaned for a moment. "Bloody hell. I sound like a right tosser. I'm sorry, Dad, I'm just being selfish. Forget I said anything." She smiled and continued in a happier tone. "I can't wait until you're both down here more often!"

Bob put an arm around his daughter. "You're not selfish, my dear. I get it. You've built yourself a wonderful life on the island with a great circle of friends and an impressive business."

AJ raised an eyebrow at him.

He waved a hand at her. "Your mother thinks so, too. She just can't help herself when it comes to business. Believe me, I know. I've built a company from nothing to an eight-figure gross, but based upon Beryl's standards, I've failed miserably every step of the way."

"Which is ridiculous, Dad. It's incredible what you've

achieved," AJ said, then laughed. "Even if I don't understand anything about it."

"That's okay," Bob smiled. "It's boring, corporate, rubbish, but it's what I've known my whole life." He swept his hand out in front of them. "But this is actually living, right?"

AJ nodded. "For me it is, but I understand we're all wired differently. I just wish Mum could accept that."

"Here's the thing with your mother," Bob said, leaning against the console and folding his arms. "Beryl's never been shy to point out ways to improve, whether we're mowing the lawn or negotiating a major deal, and most of the time, she's right. Her suggestions aren't always the most popular way of going about things, and I tend to concern myself with fair relationships over the last penny on a deal, perhaps more than I should. But, as a rule, she has a knack for seeing the important details, which makes her the best at what she does. Where your mum trips over herself is the complimenting side. For her, getting it right is the basic requirement for any task, so she has a hard time saying *well done* when things turn out as she expected them to."

Her father had an amazing knack for making everything sound like it wasn't nearly as bad as it seemed. AJ could still clearly remember when he had delivered the news that her grandfather had passed away. His own father. One of the worst days in either of their lives. At sixteen, she had been old enough to recognise when her dad was hurting inside, and yet he'd talked to his daughter about all the wonderful times they'd shared with Grandad Bailey, and joked about how he'd be telling stories and making people laugh wherever he was on the other side. AJ had cried with joy and despair in equal measures.

"Half the problem is the history, Dad," AJ said as she slowed the boat, turning across the shallower water towards the dock. "It's easy to talk about forgetting everything that's gone on before, but our memories don't have a reset button. Mum and I have a long history of getting on each other's nerves."

Bob chuckled. "You'll find as you get older and CRS takes hold, you'll find it easier to let a few of those things go, especially when you can't actually remember them."

"Reg has an acute case of CRS, according to Pearl," AJ replied. "But he thinks he has a mind like a steel trap. I tell him that's because he can't remember that he forgets all the times he forgot stuff. Which is a classic symptom when you *Can't Remember Shit*."

"I'm telling you, love, getting old isn't for the faint of heart," Bob joked. "My brain's still ready to go see Luna and the Lanterns in concert, but my body doesn't want to leave the recliner."

"Oh, hush up, Dad," AJ countered as she deftly manoeuvred *Hazel's Odyssey* against the open side of the dock. Thomas hopped ashore and tied the lines to the cleats. "You've got plenty of coins left to ride this merry-go-round."

"I hope so," Bob replied. "Just at a slightly slower pace than I used to spin."

AJ let the engines idle for a few moments before shutting them down, then put her arms around her father and gave him a big hug.

"That blood pressure business scared me, Dad," she whispered.

He squeezed her tighter. "Standard system maintenance at my mileage, love. Don't give it a second thought."

AJ took a moment to breathe in the faint but familiar trace of her father's aftershave, mixed with the stronger smell of salty, damp hair. The olfactory stimulation generated a surge of childhood memories of feeling safe, loved, and comforted in his embrace. She kissed his cheek and wiped the back of her hand across her eyes, hoping he didn't notice her tears as she turned away.

Sliding down the ladder to the deck below, AJ began helping a customer with her gear bags.

"Remember to take your kit if you're shore diving. Or leave it with us if your next dive is with us in the morning. Or, if you'd like us to sell it on eBay for a generous commission."

"Seven thirty in da mornin', please," Thomas announced. "We'll see if we can sneak around North West Point if da seas let us."

AJ slipped on her flip-flops, then amid laughter, thanks, and general chatter, she and Thomas walked to the car park, helping carry gear to their clients' cars across the road. Once they'd said their goodbyes and trotted back to the hut, Thomas went behind the little building to collect the air line and manifold to refill tanks.

"Divers were just coming up when we went by *Blue Pearl*," AJ told Reg, who was standing by the door to the hut. "They were on Memorial Reef, so shouldn't be long."

Reg nodded, then they both turned as tyres squealed from the road. A silver SUV pulled down the steep slope of their little car park and jolted to a stop beside them. The driver's door flung open and the woman AJ recognised as Sonny Watler's daughter leapt out.

"What the hell did you do?" she shouted. "You told my paps you weren't talking about all that business to no one!"

The passenger side door opened and Sonny was a little slower getting out than his daughter.

"I'm sorry, love," Reg said, looking puzzled. "I can see you're upset, but I've got no idea what you're talking about."

"Damn reporter came by when we opened at eleven this morning," the daughter shouted. "Asking all about the same people you did."

"Easy now, Tee," Sonny said, coming around the front of the vehicle. "Let's give dem a chance to tell deir side of tings."

"What reporter came by?" AJ asked, stunned that Lahaina would have done that without at least mentioning it.

"Little shit named Carlson," Tee snapped. "Said he writes for some major online news publication."

Reg and AJ both groaned.

"He's a little shit alright," AJ agreed. "We call him The Weasel."

"So why's he coming around bothering Paps?" Tee asked, standing before them with her hands on her hips, looking like she was ready to roll up her sleeves and start throwing punches.

Reg and AJ looked at each other, then back at the woman.

"We've got absolutely no clue," AJ said. "We haven't told him anything. He came by here before we even knew about the band and Sonny. We haven't seen him since."

"Told us he had it on good authority from a source that da remains on the beach were being investigated as possibly one of the band members," Tee ranted. "Can't be a coincidence dat you two came snooping around da night before he shows up."

Reg turned to Sonny. "I am really sorry Carlson came by, mate, but I assure you we didn't breathe a word to him. We stay clear of that wanker and don't tell him anything."

"I can't believe he told you he writes for a major anything," AJ added. "He has an online rumour rag, not a bloody news site."

Sonny held both hands up. "Let's all calm down a step or two, man, and I'm sorry for Tee coming at you both all fired up."

Tee shook her head and didn't look in the least bit sorry, but AJ admired her for sticking up for her dad. Even if it was misguidedly aimed at them. She noticed Thomas had continued dragging the air line down the dock and her mum and dad were staying out of the way on the boat. She had no doubt everyone had seen and heard Sonny and his daughter arriving.

"That's fine," Reg said. "I'd be upset too with Carlson running around flapping his big mouth. Did he give any other indication of where he'd got this idea?"

Tee shook her head. "On good authority from a source. Dat's all he said."

"How would he know about the connection to Sonny?" AJ asked, looking at Reg. "We only stumbled across it from the newspaper archives."

"Guess he looked at the same archive," Tee responded, in only a slightly calmer tone.

"That's the thing," AJ replied. "We have a good friend at the *Compass* who showed us. The older archives aren't public. These are from several predecessors to the *Compass*."

Tee shrugged her shoulders. "He must know your friend or someone else at the paper."

Reg scoffed. "Not likely. They hate that bloke."

"Well, he got the information from somewhere and you two are the ones snooping around on behalf of the police," Tee said.

"Calm down, girl," Sonny said firmly. "Nuttin' we can do 'bout dis now. If Reg Moore says he didn't tell no one, I'm gonna take his word for it, less I shown different."

"Appreciate that, Sonny," Reg acknowledged. "I'll find The Weasel and see what he has to say about all this."

"Best let it be, Reg," Sonny said. "No point making more of dis dan he already tryin' to do."

"Bollocks," AJ muttered, staring at her mobile. "He's already got an article up online."

"Great," Reg groaned. "Sonny, have a seat over here," he said, pointing to the chairs outside the hut. "I'll put the umbrella up. Might as well sit down out of the sun, and AJ can read the article to us."

Sonny nodded and walked over to the wood and canvas folding chair where he sat down. Tee closed the door on the SUV and joined him as Reg put the sun umbrella up. AJ pulled a fourth chair closer to the umbrella to take advantage of the shade, but it caught on the wood decking and pulled from her grip, clattering against the hut.

"Bugger. Sorry," she babbled, putting her mobile down to use both hands to pick up the chair. "What in the world…" she muttered, setting the chair aside and staring at a small black circular device no bigger than an American quarter in diameter.

AJ wiggled it, then pried it from the side of the hut where it had been stuck with a piece of double-sided tape.

"What is it?" Reg asked as AJ examined the device.

She handed it to him and put her fingers to her lips.

Reg frowned and examined the plastic device. He walked inside the hut and returned with a screwdriver. After scraping the tape aside, a quarter turn removed the battery cover on the back and Reg dropped the watch-sized power unit into his hand.

"Is that a bug of some sort?" Tee asked.

"A what now?" Sonny questioned.

"That little bastard," AJ swore, remembering watching The

Weasel leaving the day before. "He planted that when he came by here yesterday morning."

Reg nodded. "I apologise, Sonny, and to you, Tee. Looks like Carlson did find out from us."

"Yeah, but we didn't know about the Sonny connection until yesterday evening, Reg," AJ pointed out. "Only thing we talked about over lunch yesterday was Luna and the Lanterns being here on the island."

"Yeah, I suppose that's right," Reg pondered aloud, then frowned at AJ. "He better not have done…"

"Done what, Reg?" Sonny asked.

"We have to check Reg's house for another one of those devices," AJ said as Reg was pacing around in circles.

"Sorry, Sonny," Reg growled, coming to a stop, his cheeks red. "But I'm afraid I'll be having a word with The Weasel after all."

"I'd say dat's fair, Reg," Sonny replied.

"And believe me, he'll be singing like a bloody canary when I get my hands on him."

23

Rollo had Clement play more percussion with the instruments they had on hand while they waited for Sonny and Panda to return. Luna sat on the couch with Trina, who had finished her drawing for Sonny's Soggy Wreck Bar and was now working on her painting for the new album. Her *Time and Light* cover artwork had featured three lanterns as she'd created the painting before Rollo had become an official member. For the new design, Luna had warned her to include a fourth lantern or the fallout would ruin any enjoyment stemming from Trina's creativity. Trina had pointed out that technically there were only two lanterns plus Luna before, so three now would actually be correct.

"Luna and the Lanterns," she emphasised.

"That maybe so, but we're adding one from whatever you did before, which makes four," Luna insisted, then smiled. "But I love this cover, babe," she enthused, stealing another peek. "The compass rose is the perfect vibe for how we're recording this album."

"*Path and Purpose*," Trina replied. "That's what I'm calling the painting. We'll have to see if his Lordship will let us use it for the album name."

"*Path and Purpose,*" Luna echoed. "I freakin' love it. We'll just start calling the album that, and after a while it'll be too formidable not to be the title."

"Especially if you dream up a song by that name," Trina urged.

Luna rolled her eyes. "In the few days we have left?"

Trina groaned. "Yeah. I keep forgetting that's hanging over our heads, and then I see Frankenstein sitting over there," she said, nodding towards Kayo. "Such a perfectly creative environment."

Stu brought lunch into the studio in the form of sandwiches, which Kayo swiftly tucked into and ate double his share. So Stu made more. Shortly thereafter, Sonny and Panda arrived and Luna and Trina helped them haul a variety of instruments onto the yacht, including the cajón which Trina promptly sat upon and excitedly played, telling Rollo how the album couldn't be made without it. He agreed, although somewhat less enthusiastically.

"I'm not sure what all that was about earlier," Trina whispered to Luna when they sat down to eat another sandwich. "But the weird and tense vibe is back."

Panda shuffled over closer. "Doesn't help we have Thorburn's hitman hanging out with us."

"I know, I'm sorry," Luna replied.

"It's not your fault," Trina scolded her. "It's your boyfriend in there," she added, nodding toward the control room.

Rollo was busy playing back recordings and editing the best sections together.

"It's partly my fault," Luna confessed. "I sort of broke up with him."

"Finally!" Trina blurted, and Luna elbowed her friend.

"Shush, girl, you'll make it worse if he thinks we're all talking about him."

"He's not stupid. He has to know we talk about everything," Panda pointed out.

"I know, but it's one thing knowing that, and another watching it going on right in front of you," Luna replied. "Besides, we have to finish the album, so whatever we can do to improve his mood, the smoother all this will go, and maybe we'll get the sound we want."

"Fine, but let me know if I need to drop a lantern off this bloody cover," Trina said with a grin.

"It'll be four," Luna assured her. "But here's the other thing," she continued, carefully removing the sheet Rollo had allowed her to tear from his notebook. "Take a look at these lyrics."

Trina held the page so she and Panda could both read the words and Luna waited for their reaction.

"Babe, this is awesome. When did you write it?" Trina asked. "Do you have a melody figured out?"

Luna waited for Panda to finish. He smiled at her.

"I didn't write these lyrics," Luna admitted. "Rollo wrote this last night."

"Of course," Trina sighed. "Makes sense now. This is so much better than his other stuff."

Luna nodded. "That's what I told him."

"Who knew?" Trina giggled. "All you had to do was drive an axe into his heart for him to finally write meaningful lyrics. That's why I told you to break up with him ages ago."

Luna rolled her eyes.

"So, what's the melody?" Panda asked again.

"He didn't have much, just a strumming rise and fall," Luna said. "Kinda slow ballad."

"Do we have time to make this into a song?" Trina questioned. "Time might be on The Rolling Stones' side, but it's not exactly on ours."

"We have to," Luna said firmly, and the other two nodded their agreement.

"If we can figure out a decent progression, this could be really good," Panda said, and glanced up at the control room. "He onboard with making this happen?"

"Somewhat," Luna replied hesitantly. "It's all a bit raw for us both. We need to get Rollo to relax like the other day, and I think we can get our ten best songs together in time."

"This sidetrack on percussion is killing us time wise," Panda pointed out.

"Yeah, but it's too good not to use," Trina quickly replied. "And Clement throws down so fast, every song is done in two or three takes."

"Okay," Panda said, leaning closer. "You two work on the melody. I'll work on Rollo. Cool?"

The girls both agreed, so Panda picked up a couple of the few remaining sandwiches and sauntered towards the control room while Luna waved to Sonny.

"Bring my acoustic guitar over, please," and when he did, she strummed the chords Rollo had played for her.

"That's okay, but a bit boring," Trina commented.

"You building a new song?" Sonny asked.

"Yeah," Trina replied. "Let me get the cajón."

Luna handed Sonny the lyric sheet, which he quickly read through while Trina brought the wooden box closer. Sitting atop she began gently tapping the face with her palms, trying a few different-paced beats. Starting slowly, she picked up the tempo as Luna softly sung the words.

"There, babe," Luna said when the rhythm felt right.

"Dat openin' line is someting else, man," Sonny commented. "Kinda like da beginnin' of a hit song, I'd say."

"Pretty powerful, huh?" Luna said, then sung the opening again, strumming the guitar. "But Trina's right. We need a stronger melody."

"May I try?" Sonny asked.

"To sing it or play the guitar?" Luna asked.

"I ain't gonna try to sing next to you, girl," Sonny laughed. "But if you don't mind, I have an idea for da tune."

Luna handed him her guitar. "Lay it on us," she said with a smile.

Sonny began plucking chords instead of strumming and while he figured out the progression he'd come up with in his head, Luna glanced over to the control room. Through a haze of smoke, she could make out Rollo, Panda, and Clement, passing a joint around and laughing with each other. She felt a surge of hope that everything might work out after all. As desperate and ridiculous as the situation seemed, with so little time before their entire career could be pulled out from underneath them, Luna knew they could pull this off if everyone worked together.

"That's cool, man," Trina was saying and Luna realised Sonny was playing a melody.

It sounded much better than the original outline Rollo had come up with, which was more of a few basic chords he'd strummed. As Sonny played the progression again, Luna sung the first verse.

"Again, and try going up on the last note of the second and fourth lines," she suggested.

Trina slapped a soft beat along with them and they continued into the second verse.

"Nice, Sonny," Luna enthused. "Now, what do we do with the chorus?"

"Hey everyone," Rollo's voice came from the doorway to the control room. His eyes looked hazy. "Captain just called down. We have to move as someone else is coming into dock, or something like that. But we can use the tender to run anyone ashore later."

"We're in no hurry, sir," Sonny said with a broad smile. "Dis is fun for us."

"I wasn't told anything about the boat moving," Kayo said, getting to his feet from the other couch. "I need to check with the boss first. We ain't going nowhere until he says it's okay."

"Better hop off and go ask him," Rollo replied, doing a poor job of hiding his grin. "But the captain doesn't have a choice, so the boat's moving with or without you."

"Where to?" the thug asked, making for the exit door.

Rollo shrugged. "Just off the beach, I think. Wherever we can anchor."

Kayo flung the door open and headed for the bridge.

Rollo turned to Luna. "What were you just playing?"

"What did you think of it?" Luna asked.

"I only caught the very end," Rollo replied.

"Give this a listen," she said, and nodded to Sonny and Trina, who counted them in.

The three played through the first two verses again, with Luna singing in full voice. When they were done, they all looked over at Rollo. His face was blank and unreadable. Luna wasn't sure whether he didn't like what they'd played, or hearing his lyrics again had upset him.

"Play it on electric," he said after a few moments, and ducked back into the control room.

"I guess he didn't tink too much of dat," Sonny whispered.

Trina laughed. "You'll know if Rollo doesn't like it, believe me. He'll tell you."

Sonny smiled at Trina, then turned to Luna. His eyes sparkled with joy, and she wondered if any of the man's pleasure was because of her. Quickly shoving those thoughts aside, Luna kicked herself for being so silly and inconsiderate. Of Trina, and of Rollo. Their relationship might be over, but they still had to work together, and she'd be letting the others down if the break-up interfered with them getting the album finished.

"Here," she said, taking the acoustic guitar from Sonny. "Grab my Les Paul and try the verses on electric while I mess about with the chorus."

As Luna began humming the chorus and searching for the right notes, she felt the vibration of the yacht's engines rumble through the floor. Five minutes later, she'd figured out a progression she liked, and felt the familiar sway of the vessel as it moved through the ocean.

"Dat's a strange sensation, man," Sonny said, looking up from the guitar. "Like playing a sunset cruise gig, I suppose."

"But way cooler," Trina said, and gave him a wink.

"Way cooler, no doubt," he agreed, and Luna noticed the spark between the two was finally catching light. She hoped so. Trina deserved to have fun and Sonny seemed like a great guy. Luna was the odd one out who was complicating the situation, but perhaps it was all working out as it should.

The studio door opened and Kayo stomped back in with a grim expression on his face. Everyone quickly turned away and ignored him as he took his spot on the couch once more. He didn't say a word, so apparently Captain Garrison had convinced him there was little choice in the matter.

The afternoon soon flew by with Clement playing his assortment of percussion and Trina adding the cajón on any track Rollo would allow. When she wasn't slapping rhythm on the wooden box, Trina joined Luna and Sonny on the upper deck where they worked on 'Elastic Heart' under the shade of a large sun umbrella.

There had been so many moments in the past year when Luna had pinched herself to believe her life had become so different and exciting. But sitting atop a luxury yacht moored off a Caribbean island while she wrote songs felt both surreal and a snapshot in time she would remember forever.

Panda joined them and added his thoughts to the new song, and after a few hours, they decided it was ready to present to Rollo. Luna was nervous. After singing the words over and over again, she'd become numb to the meaning and the pain behind the song, but it would be a fresh wound for Rollo. They went downstairs and, with the recording light off, entered the studio. Kayo was the only one in the recording room, and he'd fallen asleep on the couch. Clement was in the control room, where Rollo was busy balancing the new percussion recordings into the mixes.

"Want to hear a run-through on 'Elastic Heart'?" Luna offered.

Rollo looked up and took a deep breath. "Sure. Give me five minutes to finish what I'm working on."

"Perfect," Luna replied. "We'll get set up."

"How do we want to do this?" Trina asked when Luna returned to them. "I'd have to figure out the drums, which might take a while."

"Let's play it just like we did on deck," Luna replied. "We'll just be mic'd, so we'll need to set one for the cajón."

"You want me to play?" Sonny asked in surprise.

"Of course," Luna replied. "Can't promise he'll have you play on the recording, but for what we're doing now. If you don't mind?"

"I don't mind at all," Sonny laughed, but then glanced at his watch. "But I do have to go soon and open da bar."

"Okay, I'll ask the captain to lower one of the tenders while you set up," Luna said and left for the bridge.

When she returned, Rollo was sitting at the mixing desk with his chin resting on his hands, waiting. Luna felt butterflies in her stomach as though she were going on stage at a big concert. Even Kayo had woken up.

"Whenever you're ready," Rollo said over the studio speakers, and Luna slipped on a headset and sat on a tall stool by the vocal microphone.

Trina counted them in and the four of them ran through the version they'd conceived of 'Elastic Heart'. When they were done, Luna caught Rollo staring at her. His eyes were moist.

Clement clapped his hands. "Dat's a fine tune."

Rollo nodded. "That'll work," he agreed.

It was hardly a glowing endorsement, but Luna knew there were far deeper emotions going through the man than his words suggested.

"Trina, why don't you work on the drums while I see Sonny and Clement off?" Luna offered, then turned back to Rollo. "They have to go open their bar, but I'll be right back so we can start recording."

"Here," Trina said, and handed Sonny the drawing she'd been working on. "Just something fun I thought you might like."

Sonny examined the illustration and smiled, showing it to Clement. She'd added palm trees around the conga player and the ocean in the background, which included an old galleon sinking in the water.

The old man laughed. "You left off all my wrinkles, and I tank you for dat."

"Dis is so cool," Sonny beamed. "Thank you. My bar have a logo now."

Rollo came out of the control room and walked over to Kayo. "Why don't you run ashore with them so you can speak to Thorburn? Captain told me we have bad weather coming so we have to find a dock, but we can't go back into George Town. He's trying to find us an alternative spot large enough to dock, otherwise we'll have to sail south, away from the storm."

Kayo frowned and stood. He towered over everyone else, which he clearly used as intimidation.

"My orders are to stay on the boat."

Rollo shrugged his shoulders. "Hope you brought plenty of underwear, then. We might be at sea for over a week."

"That wasn't the plan," Kayo replied. "You can't leave the island."

Rollo scoffed. "You'd better tell Thorburn to hop on the blower to someone higher up the chain than I can reach. If he can redirect storms, he can have at it and we'll stay right here."

Kayo's expression turned increasingly perplexed and annoyed. Decisions clearly didn't top his list of talents.

"Mr Thorburn has to give the okay before you can go anywhere," he said.

"Then go see what he says," Rollo rebutted. "The tender will wait for you."

The thug chewed the idea over in his mind and Luna watched veins pulse in his granite-like forehead.

"If this boat moves before I'm back, then you'll find out the hard way what happens when you cross Mr Thorburn. Understand me?"

Rollo held up both hands. "We're trying like crazy to meet all Mr Thorburn's demands. You've seen how hard we're working. Hurry back and I'm sure the captain will have options by then."

Kayo nodded.

"If you wouldn't mind helping Sonny and Clement with their instruments," Luna suggested. "This will go much faster."

"We'll leave the cajón," Sonny said. "It's mainly the congas we need for tonight."

Kayo shook his head and walked out of the studio, indicating he wasn't about to help with anything, and Rollo quickly pulled Luna aside.

"This is our chance," he whispered.

"For what?" Luna asked.

"To make a run for open water."

"Oh. Right," she stammered, having forgotten about her own suggestion. "I guess it is."

24

Sonny and Tee left Pearl Divers' dock in a better mood than when they'd arrived, at least towards Reg and AJ. But now it was Reg's turn to be raging mad.

"We should call Detective Whittaker and tell him about this, Reg," AJ urged as her mentor tossed the little listening device up and down in his hand. "And we probably shouldn't be putting our fingerprints all over that thing."

"Police got better things to do than deal with this rubbish," Reg muttered. "Come on. Drive me to the house and we'll check it for any more bugs."

AJ looked down the dock to where Thomas was finishing the tank fills with Bob's assistance. Beryl was out of sight, but probably in the shade under the fly-bridge.

"I need to do something with the parental units, Reg," AJ said, turning around, but Reg was already standing by her van.

She held up a finger to him, indicating she needed a minute, and jogged down the dock.

"Thanks, Thomas. I'm sorry I abandoned you."

"No worries. Almost done, boss."

"That all sounded a bit heated," Bob said, stepping to the dock.

Her mother appeared, and Bob held out a hand to assist her out of the boat.

"Yeah, we need to run around for a bit and take care of this mess," AJ replied. "Can I drop you at the cottage first?"

Bob waved her off. "It's a short walk and a lovely day. In fact, we'll just stroll along the beach. Maybe grab lunch on the way."

"Okay, thanks. And sorry, I'll be back as soon as I can," AJ said and looked up at Thomas.

"Go, boss," he said before she could get a word in. "I got dis. See you in da mornin'."

"Thank you, thank you, thank you," AJ gushed.

"You'd better get going," her father said, and nodded towards the car park.

Reg was standing with his arms crossed, glaring at her.

AJ cringed. "Yeah, someone definitely tinkled in his breakfast cereal this morning. I'll see you later."

She jogged past one of Reg's boats, which was getting ready to leave for their afternoon trip, and hurried to the van.

"We need an address for Carlson," Reg greeted her, then hauled himself into the passenger seat once she'd unlocked the doors.

"Check his website," AJ replied as she started the van.

"That'll be his PO box, won't it?"

"Probably," AJ replied, realising he was right.

The island didn't have post delivery, so everyone had a PO box of some description, either through the post office itself or an independent location who offered them.

"Call Nora," Reg grunted.

"Umm, we kinda already used that favour," AJ pointed out.

Reg frowned. "Bollocks. Call her. Tell her what's going on and she'll do it."

AJ knew he was right. Her concern was more about getting too many people involved in something she figured the police should handle. Of course Nora was the police, but she didn't need asking twice to go rogue on cases, and AJ didn't want to be the one to land her friend in more trouble than she already caused for herself. Nora had passed her detective training and was waiting for a position to open up. Which meant she needed to keep out of trouble.

"Call her," Reg growled again.

"Alright, alright," AJ muttered. "I'm also driving here. You could call her, you know."

Reg emitted a sound akin to what AJ imagined came from a grizzly bear the moment before it tore its prey apart.

Waiting for several cars to pass at the T-junction with West Bay Road, she quickly dialled Nora and put the call on speaker.

"Hey," Nora answered, and AJ could tell by the traffic noise in the background that they were also on the police car's speaker phone.

"Could we please beg another favour from you?"

"*Nei*," Nora replied.

AJ sighed. "It'll only take a minute, Nora, I swear."

"Hello, AJ," came Jacob's voice, filling the silence left when Nora didn't respond.

"Hi, Jacob. Sorry to bother you both while you're on duty."

"No problem. We just cruising our route just now. What do ya need?"

"That little wanker Sean Carlson put a bug on my hut at the dock so he could listen in on us," Reg ranted. "And we think he put another one in my house. I need his home address."

AJ looked over at Reg and smacked him on the arm. "So why couldn't you call her?" she hissed.

"I don't know that we should do dat, Mr Moore," Jacob said hesitantly. "Sounds like someting you should be reporting."

"That's what I've been trying to tell him," AJ said, rolling her eyes.

"Look up the address," Nora ordered.

"We really shouldn't," Jacob whispered, but AJ could still hear him. "We can't have him goin' by and doin' who knows what to da guy. He needs to report dis to da police."

"He just did," Nora replied firmly. "Look up the address. Carlson is a *drittsekk*."

Jacob mumbled a few complaints under his breath, but the tapping of keys let AJ know he was looking up the information. He read off the address and Reg noted it down on the back of a Mermaid Divers sticker he found in the glove box.

"Appreciate it," Reg said.

"What does he drive?" Nora asked.

"It's a little white piece of rubbish," AJ said. "I saw it the other day."

"Jacob?" Nora urged, and AJ realised she'd been asking her partner as he was looking at the DMV file on the computer in the patrol car.

"He has a 2008 Toyota Corolla registered," Jacob said.

"Okay," Nora said, and hung up.

AJ pulled into the driveway at Reg's house and parked. "Apparently Nora was done talking to us," she laughed.

"That's what I love about that girl," Reg said, opening the door. "No bullshit."

Pearl opened the front door and Coop bounded over to greet Reg, furiously wagging his tail. After one lap around the big man's legs and a quick pet, he raced around the van to meet AJ. Rolling on his back, the dog wriggled around while she scratched his belly.

"What are you two doing back here?" Pearl asked, giving her husband a kiss on the cheek.

"Looking for bugs," Reg replied gruffly, and walked inside the house.

"What is he talking about?" Pearl asked AJ. "I haven't seen any bugs. No more than usual, anyway."

Grand Cayman was a tropical island, so a variety of insects came with the heat and humidity, but air-conditioned homes weren't usually their favourite place to reside. Ants were one of the main critters to keep an eye out for.

"Not the creepy-crawly type bugs," AJ explained. "The secret agent type."

"In our house?" Pearl asked in shock. "He thinks someone broke in and planted one?"

They both followed Reg inside, with Coop on their heels.

"We found one on the hut at the dock," AJ said. "Pretty sure Carlson planted it there when he was talking to you the other day. He went by Sonny's bar this morning, asking about Luna and the Lanterns and suggesting the human remains might belong to one of the poor buggers who went down in their yacht."

They walked into the living room where Reg was lifting, moving, or looking behind every item he could reach. Coop nudged AJ's leg in search of her attention, and she reached down and stroked his head.

"He was snooping around the hut when I got there the other day," Pearl said. "And your name for him is spot on," she added, looking at AJ. "He does remind me of a weasel. It's those beady eyes always looking at everything except your face."

"I don't think he'd have the balls to break into the house, Reg," AJ said. "He's sneaky and underhanded, but I don't see him being brave enough to risk being caught breaking in somewhere."

"I haven't noticed anything out of the ordinary," Pearl said. "I don't know how anyone could get in here without smashing a window or jimmying a door."

Reg paused his search. "Then explain to me how he knew about the connection to Sonny."

"You said he'd bugged the hut," Pearl replied. "We were sitting around talking about it."

"Not the Sonny part," AJ explained. "That was here."

"Oh," Pearl murmured, looking around her living room. "Now I've got a bad case of the willies."

AJ knelt down to the absolute delight of Coop. His lips curled back into a smile which could easily be mistaken for a snarl if someone didn't know the mutt. His wagging tail sweeping the tiles was the other giveaway.

"How about you sniff the bug out, huh?" AJ said as she scratched his head, then moved her hand under his chin. "You must be part sniffer dog of some sort. You've got a slice of just about every breed on the planet... what the bloody hell..." she blurted, interrupting herself. "Hey, Reg. The Weasel didn't need to break into your house."

"No way," Reg groaned. "My bloody dog is a double agent."

AJ pulled the listening device from Coop's collar where it had been stuck and now clung to strands of hair.

"Sorry, mate," AJ apologised, attempting to hold the dog's hair while she freed the bug.

"I'm so sorry," Pearl sighed. "He made a point of fussing Coop at the dock. He must have done it pretty sharpish, 'cos Coop didn't want anything to do with him, and he's usually everyone's best friend. The bugger planted both those bugs right under my nose."

"Not your fault, love," Reg said, quickly defending his wife. "We don't call the little twerp The Weasel for nothing."

He took the bug from AJ and held it up. "I hope you're listening, you tosser. I'm coming for you. You hear that? I'm coming."

He stomped to the garage and returned a few minutes later with the battery removed from the device.

"What did you warn him for, you pillock?" AJ moaned. "Now he'll be even harder to find."

"If he's been listening, he heard all our goings-on looking for a bug, so it doesn't matter. Besides, we'll find him," Reg snarled, heading for the door. "We're looking for a weasel who just wet his trousers. Can't be too many of them in the Cayman Islands."

Pearl shook her head. "Oh, dear. Don't let him do anything stupid, AJ."

"Like I can do anything about it," AJ replied, throwing her hands in the air as she followed Reg to the van. "But it should be entertaining. For everyone not named Sean Carlson, that is."

It took less than fifteen minutes to drive from Reg's house in West Bay to Park View Court condos just outside of George Town. The complex was relatively new, and while they were tucked away between the bypass and West Bay Road, they had easy access to Seven Mile Beach and local shopping. Rents had been steadily increasing all over the island, and AJ was surprised Sean Carlson could afford a place like this from a local internet news site income.

"These can't be cheap," she voiced, driving slowly through the complex, looking for the right unit number.

"Could be family money," Reg said. "I don't know if he has a day job or if spreading bullshit on the internet is his full-time gig."

"Might be," AJ replied. "He has enough subscribers that he'll be making decent money from the ads on the site."

She pulled past the condo, which was a unit in the middle of a block, and parked in a visitors' space.

"I don't see his car," she noted as they got out. "Bet he was here until you threatened him. Probably on a plane to Thailand now."

"Job done then," Reg replied. "Good riddance."

They walked up the steps, and Reg hammered on the front door with his beefy fist. They waited, but no one came and they couldn't hear any movement inside. AJ walked around the tiny front garden to the window and peered inside. The furniture appeared to be a mishmash of second-hand bargains thrown into the same room. At the far end, she could see the dining area was being used as an office, and a triple monitor set-up rested on a metal-framed desk. The lights were off and she could see no signs of movement.

"Probably saved you from a lengthy trial and a few years doing porridge," AJ said as they walked back to the van.

"Nah," Reg replied. "They'd never find the body."

AJ laughed, but was glad The Weasel wasn't home. Reg was a gentle giant, unless anyone messed with his family, and Carlson had definitely crossed that line. Her mobile rang as she climbed into the van, so she started the engine and took the call through the vehicle's hands-free system.

"Hey Nora," she answered, seeing the caller ID.

"Where are you?"

"North side of George Town. Why? What's up?" AJ asked.

"Reg with you?" Nora asked, and it sounded by the vehicles rushing by that she was outside of her car.

"I'm here," Reg replied.

"Come to the petrol station by the four-way stop."

"Okay," AJ replied hesitantly. "What's going on there?"

"I have a 2008 Toyota Corolla pulled over for rolling the stop sign," Nora replied. "I have to check the vehicle for contraband and write a ticket. Probably take me ten minutes."

"Atta girl!" Reg said and slapped the dashboard. "We'll be there in nine."

25

Sonny helped Clement carefully climb aboard the tender, which was one of the lifeboats they'd practised lowering earlier in the trip. Luna looked around at the calm turquoise water and people lying on the beach in the distance, and found it hard to believe a storm was approaching. Lifting her eyes across the low island to the horizon, she finally noticed darkening skies to the north and east, but it still seemed unimaginable that danger lurked on such a beautiful evening.

"Thank you both again, and we'll let you know where we get moored for the storm," Luna said to Sonny as Kayo gingerly stepped aboard. "Hopefully we'll be able to keep working."

Sonny smiled. "It'll pass in a day or two. Plenty of time."

Luna forced a smile in return, but her eyes caught Kayo looking at her sternly. If only Sonny knew. This would probably be goodbye, as she doubted they'd be able to come back anywhere they might run into Lord Malcolm Thorburn. With a quick wave, Luna turned and went inside before anyone saw the sadness she knew her face betrayed. For Sonny, Clement, the Soggy Wreck Bar, and for the island as a whole. She would miss it all, and the thought she'd never be able to return felt devastating.

Rollo was waiting for her in the studio, and the moment Luna returned, he immediately led her to the bridge.

"They're heading for shore?"

"Just about to," Luna replied.

"Are you sure Sammy understands he's to drop them and come back as soon as Kayo's out of sight?" Rollo asked in the hallway.

"You told him and I told him again," Luna confirmed. She rested a hand on Rollo's arm, holding him back from climbing the steps to the bridge. "I'm scared, Rollo. Are you sure this is the best way?"

"It was your idea," he pointed out.

"Yeah, but it's one thing saying it, and another doing a runner on a bloody gangster, isn't it?"

Rollo shrugged his shoulders. "This way we'll get the record done and face Thorburn with money to pay him. He'll take the money over the yacht he'd have to deal with selling."

Luna couldn't shake the bad feeling in her stomach, but didn't have much choice at this stage. There was no radio on the tender, so they couldn't tell Sammy a change in plan, even if they wanted to. Rollo slipped away from her hand and mounted the steps to the bridge, so Luna followed.

"What are our options, Captain?" Rollo asked Garrison, who had several nautical charts spread out before him.

"I wish we could pull back into Hog Sty Bay where we came from, but according to the port authority, that's not an option. Their inter-island freighter took our spot."

"What if we started back for Miami?" Rollo asked.

Garrison looked at him quizzically. "I thought you wanted to stay here for at least another week or two?"

"Just looking at options," Rollo replied.

Luna gazed out the window of the bridge to see the tender motoring towards George Town where Sonny had left his uncle's car. The figures sat crowded in the little boat amongst the instruments.

"We'd have to leave immediately to get out front of the storm," the captain replied, rubbing his chin. "But I'd advise against that. I can't guarantee we'd outrun the weather."

"But we could head farther west and dock in Mexico," Rollo said, pointing to the Yucatan Peninsula on the chart.

"They think the storm is turning north over Cuba," Garrison countered. "Which would give us a bumpy but achievable run around the west end of Cuba ourselves, but then we'd meet the storm on the other side of the land mass. If they're wrong and it stayed west or even turned slightly south, we'd be caught in it."

Rollo sighed and thought for a moment. "We need five days away from Grand Cayman to complete this album, and then a major port from which I can air-freight the master tapes to the UK."

"We could head east and dock in Jamaica," the captain offered. "That's away from the storm, and you should be able to find air-freight out of Kingston. Or we can return to Miami that way. It's the longer route, but you're looking for five days at sea. We can make it all the way to Miami in less than five days, including a refuelling stop."

"That might be our best option," Rollo agreed.

"Latest predictions show this storm has the potential to become a tropical storm or even a hurricane," Garrison added. "If we can't find safe harbour, then our best bet is to run away from the weather."

"It's decided, then," Rollo replied. "When Sammy returns with the tender, we need to leave immediately."

"Right away, Mr Fletcher?" Captain Garrison asked. "I'm afraid we're not provisioned for that length of journey. Stuart usually stocks fresh food the day before we leave."

"I thought we always had supplies for several weeks out of port?" Rollo questioned.

"We do, sir, but that's canned and dried foods, not fresh fruits and vegetables."

Rollo scoffed. "We'll manage, Captain. We can stop in Jamaica if need be. Please ready the yacht for a rapid departure as soon as Sammy is back."

"As you wish, sir," Garrison replied and glanced at Luna.

She wasn't sure quite what he was looking for from her, so she turned away. Perhaps he needed affirmation that the whole band was happy with the decision, but she couldn't be enthusiastic about it. Even if it was what they needed to do, Luna was still disappointed and frustrated they'd put themselves in this position. That Rollo had put them in this position.

"Let's work until Sammy gets back," she said and started down the steps for the studio. She needed the separation of the wall to the control room to keep her from lashing out at her now ex-boyfriend.

The afternoon had been a breath of fresh air for her. The joy of creating music with people she loved to be around. Rollo had provided the lyrics which had become the backbone of a wonderful collaboration, but in typical fashion, he'd turned the day on its head.

Trina was ready, so Luna was able to take her guitar to the upper deck and try to repeat what Sonny had played while Rollo recorded the drums. Right away, she noticed the ominous clouds in the distance were already closer. To the west, the sun was beginning to set, throwing gorgeous yellow and orange hues across the horizon and shooting colourful rays past distant clouds. The two polar opposite views were a startling reminder of how the weather could shift in the blink of an eye.

Thirty minutes later, with the sun dipped below the deep blue ocean, Luna watched streaks of lightning crack the darkness to the north and east. The usually calm west-side water was beginning to rock the big motor yacht, and she searched the water for the tender. Maybe she could see the white curls of disturbed water from the bow of a boat, but couldn't be sure it was theirs. She hurried down to the studio and waited for several minutes until the red recording light went out.

"The weather is turning nasty," she announced nervously to Panda and Trina.

"Is Sammy back?" Trina asked, although Luna didn't think anyone but Rollo knew the plan to abandon Kayo.

"I think I saw it approaching, but it's getting dark. It was hard to see."

"Want to record the guitar?" Rollo asked, standing in the doorway to the control room. He looked far calmer than she felt.

"Sure," she said, glad of the distraction.

Luna plugged in the Les Paul and sat on a stool, noticing the boat was now rocking enough to feel the movement in the studio. She made two passes through the guitar track, which she didn't feel were great, but good enough to use alongside the drums as a guide so she could record the vocals. Just as Rollo told her over the headphones that he was ready, they all felt and heard a bump against the yacht.

"Tender must be back," Luna said, and Rollo nodded from the control room.

"Let's get one run recorded while they stow the tender and pull anchor," he said, and a moment later Luna heard the music start in her headphones.

Halfway through, she stopped singing, and let out a long breath.

"Just relax, babe," Trina said, handing Luna a glass of water. She leaned in closer and whispered. "Just imagine we're back on the top deck, jamming with our mates."

Luna smiled as the memory of the afternoon came flooding back. She felt the warmth of the Caribbean sun tempered by the ocean breeze. The laughter, the creativity, and the tight bond between them, which Sonny had seamlessly become a part of. A bond Rollo had never managed to cement with the group.

Waving a hand to indicate she was ready, the music started over, and Luna sang the song that Rollo had written the night before. She held the lyric sheet in her hand, but she knew all the words by now, and while her eyes remained on the paper, her focus was somewhere else. A no-man's-land between the pain of the break-up and the joy of creating the music. Her soul and her voice dragged back and forth by the story behind the song.

When the music fell silent in her ears and all the lines had been sung, a strange stillness fell over the studio. Trina held her face in her hands, and Panda sat on the couch with his mouth slightly open. Had she been way off key and too absorbed to hear it? Luna glanced at the control room window. Rollo stood behind his chair with head hung, and a knot gripped Luna's stomach. Everyone missed a note or two or even had bad days, but she'd never had this reaction before.

"Babe," Trina said softly as Luna slipped her headphones off. "That was incredible."

Luna let out the breath she didn't realise she'd been holding. "It was okay, then?"

Panda laughed. "Are you kidding, Luna? That was from another planet."

"I don't think I've ever heard you sing like that," Trina said. "Seriously, babe. He better not have buggered up the recording on that one."

Luna looked over at the control room again. Rollo was spooling the tapes and preparing for whatever he wanted to do next. She finally allowed herself a smile.

"Tender is secured," Captain Garrison announced, opening the door and making a rare appearance in the studio. "We're about to pull anchor. The storm is building quickly, and it's already over the northern part of the island. I need to move out to deeper water sooner than I'd like, so you should secure all your equipment. It will get rougher until we get farther south-east."

"Thanks, Captain," Luna said.

He nodded and quickly left.

"Hey, can we record the bass before we have to stop?" Panda asked.

"I'd like to if we can do it quickly," Rollo replied over the speakers. "Let me know when you're ready."

While Panda set up, Trina and Luna began tidying the studio, breaking down mic stands and packing the drum kit into protective travel cases.

"What do we do with the cajón?" Trina asked.

"Oh, bugger," Luna muttered. "We should have had them take it, too."

Trina shrugged her shoulders. "I just meant for tonight while we dodge the storm. We can give it back in a couple of days when we dock again."

Luna hesitated. Neither Trina nor Panda had been involved in the conversations about leaving, or the details regarding Thorburn and Rollo's debt. Which, by default, had become the band's debt. Luna had intended on filling them in earlier that day, but the right moment hadn't presented itself and then time had slipped away.

"I don't think we're coming back," Luna said quietly. "We'll have to send them some money for it and anything else they left."

"What do you mean?" Trina blurted.

Luna held a finger to her lips. "Keep your voice down. I'll tell you and Panda everything when we're alone, okay?"

Trina understandably didn't look pleased, but Panda was ready, so the girls took a seat on the couch and made sure all was quiet for the recording to start. Halfway through his third time playing, the yacht lurched, and the girls sat up straight.

"Pulling the anchor," Rollo said over the speakers in way of an explanation. "We'd better wrap everything up."

The sound deadening kept the noise of the diesel engines at bay, but a subtle vibration emanated through the yacht, letting Luna know they were under way. They were also being rocked around more and more as they motored across the increasingly turbulent incoming swells.

Luna stood by the control room door and watched Rollo finish labelling the reel he'd pulled from the tape machine and place it in the secure locker.

"Mind putting this in there too?" Trina asked, holding out her painting for their new cover.

"Is it dry?" Rollo asked before taking the art board.

"Dry to the touch," Trina replied. "I wouldn't stack anything on top of it, but it'll be fine if it's face up."

Rollo reluctantly took the artwork, giving it an appreciative smile as he locked it away on top of the tapes.

"Hopefully, we'll be able to work again by the morning..." he began, but didn't get to finish his sentence.

Soundwave jolted, and they all took a step to keep from falling as the yacht slowed. Luna swung around as the studio door was flung open.

"I don't know what you're trying to pull," Kayo barked. "But you lot aren't going anywhere!"

26

AJ drove faster than she should have, but the trip still took almost fifteen minutes to make their way along Seven Mile Beach in the afternoon tourist traffic. When she arrived at Nathaniel Merren's little petrol station, chaos best described the scene. A tow truck was backing up to the rusty white Toyota Corolla belonging to The Weasel, while the internet reporter shouted and complained to the driver. Who, in turn, paid no attention to him. Merren's granddaughter stood outside the office with one hand on her hip and the other holding her mobile while she recorded a video of the mayhem blocking anyone from reaching the pumps.

"It's going to be tricky to pull this off without attracting attention," AJ pointed out, seeing at least a dozen people watching from the street.

She pulled into the convenience store across the road and parked.

"Where's Nora and Jacob?" Reg asked, looking around for the police car.

"As far away from here as they can get would be my guess," AJ suggested. "They can't be associated with us questioning Carlson."

Reg grunted and opened the passenger door.

"Reg, you can't go charging over there with all these people watching," AJ said, opening her own door and jumping out.

"Watch me," he growled in response and marched across the road to where Carlson had his back to them as he now threatened the tow truck driver with legal action.

"Reg!" AJ hissed, but there was no stopping him.

She waited by the back of the van and crossed her fingers. Her concern was for the trouble Reg would get himself in if he broke parts off The Weasel, but also the ramifications of Nora and Jacob's involvement, which would be hard to deny when Carlson started squawking.

To AJ's surprise, all Reg did was put an arm around The Weasel's shoulders once he reached him. The scrawny man flinched, but couldn't go anywhere while Reg had him clamped to his side. The tow truck driver grinned, nodded to Reg, then continued doing his job. AJ couldn't hear exactly what was being said, but when the rumble of Reg's quiet voice finished reverberating around West Bay, Carlson nodded his head a few times and the two of them turned and walked towards the van.

"Mr Carlson needs a ride home seeing as his car's being towed," Reg announced loudly for all to hear, although he was looking at AJ. "I told him we happened to be going that way and would be happy to drop him off."

AJ fought back a smile. She was sure if Grand Cayman had a cliff more than ten-foot high, then that's where The Weasel would be dropped, but Reg had surprised her once again with his quick thinking.

"Hop in the back and make sure to buckle up," she said, then climbed into the driver's seat.

Reg opened the sliding side door and practically picked Carlson up by the scruff of his neck and tossed him across the back seat. Instead of getting in the front, he then stepped up and sat next to his captive, who struggled into a seated position. AJ started the van and swiftly drove away, leaving the prying eyes behind them. Reg stayed silent, so she did too, focused more on the best place to drive to.

"Technically, this is kidnapping," The Weasel began babbling, pushing his glasses up his nose. "I can report you to the police."

"I can call them right now if you like?" AJ replied, glancing in the rear-view mirror.

Carlson's eyes widened as he realised the implication behind her words. He shook his head. Apparently, he'd had enough of the Royal Cayman Islands Police Service constables currently on duty in West Bay.

AJ turned left past their dock and kept going. Farther away from George Town and Carlson's apartment.

"Here'll do," Reg said, leaning forward and pointing to the church car park on the inland side of North West Point Road.

The lot was empty and AJ parked in the back by a tall hedgerow separating the church from the neighbouring house. Hitting the door lock, she left the engine running with the AC on, and turned around. Reg reached into his pocket and Carlson cowered against the side of the van, expecting the big man to pull out a weapon of some description.

He didn't. Opening his big paw, Reg held out the listening devices for Carlson's to see.

"Want these back?" he said.

"I've no idea what those are," The Weasel replied, staring at the small plastic bugs.

"Got your fingerprints all over them," Reg said, his voice surprisingly calm.

Carlson frowned but didn't say anything.

"Couldn't wear gloves in front of my wife when you placed one on the hut and one on my bloody dog, huh?"

Carlson's eyes darted around the inside of the van. "I've no idea what you're talking about."

"Of course you don't," Reg replied, handing the bugs to AJ. "When Detective Whittaker traces the serial numbers on those little gems, he won't find your name on the purchase then, right?"

"If Whittaker was involved, I'd be talking to him instead of being kidnapped by you two," Carlson snapped. "You haven't gone to the police with this."

"Yet," Reg replied. "And you know why?"

"Because you don't have any real evidence," Carlson grinned, gaining confidence. "You're just guessing."

Reg shook his head. "Nah. We have no problem calling up our mate and handing you in. But the thing is, he has to play by the rules, doesn't he? And seeing as you didn't play by the rules, I figured you wouldn't mind if I didn't."

"What do you want?" Carlson asked, losing the grin as he realised he was still trapped in the back of a van with a man twice his size.

"You crossed a line," Reg said.

"What do you mean? I just write stories as I see them. It's not my problem if you don't like them."

"I don't give a toss what fairy tales you tell on your little internet site, Weasel," Reg said, leaning closer.

Carlson flinched and AJ couldn't tell whether it was in reaction to Reg's close proximity or hearing himself being called a weasel to his face. He had to have heard them say it over the listening device. Apparently, the insult had hit the mark.

"But you crossed the line when you violated my privacy and used my wife and dog to do it," Reg continued. "Now it's time to pay the piper."

"I already told you I had nothing to do with…"

Carlson didn't get to finish his sentence. Instead, he yelped as Reg's giant hand flew past the end of his nose and slapped against the window. AJ was amazed the glass didn't shatter, but she jumped nearly as much as The Weasel did.

"Stop lying Carlson," Reg growled. "And stop harassing my family and friends. You're inventing a story out of nothing with no regard to anyone involved."

"I'm just following creditable leads," The Weasel said nervously. "The public has a right to know."

"They have a right to know facts, not your flights of fantasy!" Reg snapped back.

"You followed the same path," Carlson pointed out.

"But we're not blabbing about it in a news article, which is nothing more than speculation. We spoke with Sonny and he verified he knew the band and as far as he knows they were all lost out at sea when the yacht went down," Reg raged on. "Which was well out of Cayman waters or it would have been scanned and found by now. So we're moving on to searching for more bodies floating out of cemeteries, which is most likely where the remains came from."

"You already ruled that out," Carlson said, before realising his error.

"We ruled out one incident, which you only know about because you illegally bugged me!" Reg poked a finger in Carlson's chest and the man covered his face with his arms and whimpered. Reg swatted The Weasel's hands away.

"Listen to me. Here's how this is going now. Until the authorities verify the identity of the remains from Cemetery Beach Reef, you're not going to post any more articles spreading your bullshit rumours."

"There's such a thing as freedom of speech," Carlson muttered.

"There's such a thing as people going missing never to be found again," Reg seethed. "It's a big ocean out there. Ask all the poor buggers on *Soundwave*."

The Weasel sucked in a breath.

"And if you ever plant any form of spying device anywhere near me or my family again, you and me are taking a long boat ride and you ain't coming back. Is that crystal bloody clear?"

AJ winced. She'd been sure her mentor would take the calling Detective Whittaker route rather than resort to violence, but even knowing Reg as well as she did, doubt now entered her mind. Carlson's terrified face revealed he was wholly convinced Reg meant what he said.

"I asked you if that was clear?" he repeated and The Weasel frantically nodded.

"And I know where you live," Reg added. "Now get out."

The big man shuffled across the seat and AJ hit the unlock button. He slid the side door open, stepping outside. Carlson sat up but didn't get out.

"Here? My car's a mile away."

"Your car is more than a mile away, numb-nuts. I'd say it's in the police pound in George Town by now," Reg laughed. "Take the bus."

Realising he had limited options and at least he'd be away from the bear who was threatening him bodily harm, The Weasel wisely hopped out of the van and moved away, pulling his mobile from his pocket. Reg quickly snatched it from his grasp and tossed it over the hedge.

"My phone!" Carlson yelped. "My life is on that phone!"

"That thing must be worthless then," Reg scoffed, slid the side door closed and got in the passenger seat. "Let's go," he told AJ. "Before he takes a picture of us."

Wasting no time, she turned the van around, and they watched Carlson scrambling around the hedge into the neighbouring front garden to retrieve his device. The last they heard was a dog barking and snarling as they drove south on North West Point Road.

"What can we tell Sonny?" AJ asked once they were turning into their little car park by the dock.

"Nothing," Reg replied. "What just happened never happened, so there's nothing to tell. Besides, words don't mean anything at this stage. He needs to see the dust settle and the bullshit stories go away. That's the only way he'll trust us again."

"Pearl agreeing to play at his place might help." AJ pointed out.

"I suppose it might," Reg agreed. "And I feel bad that I've been the one all this time to stop that happening."

"The Soggy Wreck Bar is pretty cool," AJ laughed. "I can't wait to go back there."

Reg nodded. "Yeah. Foolish of me to believe the rumours about the place. Sonny's been a part of the Cayman music scene since he was a lad. I should have known better."

"Well, things should calm down now if The Weasel values his life," AJ chuckled. "Give it a week or so and then see if Sonny's offer still stands."

"Yeah," Reg grunted and opened his door.

AJ went to turn off the van, but her mobile rang and she fished it out of her pocket.

"Hey Reg, it's Lahaina," she said and answered the call through the van's speakers.

Reg got back in and closed the door.

"What kind of madness have you two got started on our sleepy little island?" the reporter asked.

AJ groaned. "Are you referring to The Weasel's Pulitzer-winning article tying missing musicians to our Cemetery Beach find?"

"How come you didn't come to me about this?" Lahaina complained. "I gave you the bloody research material!"

"It's all BS, love," Reg said. "We didn't tell that wanker anything."

"Well, actually, we sort of did," AJ pointed out.

"The little tosser bugged us," Reg said. "Can you believe that?"

"That Carlson would bug you for info?" Lahaina scoffed. "He bugs the crap out of everyone."

AJ laughed. "We don't mean bugged as in annoyed. We mean bugged as in James Bond spy-like listening devices."

"Seriously?"

"Seriously," AJ confirmed.

"Did you go to the police?" Lahaina asked.

AJ rolled her eyes at Reg. "No. One of us decided it was better to handle it more directly."

"Oh dear," Lahaina muttered. "Why on earth did you do that?"

"'Cos I needed to handle the situation for Sonny Watler too," Reg replied.

"Okay, but you realise if you'd involved the police, then I would have a story to run about Carlson and his ridiculous internet news site and its far too many readers. We could have discredited him."

"People would still read his rubbish," AJ said despondently. "These days it seems people pick and choose what to believe based on what they already want to be true, regardless of the source or the actual truth."

Lahaina sighed. "Unfortunately. But you're telling me there's nothing to this connection with Sonny Watler and this band from the late 60s?"

"We doubt there is," AJ replied. "We were more interested in chatting with Sonny about Luna and the Lanterns than believing the skull could be one of the people lost with their yacht."

"Oh dear," Lahaina said again.

"Why? What's up?" AJ asked. "You didn't run a story on it too, did you?"

"No, I was calling to see if I should be investigating the angle," the reporter replied. "But a big-time freelance reporter from New York just stopped by our office. Sent here earlier today by a national magazine in America to follow up on the story of the disappearance of Luna and the Lanterns. Someone must have decided their story is internationally newsworthy."

AJ and Reg looked at each other.

"Oh dear," AJ mumbled.

27

"How did you get back here?" Rollo blurted, looking more surprised than anyone.

"I never left," Kayo grinned. "I could smell you were up to something."

Rollo glared at Luna, who shook her head.

"I'm sorry! He was on the tender when I came inside. He must have got off afterwards."

Kayo reached inside his jacket and pulled out a handgun.

"Bloody hell," Trina muttered.

Luna wondered how they'd all missed the fact that the man had probably been carrying the weapon the whole time he'd been onboard. Maybe because they didn't expect him to have a firearm. The island followed England's restrictive laws regarding guns, and Luna simply didn't think about them.

"Fletcher, come with me. We need to talk to the captain," Kayo ordered. "The rest of you stay here. Give me any trouble and I'll start shooting people until you realise how serious Mr Thorburn takes this situation."

They all held up their hands.

"Chill, mate," Panda said. "We're a rock 'n' roll band, man. We don't do guns and killing and shit."

Kayo waved the gun at him. "I bet you don't, you puny streak of piss. But I do, and you'll probably be first just because you annoy me." He turned to Rollo. "Let's go."

Rollo complied, leading the way through the door towards the bridge. The others dropped their hands and moved closer together.

"What are we gonna do?" Trina whispered, despite the sound-proof room.

"Anything he says," Luna replied. "He's got a bloody gun."

"I had no idea I annoyed the wanker," Panda moaned. "I didn't think he even noticed we existed."

"He can't take us all on," Trina said. "If we rush him."

"That might be true, but he'll pop off one or two, won't he?" Luna countered. "Personally, I don't want to get shot and I really don't want to see either of you get your heads blown off."

"What if one of us hides behind the door and whacks him over the head when he comes back in?" Panda suggested.

Luna groaned and shook her head. "You already said it. We play music for a living. He beats people up and no doubt murders them when Thorburn tells him to. We're way out of our depth here."

The yacht was rolling noticeably more and more by the minute. Enough that the three of them rested a hand on something fixed to maintain their balance. It surged forward and Luna could tell the captain was back in motion and turning in a new direction. Luna wished they had portholes to see what was happening outside, but then she remembered it was dark so it didn't matter.

"He's probably coming back, so let's chill and see what he has to say," Luna said, clutching the corner of the couch. "Hopefully Captain Garrison has talked sense into Kayo and maybe we can overnight offshore, or even make for a marina somewhere else on the island."

"I really don't think there are any marinas we can get to," Trina said. "The captain told me the only other place we could fit *Sound-*

wave was around the other side of the island, and it meant going through a break in the barrier reef."

"That's where the storm is coming from," Luna pointed out.

"Exactly," Trina agreed. "So we're buggered for options."

"Maybe the captain can talk them into letting us pull back into the harbour by the town," Panda said. "Surely they can't leave us stuck out here?"

"He said there was no room," Trina replied as the door opened and Rollo stumbled in, shoved by Kayo, who followed.

"All of you," the thug ordered. "Downstairs. I'm locking you in a cabin for the night."

"Where is the captain taking the yacht?" Luna asked.

"Kayo here insists we make for port," Rollo replied.

"Shut the hell up," the man snapped, and a moment later, the lights went out.

Luna felt the vibration through the hull recede and knew the engines were shutting down. Maybe the captain was rebelling on his own?

"What the hell?" Kayo shouted. "Everyone stay where you are! If I hear you moving, I'm gonna shoot."

"Damn," Rollo cursed. "The power's out. They have to get the reserve system going. We need the air conditioning for all the equipment."

The yacht violently bucked and rolled in the swells as the seas turned the unpowered vessel at will. The lights flickered for a moment like a strobe, illuminating the room as though in a stop motion animation. Only two people were moving. Kayo swung the gun around, unsure where to aim as sounds came from all around him. The other was Panda. A dull thud resounded through the studio just as the lights came back on. Panda wound up his bass guitar by the neck, and brought it down again on Kayo, who was already crumpled across the couch.

The second blow sent blood splattering across the furniture, and Luna screamed.

"Panda!" Trina shouted and grabbed his arm before he could club Thorburn's man a third time.

Luna's heart thumped in her chest. In a matter of hours, their serene island visit to record an album had spiralled into a terrifying storm, violent threats, and now a man bludgeoned before her eyes. Panda heaved and panted, his eyes wide like a wild beast.

"Calm down, mate," Trina urged. "Let me take that from you."

She removed the bass guitar from his grasp and guided him to the other couch, with them both swaying and staggering as the boat lurched back and forth.

"Shit," Rollo muttered, staring at Kayo's limp and bloody form. "I'd better see what the captain's doing. We don't need anyone coming in here."

His words shook Luna out of her stunned paralysis, and she nodded. "Okay. I'll find a medical kit."

"What the hell for?" Rollo asked, starting towards the door, clutching at the back of the couch to hold himself steady. "He's done for, babe."

"You think?" Luna gasped. "He's dead?"

"Check his pulse," Trina said, making her way back after leaving Panda in a trance.

Luna touched Kayo's neck and flinched when blood ran down her fingers. "Oh shit. This is awful," she stammered, but hunted for a heartbeat. "I can't feel a pulse. You try, Trina."

"Don't let anyone in but me," Rollo said, and slipped out the door, closing it behind him.

"Surely we have to head for the port now?" Luna wondered aloud. "We have to call the police."

"No!" Panda moaned from the other side of the studio. "I'll go to prison, man. I can't go to prison."

"No way," Trina replied. "It was self-defence. The tosser pulled a bloody gun."

"He fell overboard," Panda said, getting to his feet. "We don't know what happened. He went outside, and we never saw him again."

Luna and Trina looked at each other. Luna couldn't believe they were even talking about throwing a man's body off the yacht. But Panda might be right.

"Could have bashed his noggin on anything, right?" Trina offered. "I'm just saying, you know? If he washes ashore. Smacked his head falling off the boat, or on a piece of driftwood."

"There's blood everywhere," Luna pointed out, feeling bile rise in her throat as she looked at the man's battered face.

"We'll mop all that up, or throw the cushions out," Panda urged, already wrapping a skinny arm under Kayo, testing his weight. "This'll take all three of us. He's heavier than hell."

"Where do you think we're taking him?" Luna asked. "We can't march his body past the bridge."

She shook her head, dumbfounded that she was even contemplating this madness.

"Out the back," Panda said, pointing towards the control room.

They all scrambled to hang on as the yacht rolled hard to starboard and Luna realised she still couldn't feel the engines running.

"There's a door out of the control room to the low rear deck where we get on and off the tenders," Panda continued. "Rollo has the tape storage in front of it, which we'll have to move."

"Rollo told us to never open that door," Luna said. "It'll let all the moisture and humidity in. He said it'll ruin the equipment."

"Sod Rollo," Trina retorted. "We can buy new gear, but we can't get us a new Panda, can we?"

Luna groaned in despair. "I know, but we should wait and see what Rollo thinks," she urged. "We still don't know what's going on. I don't think they've got the engines running yet."

As if to confirm her point, the lights flickered again.

"Rollo won't give a shit about me," Panda scoffed. "He only cares about whatever deal he has going on with Thorburn and this goon."

Luna opened her mouth to argue, but her friend had a point.

"Come on," Trina said, taking Kayo's legs. "We can't let Panda do time over this wanker. He's dead whether we leave him here or toss him over the side, so I vote he goes."

"He wouldn't give it a second thought to throw us overboard," Panda added, and tried lifting the man.

"This is crazy," Luna muttered, but scooped up Kayo from the other side, and the three of them lugged his still form towards the control room.

Another jarring wave sent them sprawling to the floor, dropping Kayo with a thump.

"Eww," Trina yelped as more blood spilled across the floor from the thug's head wound.

They got to their feet and Panda thrust the control room door open, pulling on Kayo's shoulders, his body sliding in the blood.

"Move the tape locker," Panda ordered the girls, as he dragged Kayo closer.

Luna and Trina took a side each and heaved Rollo's precious tape storage across the cramped control room, setting it down by the mixing console. Trina rushed back to the door, which was locked in place with a long handle. Pulling up released the seal and wind immediately rushed inside the room, swirling papers around in a fury.

"Bloody hell!" Luna gasped as rain and seawater sprayed her and the other two.

"Quick!" Panda shouted. "Before we drown the place."

The three took hold of Kayo and hauled him through the slender opening, slipping and sliding on the mixture of blood and salt water. The long, teak swim step bounced up and down in the darkness, with the only light coming from the open door. On her hands and knees, Luna tugged on the man's arm, while Panda dragged his other hand. Trina shovelled Kayo's feet along and, bit by bit, they scooted him towards the ocean.

"Nooo!" Luna yelped and sat back. "He's still alive!"

"Just a nerve twitch or something," Panda shouted to be heard over the crashing waves and whistling wind. "You know, like the headless chicken thing."

"I swear he grabbed me," Luna cried.

"Bugger him," Panda said through gritted teeth. "I either killed the bastard in there, or he died out here. It doesn't matter which. Better him than me is all I say."

Kayo's head rolled to his left, and his eyes blinked at Luna.

"See, he's awake!" she yelled.

"Screw him!" Trina shouted, lifting the man's feet and pushing with her body.

Kayo reached out with his left hand and tried to grab at Luna, but she pulled clear of his fingertips. His right arm lay limp and useless in Panda's grasp. Trina screamed into the tempestuous night and shoved with all her might. Kayo's good hand swept up, and Luna watched in horror as the wounded man grabbed Trina's hair as he slipped from the swim step into the raging sea. Trina tumbled helplessly after him, her scream instantly lost as both figures disappeared from sight.

"Trina!" Luna yelled, perched precariously near the edge.

Rain and seawater, whisked in her face by the powerful wind, blinded her vision as she sobbed and hoarsely shouted her friend's name.

"Trina!" Panda joined in, one hand holding Luna from falling in, the other grasping a cleat on the swim step.

"No, no, no!" Luna cried into the night.

"What are you doing?" came Rollo's voice from the doorway. "Why the hell is this door open? Get back inside!"

"It's Trina!" Luna shouted. "She's gone overboard!"

Rollo stared at them in disbelief. "How on earth? Why were you out here?" he asked, and then his expression suggested he'd connected the dots. He frantically beckoned to them both. "Get back in here."

"We have to search for her!" Luna screamed, gritting her teeth against the driving rain and surging sea.

As best she knew, they hadn't made it far under power, yet she couldn't see a single other light through the storm. She crawled back across the swim step and Panda came with her.

"We have to launch a lifeboat and search for her," she said, reaching Rollo.

He pulled her inside by her soaking wet shirt. Once Panda scrambled into the control room, he closed and latched the door.

"I'm launching a tender whether you help me or not," Luna told Rollo.

"It's hopeless, love. Hopeless," he replied.

She pushed past him.

"Luna, wait," he said, taking hold of her arm.

She flinched, but he didn't grip her like he'd done in anger before. His hold was firm, but not painful.

"The crew are trying to sort out the power," Rollo explained. "We've lost everything but essentials. Which means the studio will be ruined, and maybe the tapes if we don't restore power."

"I don't care about the yacht, the studio, or the tapes," Luna cried. "All I care about is finding Trina."

"If they can't restart the engines, the yacht will be swept ashore and run aground, won't it?" Panda asked.

"Most likely," Rollo replied. "If it doesn't capsize on the way."

"Then why wouldn't we take to the lifeboats anyway?" Panda asked, wiping strands of long wet hair from his face.

"Because those tenders are really just that," Rollo replied. "Runabouts to get us to shore and back in calm seas. They're not built for seas like this. The safest thing is to get the engines running and head south. Farther we get, the better the conditions will be. The captain has been in radio contact with the authorities and they said it's building into a tropical storm."

Luna pulled away from his grip. "I'm launching one of the tenders."

Rollo turned to Panda. "Damn it. Help me with the tape storage. I'm taking it with us. We'll search as long as we can for Trina, then make for shore."

"I don't think that's a great idea for me," Panda responded. "I'll help you get going, but I can't go with you. I can't swim, man."

"That's your choice, mate," Rollo replied.

Luna flung her arms around her friend. "I understand."

"It's my fault she's gone," Panda sobbed, clutching Luna tightly. "It's my fault, but I'll be a liability out there."

"It's okay, Panda. We'll find her," Luna cried. "You know I love you, right?"

"I love you too, babe," Panda gasped. "Please find her."

28

"What do we do about this new reporter?" AJ vented. "This whole thing is becoming a train wreck."

"What can we do?" Reg replied. "Hopefully, the bloke will sniff around, realise there's nothing in it, and bugger off home."

AJ scoffed. "That's not happening. They spend the money to send someone over, then they'll want a story out of it, even if it's just a *whatever happened to the long-lost rock band* headline."

Reg grunted and thought for a moment. "Okay. In that case, let's meet with him."

"And give him more to write about?" AJ said sceptically.

"Like you said, he's going to write a story regardless," Reg responded. "Might as well give him the facts as we know them. Better than him getting his information from The Weasel."

It was AJ's turn to ponder the dilemma for a few moments. Then she picked up her mobile and called Lahaina back.

"Yes?" the reporter answered with trepidation. "I'm about to go into a meeting with my editor, so make it quick."

"We want to meet with this reporter from America," AJ said. "Can you arrange it?"

"A minute ago, you two were doing your best to sweep all this chatter under the rug, and now you want to meet them?"

"They might as well hear exactly what we know and don't know, right?" AJ countered. "Or Sean Carlson will be their source and we know how that'll go."

Lahaina groaned. "Jeez. I'd better end up with an article of my own out of all this."

Reg laughed. "You can write about how a big-time New York journalist came to the little island of Grand Cayman, and left with nothing but a tan and a bottle of the finest Seven Fathoms rum."

"Just in case you were unaware of this, Reg Moore," Lahaina replied. "You're of no use whatsoever to me."

Reg laughed again. "Let's hear you say that next time you want your tanks filled."

"Fair point. Give me a few minutes to talk to my editor and I'll call you back."

"You're the best, thanks," AJ said, and ended the call.

"I'm bloody starving," Reg announced. "We missed lunch."

"Wouldn't do you any harm to miss a meal or two, old man," AJ replied, raising an eyebrow at him.

"Don't give me that, you skinny little smart mouth. You know I get grumpy if I don't have my lunch on time."

"Opposed to your regular and consistent state of grumpiness?" AJ queried. "I must say, I find it hard to tell."

Reg stared at her. "You're still not driving."

"Hold your horses, dustbin," she said, opening the driver's door. "I need a change of clothes."

"We don't have time for that," Reg complained.

"Too bad," she replied, getting out. "These damp and salty clothes are playing havoc with my unmentionable parts."

Reg moaned. "Bloody hell. You didn't have to say that out loud. Completely out of order."

"Still hungry?" AJ laughed as she jogged to the little hut.

Five minutes later she returned, wearing a pair of shorts and a

Fox and Hare T-shirt advertising Pearl's Friday night appearances. She held up her phone as she crossed the car park.

"Lahaina called back. We have to meet her at the Compass office as soon as we can get over there."

"Alright, but we're stopping for grub on the way," Reg insisted as AJ climbed in and started the van.

"What part of *as soon as we can get there* didn't you get, deaf ears?" AJ retorted, backing up and pulling up the steep slope to the road.

"After stopping for food is as soon as we can get there," Reg replied. "Whether you're still driving or sat by the side of the road on the way."

AJ chuckled. "Fine. But only because I can barely handle the regular grump."

After bickering all the way about which place would delay them the least, AJ won out as she was behind the wheel. She pulled into Cafe Del Sol, one of her favourite coffee shops, and ordered a caramel latte and a pastry. Reg bought a grilled cheese and a chocolate croissant with decaf coffee, as he couldn't sleep if he had caffeine in the afternoon. They were back on the bypass to George Town in a few minutes, and neither said a word as they wolfed down their late lunch.

Lahaina met them in the reception area and led them back to a small conference room where a thirty-something woman waited for them. She was tall, slender, with long brunette hair, and wore a flower print blouse. AJ presumed it was the paper's editor who she hadn't met before.

"Reg Moore and AJ Bailey, meet Meadow Blake," Lahaina said by way of introduction. "Meadow is here looking into the disappearance of Luna and the Lanterns in 1969."

Reg shook her hand. "Nice to meet you."

AJ did the same. "I don't know why, but I was expecting a man. Isn't that terrible?"

Meadow laughed. "You'd be accurate more often than not in my field. And to be honest, when Lahaina told me I was meeting with a pair of divers, Reg and AJ, I expected a couple of blokes as well."

"I get that a lot," AJ replied with a smile.

The woman wasn't only the opposite sex to what AJ had imagined, she also spoke with an English accent, with a relaxed smile and a gentle manner. Not at all the aggressive reporter she'd feared. At least, not on first impressions.

They all sat. "I've shown Meadow the various clippings we have in our archives," Lahaina began. "And I mentioned that you've been privy to them as well. So, perhaps you can share anything you've discovered in the past few days that you think might be related to the band."

AJ and Reg looked at each other. The woman seemed nice, but she was still there to write a story, and they were already in the doghouse with Sonny. Silently, their exchanged glance was a warning to err on the side of caution.

Reg spoke first. "May I ask why the sudden interest in the band?"

Meadow nodded and replied in a barely noticeable London accent, which AJ guessed had been softened by living in other places. "Sure. So we have software these days which flags stories on the internet from around the world. An article caught my eye, and I happened to know a little background on the band, so I pitched the idea of coming down here to an editor at a magazine I do freelance work with. He said yes, so here I am. From what I could see, nothing serious has been written about Luna and the Lanterns in decades, and their disappearance is still a mystery. If I can find any new answers, then that's fantastic. If I can't, I can still write a piece around the fact that it remains an unsolved mystery. You never know, maybe we'll inspire someone to search for the wreck."

"It's a big, deep ocean out there," AJ pointed out. "And from what we could find, no one knows exactly why or where the *Soundwave* headed. It would be beyond a needle in a haystack."

"Probably wishful thinking on my part," Meadow said with a

smile. "But I'll start by seeing if there's any new information available, or something that may have come to light after the story died down five decades ago."

"Can't say we've been able to find anything useful," Reg said. "It's a long shot that the skull AJ found on Cemetery Beach Reef is in any way related. We were following the theory that the body came from the cemetery during a storm. As you probably saw, the archives aren't easily searchable, so we looked up the sort of hurricanes and tropical storms which caused enough flooding to dislodge one of the old graves."

Meadow winced. "That's awfully creepy, isn't it?"

AJ laughed. "Just a bit. But they started using different methods of concrete crypts and cover stones to secure the sites, so it's most likely the body I found was from before the newspaper was even around."

"I'm hoping to meet with a representative from the local police tomorrow," Meadow said. "Maybe they can shed more light on the remains and tell me when we might have lab results."

"That'll be a while," Reg said. "A lot of our lab work has to be sent to the US to be processed by independent labs. We have some capacity on the island, but they're always backed up."

"And this is relatively low priority as obviously this poor bugger died a while ago," AJ pointed out.

Meadow smiled again. "I'll talk to them. Perhaps I can help expedite things through a connection or two in the states."

AJ wasn't sure how she felt about that. She'd gone from incredibly curious to overly protective of her find. Mainly because of the Sonny angle. As she chewed it over, it seemed the best solution would be for the results to come back as quickly as possible. The sooner they were able to determine who the remains belonged to, the sooner all the fuss would die down. If they could determine anything beyond an age and sex.

"What can you tell me about Mr Sonny Watler?" Meadow asked. "Is there any truth to his connection with the band?"

AJ looked at Reg again. She could tell he was weighing up how to answer.

"I can tell you he was mighty upset by what Sean Carlson wrote," Reg replied.

"I'm told Mr Carlson isn't very popular with many of you," Meadow said with a grin.

"He might be the next disappearance mystery if he keeps up his BS," Reg muttered.

Lahaina laughed nervously. "Reg isn't serious, just to be clear. But Carlson has rubbed many people the wrong way. He's prone to printing any rubbish he dreams up."

"Lot of that going around," Meadow agreed. "The internet is a wonderful thing. Mostly."

"But it was his article that brought you here," AJ said. "Have you spoken with him?"

Meadow shook her head. "No. I could tell from that article and a few others of his I looked at that…" she paused, searching for the words she wanted.

"They're a load of bollocks," Reg finished for her.

Meadow laughed. "Something like that."

They fell silent, and AJ knew there was still an unanswered question hanging over the table.

"Sonny's a lovely man who values his privacy," she said, and caught Reg nodding his agreement.

"I doubt you'll have much luck dropping by his place."

"Would I be right in saying he's a bit touchy after Carlson's article, then?" Meadow asked.

AJ raised an eyebrow. "If by 'a bit' you mean steaming mad, then yeah. He's a bit touchy."

"That's a shame," Meadow responded. "I mean for him, you know? It's not ideal for me either, but it's never good when people have their privacy invaded."

"Unless they're wankers like Carlson," Reg grunted. "I don't mind him having his dirty laundry thrown about the place."

Meadow laughed. "He really has got on the wrong side of you, hasn't he?"

"He bugged my bloody dog," Reg replied. "And our dock where we run our boats from. Carlson never would've known a thing about Sonny unless he'd listened in on us."

"Bloody hell," Meadow sighed. "He bugged your dog?"

"Put a listening devise on his collar so he could hear what we talked about at Reg's house," AJ explained. "There's good reason we call him The Weasel."

"The Weasel?" Meadow echoed. "That does sound appropriate."

"So, now you can understand why we're a bit wary, and Sonny is really cheesed off," AJ said.

Meadow thought for a few moments, then glanced over at Lahaina, who'd remained quiet throughout the conversation. But now she spoke up.

"I told you, Meadow, you can trust these two."

The woman smiled in return, but still thought things over a little longer.

"I think Sonny may be okay talking to me if you introduce me to him."

Reg laughed. "We're hardly in his good graces just at the moment, love. We might need a week or two before we butter him up enough to hear anything we have to say."

Meadow smiled. "Perhaps if he knew who I was, it might make a difference."

"You have a lovely name, don't get me wrong," AJ replied. "But the problem is you're a journalist, and they're not too popular in his bar this week."

"I understand that," Meadow continued. "But do you know who Billy Hastings was?"

Reg frowned. "I know that name from somewhere."

"Panda," AJ blurted. "Wasn't he the bassist in the band? His nickname was Panda."

Meadow nodded. "He was my uncle."

"Stone the crows," Reg muttered.

"That's why you knew so much about the band already," AJ said as she recalled Meadow's earlier words.

"My mum is his younger sister. She was only ten in 1969 when the yacht went missing. I grew up hearing all about my Uncle Billy."

"Yeah," AJ said. "I think you're right. Sonny might want to chat with you after all."

29

"We've found the problem and we'll have the engines started in five or ten minutes," Captain Garrison said with sweat glistening on his brow. "We're constantly blowing breakers and fuses. The electrical system is so much more complicated with all the power required by the studio. Something is fundamentally wrong in the way they've wired it, but we think we've found a workaround."

Rollo and Luna had stopped on their way up to the top deck and explained their plan. Panda hovered in the hallway instead of further crowding the small bridge.

"Your best bet is to stay aboard," the captain urged.

"We have to search for Trina!" Luna responded, feeling more desperate as the minutes ticked by.

Garrison's brow furrowed in sympathy, and he shook his head. "I can't lie to you, Miss Skye. Her chances are not good in these conditions. How did she go over? Why would anyone go outside in this weather?"

"Thorburn's man, Kayo, panicked," Rollo said, and Luna looked at him in shock. Why would he even bring up the thug's name?

"Seems he was terrified of storms. He opened the rear door

from the control room and went out," Rollo continued, and Luna realised what he was doing. "Trina was closest and tried to stop him. They were both swept overboard."

"So we have two people in the water?" Garrison asked.

Rollo nodded. "Yes, sir."

"He went bloody loopy," Panda shouted from behind them. "Said he couldn't swim and was losing his mind. He took a nasty tumble in the studio and bashed his head. I don't think he was in his right mind at all."

And just like that, between the two men, they'd fabricated a cover story that would be hard to refute. Providing the bass guitar covered in blood went missing, which Luna assumed Panda would take care of once she and Rollo had gone. Luna's head was spinning and she couldn't believe the other two could think clearly enough to invent such a tale.

"When we get running again, we can make a circle and use our spotlights to search for them," Garrison said. "Sammy and Stuart will be done soon."

"I can't wait," Luna pleaded. "We're wasting time."

Rollo nodded. "When you get running, captain, take *Soundwave* south and get clear of the weather. We'll search the water, then make for shore in the tender."

The captain shook his head. "That's madness, Mr Fletcher. If you get the tender turned in the wrong direction, these seas will roll you over in the blink of an eye. I beg you to reconsider."

Luna pushed her way past to the steps leading up, and Rollo struggled behind her with his tape storage box.

"Keep everyone else safe, Captain," Luna heard him say. "Come get us after the storm passes."

"Wait!" the captain shouted, and Luna stopped.

Garrison handed Panda a compass he pulled from a drawer. "The shore is directly east. The seas are sweeping around the northwest point, so they'll be pushing you south. I know you feel the need to search for your friends, but believe me when I tell you, it'll be a waste of time. Their only hope is to be washed ashore, just like yours will be. Under the bench seat above us are life jackets," he added, pointing up. "Put them on before you do anything, understand?"

"Thank you, Captain," Rollo replied.

The upper deck felt worse than being exposed on the swim step with the yacht's movements further exaggerated up higher, and the wind hit them unabated. Luna lifted the top of the bench seat and pulled three lifejackets from the storage. The two men were already carrying the tape locker across the deck, so she staggered after them. They chose the davits on what appeared to be the lee side, but Luna knew that could easily change as the seas moved the big yacht around. Rollo and Panda manhandled the box into the tender once Luna had pulled back the cover, and she threw two lifejackets in behind it. The third she gave to Panda, who quickly slipped it over his sopping wet, skinny frame.

"Climb in!" Rollo yelled at Luna.

"Let's get the winches started first," she called back.

"They're not working!" Rollo shouted, pushing the button repeatedly.

"We can wind the handles," Panda said, already releasing the lock at the stern end.

Luna could see her friend was terrified, with the roiling seas bashing the yacht around and the powerful wind making it impossible to stand without hanging onto something.

"Let me get it started, then I'll get in the lifeboat while you finish," she shouted, her teeth beginning to chatter despite the temperature.

Panda relented and clung to the davit while Luna cranked the handle. The tender slowly lowered towards the fierce surf, slightly raked as Rollo had made more progress at the other end.

"Get in, Luna, and start the outboard!" Rollo ordered, and she peered over the side.

It was already a long drop into the lifeboat and it was only halfway to the water.

"A little lower and I'll run down to the lower deck and climb in," she replied, and Rollo nodded.

Panda took over on the handle while Luna clung to the davit with one arm and a firm hand on her friend. Looking out into the darkness, a knot formed in her stomach. Only hours before, she'd been staring at calm turquoise water and people lying in the sun on the beach. How could anyone survive in the tempest that had consumed the island since then? Tears fell down her cheeks, both for the fate of Trina, but also the terror she now faced herself. Luna respected the captain, and he'd tried everything short of physical force to dissuade them from launching a tender. Now, outside in the midst of what must be a tropical storm, she trembled and yearned to be safely inside the big yacht. But inside was hardly safe. With no engines, *Soundwave* would surely succumb, eventually. What would be worse? Crushed against the shore in the larger vessel, or tossed into the sea from an 18-foot lifeboat?

"Go now!" Rollo screamed into the howling gale, and Luna looked over the side as the tender clattered against the yacht.

It was below the lower deck, still three to six feet above the surf, depending on the waves. Luna wished she and Rollo had donned the lifejackets as the captain had ordered, but now she'd have to do it first thing once she was in the lifeboat. The closest steps were at the rear, and she carefully clung to the railing as she made her way down, a mix of rainwater and seawater flowing down the stairs beneath her feet.

The tender swung from the lines and bounced off the fenders protecting the two hulls from each other and Luna realised getting in the lifeboat would be treacherous in itself. She'd pulled the cover back enough to slide the tape storage box and lifejackets inside, but now it flapped violently in the wind. Its freed tethers thrashed like whips.

"Hurry, Luna!" Rollo called from above. "Get in!"

Stepping over the railing of the *Soundwave*, Luna felt gravity pull her over as the boat rocked in the swells. The dip brought her closer to the hanging tender, and she threw herself into the lifeboat, landing awkwardly across the box and wooden seat.

"Start the outboard!" Rollo yelled.

Pulling herself to her knees, Luna couldn't tell if they were still lowering the tender or if it was simply the rise and fall of the ocean and the yacht. Her ribs stung, but she pushed the pain aside and turned to the stern. Before she could start the engine, she needed to clear the cover as she held her arms in front of her face to protect herself from the flailing lines.

"Argh," she groaned as the thin rope slashed across her body.

Grabbing the cover, she balled it up and managed to subdue the lines while freeing the others, which held the tarpaulin in place. Once it was loosened, she had no choice but to release the cover, letting it fly off into the darkness. To her terror, with it went the two lifejackets, ripped from the boat by the wind.

Frustrated and dismayed, Luna shuffled to the stern, crawling awkwardly over the wooden plank which served as a seat. Facing the outboard, she tried to remember the sequence Captain Garrison had repeated to them on how to operate the engine. She found the fuel valve and discovered it had been left open from the earlier venture to shore. Flicking the ignition switch on, she wrapped her hand around the pull-start and yanked it as hard as she could. To her amazement, the little engine came to life. And then immediately died.

What had she done wrong? Something thumped the bottom of the tender, tipping it against the hull of the motor yacht and throwing Luna off balance. The little boat was now in the water. Getting back to her knees, she squinted against the driving spray and fumbled in the dim light from the yacht to find the pull handle again. Pulling as hard as she could, the engine spun over, but didn't fire.

"Choke!" Panda yelled from above.

She looked up at him, wondering what he was talking about.

"Open the choke!" he repeated, and Luna remembered the little knob the captain had shown them. She cursed herself for not paying better attention, amazed that Panda, of all people, had. It had all seemed so unnecessary in the calm, beautiful days they'd savoured on the trip down.

The lifeboat was now lifting and moving separately from *Soundwave*, smacking against the bigger boat, then yawing and bashing the side again. When the sea lifted the tender, the winch lines went slack, snapping taut as the wave receded. Luna searched for the black choke knob and once found, she pulled it out. This time, when she ripped the chord, the little engine started and kept running.

"Move the box!" Rollo shouted from the lower deck railing.

Luna shoved the tape storage towards the bow, then scurried to the stern, leaving room for Rollo to drop into the tender. He landed with a thud, meeting the boat as it rose on a swell.

"We have to release the clips at the same time!" he shouted as he shuffled to the stern on his hands and knees, clambering over the thwarts and seats. "Go to the bow. I'll need to get us away from *Soundwave* as soon as we're free or we'll be crushed against her."

Luna was thrown from side to side and dumped on her backside several times as she moved forward once more over all the obstacles. Once she found the clip at the end of the davit rope, she gave Rollo a thumbs-up. She could barely see him at the stern, but his motion suggested he'd returned the signal.

"Be ready! When I say go!" he bellowed, and she repeated the thumbs-up.

The lifeboat rose on a swell, jolting against the yacht, but Luna hung on to the large stainless-steel clip.

The line went slack. "Now!" Rollo shouted, and Luna pushed the safety lock with her thumb and tried to disconnect the clasp from the eye on the bow of the tender.

A wave violently rocked the boat, throwing her to one side, and she lost her grip on the clip. By the time Luna had recovered, the davit line was stretched and the stern of the lifeboat dropped as the yacht rose on a swell. Rollo had freed his fastener and now they were only tethered to the larger vessel by her clip. Gravity pulled her towards the stern, but she clutched the gunwales and gritted her teeth, desperately hanging on.

"You have to release the line!" Rollo screamed into the howling wind.

The boat now kicked and bucked in the storm far worse than before, and Luna grimly held tight, certain she was about to be tossed into the surf. Terror seized her as the captain's warnings played in her head. He was right. This was suicide, but there was no way back now. Feeling the tender slam upwards once more and gasping with her heart in her throat, she lunged for the line and the clip, knowing this would be her last chance. The line went slack, and she pressed open the safety latch. The line tugged on her hand, wrenching her up like she was being shot from a cannon. Realising the clip was no longer attached to the eye, Luna released her grip and fell back into the little boat as the engine note screamed into the maelstrom.

In the blink of an eye they were free of the yacht, which she watched vanish from sight, clutched by the driving rain and manic surf. As it faded into the darkness, she heard what she hoped were the diesel engines coming to life, but in a matter of seconds, they were tossed too far away to hear anything except their little outboard and the storm.

"The compass!" Rollo shouted. "Take the compass!"

Luna struggled to her knees and reached out, taking the compass which Panda had passed on to Rollo.

"Point east with your arm!" Rollo instructed. "Keep pointing east!"

Luna fell back to the bow and wiped the stinging seawater from her eyes. In the pitch-black darkness, away from the lights of the yacht, they were blind. With no idea from which direction the swells were coming, she found herself being knocked around as though blindfolded in a boxing ring with a heavyweight champion, punching her from all directions. She looked down at the compass in her hand and noticed one side of the needle was luminescent.

She could also see four dots around the compass face, one of them twice as large as the others.

"North!" she muttered to herself. The large dot had to be north.

Never eat shredded wheat, she repeated in her head, recalling the phrase a teacher had drilled into his students in school. Which meant east was to the right of north. Lining up the needle with the large dot, Luna raised her arm to the east. Which was off the port side of the lifeboat. They were heading south, which had to be away from where Trina had gone in.

"We have to go north to search!" she yelled at Rollo. "The waves are driving us south!"

Rollo shook his head, wiping his long wet hair from his face as he tried turning the boat with the tiller.

"Babe, there's no chance in this storm! We have to get to shore!"

Luna screamed into the night. He was right, and she knew it. They had more chance of running Trina over than ever seeing her. A bright light suddenly flashed in Luna's eyes, blinding her, and she almost dropped the compass.

"Sorry!" Rollo shouted. "I found a torch."

Clutching the light in one hand, which he pinned to the gunwale, Rollo steered the tiller with the other. At least now they could see the swells rising in front of them. Swirling rain soaked up the light no more than twenty feet in front of the tender, but at least they could see something.

Reluctantly, Luna checked the compass and raised her arm again, pointing east, resigned to the fact that all she could do was search the beach with the torch if they made it ashore in one piece. Rollo turned until the bow faced east, then rode along the faces of the incoming swells, until forced to veer over the crests into the following trough.

Luna began to believe they could make it. Rollo was surprisingly adept at manoeuvring the little craft, and although the seas were confused and wind driven, he was finding the troughs to run along, which carried them in a generally easterly direction. She noticed he was taking them slightly north whenever he found the chance to cross over the crests, compensating for the swells pushing them south. Luna clung to a glimmer of hope that Trina had kept her head above water for long enough to make it to land. If she had, they might hit the island near where she'd been washed ashore if they kept edging north while trying to reach Seven Mile Beach.

Luna thought she heard the outboard falter as the tender yawed to starboard, rising up a trough, right before a crack of lightning momentarily illuminated their surroundings. Ahead and slightly to their right, Luna saw the silhouette of trees being bent over by the wind.

"Land!" she screamed. "I saw land!"

"I did too," Rollo replied with determination in his voice as he steered to port over the next crest.

As the tender's bow rose over the peak and Luna clutched hold of the gunwales, the little engine coughed, spluttered and died. Certain they were about to be flung over backwards, Luna screamed. But the bow finally fell, and they plummeted into the next trough. Rollo pulled like a madman on the rope, but the outboard spluttered and wouldn't start. The next wave bore down on them like a towering cliff, the daunting wall of water illuminated by the torch.

"The choke!" Luna suddenly remembered. "Turn off the choke!"

"Bugger," Rollo swore, and fumbled for the black knob as the bow rode up the face of the incoming wave.

He shoved the knob closed and yanked the pull-start again and again as the swell lifted them like a bathtub toy. Luna heard the outboard fire, but she knew it was too late. She clung to the sides of the tender for as long as she could, but when the bow swung over her head, she felt her body flung from the boat. For a moment, she was suspended in air, and the world slowed to a crawl. The blasting noise of the wind subdued and the crashing of the surf ebbed away. A split second later, she hit the water, followed by the crushing blow of the lifeboat smashing down on top of her.

30

"What do you want?" was how Tee greeted AJ and Reg when they walked into Sonny's Soggy Wreck Bar.

Lahaina and Meadow waited outside in AJ's van, based on the theory that all four of them marching into the little place at five o'clock in the afternoon would look like an intimidating onslaught. Which was also partly centred around the idea that Sonny's wouldn't be busy in the late afternoon. But that wasn't the case. The bar was already half full and it took a while for Tee to stop ignoring Reg's large frame towering over everyone else. The older woman AJ had seen before stayed at the other end of the bar and ignored them even more. AJ guessed she was probably the owner's wife.

"We have someone Sonny will want to meet," Reg said loudly over the hustle and bustle of the dimly lit and crowded place. "Can we have a quick word with him to explain?"

Tee shook her head. "He's not here," she said and turned away.

"This woman's the niece of one of the band members," AJ blurted, and Tee paused and turned back.

"Bullshit."

Reg held up both hands. "I swear to you, love. We were as surprised as you are."

"Why is she here?" Tee asked.

That was a harder question to tackle, and AJ had hoped they'd be all sitting around Sonny's reserved table before it came up.

"She came across the story and wants to talk to anyone who might have met her uncle," Reg replied.

He'd carefully told the truth while omitting the detail which would have them both thrown out. The word *journalist* wasn't currently popular in the Watler household. Tee thought it over and served another customer to buy herself time.

"You're sure she's telling the truth?"

"About being who she is?" Reg replied.

"Yeah. I mean, anyone can waltz in and say dey are John Lennon's cousin's granddaughter. Doesn't make it true. Have you checked her out?"

AJ and Reg looked at each other. The simple answer was no. But they trusted Lahaina and had to believe she'd verified the woman in some way.

"We're confident she's who she says she is," Reg replied with more conviction than AJ felt.

Tee thought it over for another minute while she served more drinks to locals who were beginning to look at the strangers taking up space at their drinking hole with something more than curiosity.

AJ smiled at the man next to her. "Afternoon, mate."

He gave her a toothy grin in reply and seemed satisfied as he left with his fresh beer.

"Wait here," Tee said and walked to the other end of the bar.

"Wat a man gotta do to get a drink?" another patron shouted, leaning over from beyond Reg.

Tee barked something back so heavy in local dialect, AJ couldn't understand the words. But the meaning was clear. The man mumbled under his breath.

"She'll be right back, mate," Reg assured him.

The man was 60 if he was a day, skinny, and the top of his head came level with Reg's shoulder.

"Hey dere, big fella. Reach over dere and get me a Caybrew," he said, looking up at Reg.

Who laughed. "If you think I'm going up against Tee, you must be barmy, mate."

"Ya big chicken," the old man grumbled, but then grinned. "But wise enough."

AJ looked towards the other end of the bar where Tee was huddled in a whispered conversation with the older lady.

"I think that's his missus," Reg confirmed. "Not sure how keen she'll be to keep bringing up this band from half a century ago. Especially if she knows Sonny had a thing for Luna."

"You wouldn't think she'd be bothered by something so long ago," AJ replied, watching Tee return to the customers as Sonny's wife walked through the door to the back. "Sounds like he only knew the band for a couple of days."

Reg laughed. "Don't underestimate the bounds of a woman's suspicion when it comes to her bloke."

AJ frowned at him. "You know I'm a woman, right?"

Reg frowned back. "Well, yeah. Then you know what I mean."

AJ shook her head. "First of all, when did you become Yoda of the opposite sex? And two, Pearl doesn't have a jealous bone in her body."

"That's because she trusts me."

AJ laughed. "That's because she trusts no other woman will have you."

Reg chuckled behind his thick beard, and then stopped, standing up straighter. AJ turned to see Sonny in the doorway from the back. He nodded towards his reserved table. Reg and AJ hurried through the post-work crowd.

"Thanks for seeing us, Sonny," Reg said, and AJ was pleased to see the old man shake his hand.

He offered the same to AJ. "Miss Bailey."

They all sat.

"Who dis lady Tee say you have wit you? Where is she?"

"In the van outside," Reg explained. "We wanted to make sure it was okay with you first."

Sonny eyed them both. "If you sure she's for real, den I'll meet da woman."

"I'll go get her," AJ offered and slipped from her stool.

By the time she returned with Meadow and Lahaina, Reg appeared to have softened Sonny's cautious demeanour, and the two were laughing about an old story.

"Sonny, this is Meadow Blake," AJ said as they walked up. "She's Billy Hasting's niece. He was the bassist in the band."

"You're Panda's niece?" Sonny said, politely standing and shaking her hand.

Meadow nodded and smiled. "I am. Unfortunately, I never met my uncle as my mum, his sister, was only ten when he went missing. But I grew up around stories about him. According to my family, he was an interesting and loveable man."

Sonny's eyes shot to Lahaina. "Don't you write for da *Compass*?"

Lahaina offered her hand, which Sonny shook.

"Lahaina Jones, sir. Pleasure to meet you. I'm only here because Meadow contacted us when she arrived."

Sonny murmured something under his breath and shot a glance towards his daughter behind the bar. She was by his side in a moment.

"Everything okay, dad?"

"I didn't know we had a reporter visiting, too," he said, giving Reg a stern glance.

"Neither did I," Tee replied, and doubled the annoyed looks coming Reg's way.

Meadow held up both hands. "In full disclosure, I'm a journalist as well, but I promise you both, nothing you say goes in print unless you tell me it's okay. I'm not here to make a sensational splash or rake up any painful memories, if there are any. My primary interest is to learn more about my uncle."

Tee looked at her father, and he softly nodded. She rested a hand on his shoulder, which he patted and nodded again.

"We're okay," he said, and Tee threw Reg and AJ one more stink eye before she returned to the bar.

Tee paused to whisper an update in Sonny's wife's ear as she passed by. The older woman said something back, and the two returned to serving drinks to their patrons.

"We can talk some," Sonny said. "At da end, I tell you what's okay to print. May be none of it. May be some. Dat understood?"

"Yes, sir," Meadow agreed, and Sonny looked at Lahaina.

"Sure enough, Mr Watler," the Irish woman replied.

AJ wondered whether either of them could truly stick to that deal, but her hope was actually that Luna and the Lanterns' story could be told again. She'd discovered an emotional fascination with them and their connection to the island. Her other hope was that the skull didn't turn out to be one of them, as the idea felt sad. Which she knew was ridiculous. They were all dead, so their bodies were most likely in the wreckage of the *Soundwave* wherever that might be. *Why should that be any better?* AJ couldn't come up with a tangible reason. Maybe the thought they'd been interred in some way felt better than being tossed around the ocean floor.

"Then yes, I met your uncle, and he were a nice fella, best I could tell," Sonny said. "Handy on dat bass, too."

Meadow smiled. "Can you tell me a little about how you came to meet him?"

Sonny settled in and retold the story he'd relayed to Reg and AJ. The more he spoke, the more he relaxed, and dropped in several details that had probably come back to him, having thought about them over the past 24 hours. Meadow let the old man reminisce and only asked questions to keep his stories going or over a few curiosities. The other three stayed silent and listened in. Tee returned after ten minutes with waters for everyone, and even she seemed more at ease.

After forty minutes, Sonny came to the end of his tale, and

finished with telling how he and Clement had been ferried to shore in the late afternoon of the day of the storm.

"Camille blew much harder dan anyone expected. Tropical storm over da island, dey say, but sure made a mess of da place."

"And that was the last you saw of them?" Meadow asked.

Sonny nodded.

"So what happened to this fellow, Kayo, who told the crewman to take you back without him?" she asked.

Sonny shrugged his shoulders. "Lost wit da rest of dem."

"And why was he there?"

The old man took a sip of water before replying. "Can't say I rightly know."

For the first time since he'd began recalling his story, AJ felt as though Sonny was holding back. Meadow must have thought so too, as she pressed on.

"He wasn't a friend of the band's?"

"Like I said, dat's how dey introduced da man."

"But you don't think he was?" Meadow continued.

Sonny shrugged again. "I really don't know. But he weren't important. It da band and da crew lost dat day. Dat's da real shame."

AJ could see Meadow wanted to ask more, but wisely let it go. "I can't thank you enough for talking to me, Mr Watler."

"Just Sonny is fine, miss."

"Well, thank you, Sonny," she said. "And can I ask how you feel about me telling this story in a proper article about the band?"

Sonny thought for a moment. "You tying tings into these remains young AJ here found?"

Meadow shook her head. "Not unless there's irrefutable proof the remains belong to someone from the yacht. Which I seriously doubt they'll be able to do, even if it is one of them. They don't have DNA samples of the victims from 1969 to compare to."

"Can they use relative's DNA to compare?" AJ asked, as the thought occurred to her.

Meadow nodded. "That's definitely a possibility. As long as

they're a direct blood relative. The farther away the two samples are by generation, the less they're likely to have in common, so it's not perfect. But my mother's DNA compared to the skull would determine if the remains belonged to my uncle."

"And to yours?" Reg asked.

"A generation away, but I'd say it would still be conclusive based on the fact we don't have any other family members in this region," Meadow replied. "It wouldn't be with one hundred percent certainty, but extremely likely if we had a large proportion of matching DNA."

"Might be worth leaving a sample with the police when you meet with them," AJ suggested.

"I plan to," Meadow agreed. "And I'll look into tracking down relatives of the others on the yacht. Although that Kayo fellow might be harder to figure out."

She turned to Sonny once more, and he caught her questioning gaze.

"It's fine you sharin' what we talked about today," he said. "I just don't want a line of people stompin' through here tinkin' I got more to say on da matter."

"I think I can word this portion of the article appropriately, so it won't invite more journalists thinking there's more to be had. I really appreciate your time, and to hear the stories about my uncle."

Meadow rose from her stool, and Sonny stood as well, shaking her hand.

"Nice to meet you," he said. "And safe travels."

"I plan on being here for a few more days, Sonny. If I have another question or two, would you mind if I stopped by?"

"I suppose dat be okay," Sonny replied, and Reg and AJ both thanked him for his time.

They were about to leave when AJ noticed Sonny's wife had joined him.

"These folks are just leaving, love," her husband said. "Best you stay behind da bar. We're gettin' busy."

It struck AJ as strange that the old man would send his wife away in such a short manner. He'd been nothing but polite to all of them, even when he was angry at the dock.

His wife leaned over and kissed his forehead, then whispered something in his ear. Sonny's brow pinched, and he cupped a hand around his mouth to hide his reply. The others realised AJ hadn't walked away and turned back to the table. Sonny's wife kissed him again.

"I don't know 'bout dis, love," Sonny said with a pained expression.

"It's time, babe," she replied, then extended a hand across the table to Meadow. "I'm Sonny's wife, Louise Watler."

AJ gasped and put a hand on Sonny's shoulder while staring at the woman with the long grey hair. "You're her, aren't you?"

"She's who?" Reg asked, and the two journalists turned to AJ in confusion.

Sonny's wife sighed, then gave them a smile, and AJ swore she detected relief on the woman's face. "You may know me as Luna Skye."

31

Luna kept her eyes tightly shut as she pounded against the sandy sea floor before being spun like a washing machine with pieces of the wooden boat and other detritus bashing her bruised body. Stunned and barely conscious, she instinctively held her breath as the beating relentlessly continued. Plucked from the sand, she was tossed to the surface, where she caught a brief gulp of air mixed with seawater before the roiling seas dragged her under and tumbled her once more. Grains of sand scratched and peppered her skin, and she could taste the granules in her mouth.

Slammed into the sea floor even harder, all the wind crushed from Luna's lungs and this time she had no choice. Gasping, she waited for her throat to fill with salty water. Rolling across the sand, she landed on wooden debris and realised it was air she was sucking in. The ocean roared, and the next wave hammered down behind her, sweeping her up and throwing her farther up the beach. This time, when the powerful swell released its grip, Luna crawled on all fours away from the sound of crashing surf.

The wind howled all around her, whipping seawater and rain like a constant barrage of tiny bullets, stinging her flesh. Her hands and knees burned from cuts picked up from the carnage scattered along the beach. Luna could barely open her eyes and couldn't see much in the darkness when she did. Her head throbbed, and she felt a stickiness amongst her soaking wet hair, which she presumed was blood.

Occasional cracks of lightning created terrifying silhouettes of trees being bent over and tall waves threatening to break over her battered body. Exhausted and scared, she was physically unable to do anything more than inch farther up the sodden sand, finally bumping into something solid. Luna curled around the object, taking the little protection it offered, and after coughing and spluttering for several minutes, she passed out.

The wind had dropped considerably. It was also cooler. Luna's body felt like it had been scuffed with coarse sandpaper, and she welcomed the fresh air blowing across her skin for brief moments of relief. She cracked her eyes open, the dried salt making her whole face seem crusty. Daylight was breaking across the island, and she stared down the curving beach at a mass of branches, driftwood, and other rubbish which had either blown or washed onto the sand.

Luna pushed herself to her feet and looked around. What had been a sunny paradise the day before now looked more like a bomb had gone off. Dark, threatening clouds still hovered low over the island, but in the distance to the south and west she spotted clearer skies. For as far as she could see, she was alone. *Soundwave* had gone. Hopefully, they were under the blue skies in the distance. Safe. She recalled hearing the engines running as the lifeboat had sped away from the yacht.

Looking down, Luna studied the box she'd held on to throughout the night. It was the tape storage locker, complete with *'This Way Up'* painted on the side. Scratched and upside down, but still legible. But where was Rollo? Surely if she'd made it to shore, he would have too. He wasn't a burly man, but he was bigger and stronger than her, so he must have survived. Luna fought back the bile in her throat. She was standing there, considering whether her boyfriend was alive or dead. Ex-boyfriend, she corrected herself. *What about Kayo? He'd been barely alive when he went over the side. More importantly, what about Trina?*

"Trina," she tried yelling, but her voice was hoarse and barely louder than a whisper.

Luna coughed and cleared her throat, but she desperately needed fresh water to wash away the remnants of salt and sand.

"Trina!" she tried again, managing a sound, but it hurt like crazy.

Had she damaged her singing voice? What did it matter? Her friends were all gone. The Lanterns were dead. Except Panda. She glanced to the horizon once more, hoping to see the silhouette of the yacht, but there was nothing out there. The big motor yacht would have made it safely to calmer water, she felt sure.

Her head ached and Luna tentatively probed her scalp with her hand, wincing when she found the wound. She needed help, and she wondered where exactly she was on Seven Mile Beach. She'd only been there once, but had looked at the coastline from *Soundwave*. The main town was to the south. So was Sonny's bar. If there was anything left of it. She could also see a beachfront hotel. Torn between looking for Rollo and Trina along the coastline to the north or searching as she trekked south, Luna stood there with her mind running at half speed. She looked at the tape box again. Could anything have survived inside?

Luna dragged the locker into the trees behind her, rolling it upright. Covering it with broken-off palm fronds, she found a dirty and faded red shirt nearby and tied it around a tree. Her legs felt like lead and her bare feet were sore, but she carefully began picking her way down the beach towards civilisation. Constantly searching amongst the mess on the sand, she also scanned into the trees for any signs of life. Or a body. The idea sent shivers through her soul.

After half an hour, Luna reached the hotel, where she began

seeing workers picking up trees and foliage from around the patio and pool. The wind seemed to abate even more as the sun rose, and the early-morning coolness was soon replaced by a building heat.

"You okay, miss?" a man with a rake called to her. "Can I help you?"

Luna looked along the shoreline. Up ahead, maybe a half mile, she could see what she thought was Sonny's bar. She needed fresh water, but something told her to press on. Waving her thanks to the worker, she continued walking. The man watched her, but didn't say anything more, and soon she was out of his sight.

Sonny's Soggy Wreck Bar now lived perfectly up to its name. It was a sodden pile of colourfully painted wood and bar furniture. Luna couldn't see any of the instruments, so she hoped they'd managed to take everything to safety in time. She heard movement amongst the carnage and braced herself, in case it was a stray dog looking for food. From where a door hung limply from one hinge, Sonny emerged and stared at her.

"Luna!" he shouted, and ran towards her, hopping and jumping over the mess on the way. He stopped short and gently threw his arms around her. "I didn't know what to do," he said softly. "Dis storm much worse dan dey tink." He pulled away and held her at arm's length. "What happened? You're hurt. Where all da blood comin' from?"

Luna pulled him back to her and squeezed him tightly. "She's gone, Sonny," she cried. "Trina's gone."

32

AJ sat on her stool, mesmerised by Louise's story. The incredible loss she'd endured. The painful waiting to hear from *Soundwave*, which never came. By AJ's calculation, the woman had to be in her mid-seventies, but she didn't look a day over 55. She had beautiful, long, silver-grey hair and an elegance to her slender frame. She wore very little makeup, peace sign earrings, and a delicate pendant on a chain around her neck. Which AJ could now see was a lantern.

"Is your daughter named after Trina?" AJ asked.

"Catrina Anne Watler," Sonny replied proudly. "Tee instead of Trina, so we didn't raise no suspicions."

"So what was the story with the Kayo bloke?" Reg asked. "How did he fit into all this?"

Louise looked at Sonny, and he gently held her hand.

"He was the reason I never came forward after the storm," she said. "Not him, to be accurate, but the man he worked for. Lord Malcolm Thorburn had funded Rollo's project to build *Soundwave*. It was all under the table, and he was calling in his note. Kayo was his heavy who he put on the boat to watch us."

"Who you said my uncle killed?" Meadow questioned.

"Turns out he didn't, but he'd incapacitated him enough that the man didn't stand a chance in the water," Luna confirmed. "I'm not sure you want to print that part, but yes, it was Panda who hit Kayo over the head to save the rest of us."

"Okay, so who's this Thorburn fellow?" Reg asked.

"I only met him on the yacht and had no idea Rollo had used him to bankroll the fit-out for the studio," Louise continued. "He was actually a lord, but he was also a shady bloke. A loan shark, among other things. He had a place here on Grand Cayman where he spent time when he wasn't in London. That's why Rollo brought us to the island, because Thorburn had insisted."

"Why was it because of him you went into hiding?" Meadow asked.

"Initially, because I thought *Soundwave* would come back, and he'd seize her," Louise replied. "I was scared to death of the man. But when the yacht never showed up, the only asset worth anything was me and the music."

"The new music," AJ said excitedly. "In the storage box thing, right?"

Louise nodded.

"It all survived?" Meadow asked.

Louise nodded again.

"And you still have it?" AJ asked, bursting at the seams.

"We do," Louise replied. "And Thorburn is long gone. But even when he died, we decided to continue to keep quiet. We'd built a life here, and it didn't seem worth tipping everything upside down to come forward. I was mourning the loss of my friends, and I didn't mind leaving the music business behind me. The music, yes, but not the business."

"So why now?" Meadow asked. "I mean," she quickly clarified, holding up her hands, "I'm ecstatic about this, but still curious why after all this time."

Louise shook her head. "I don't know, really. The recent fuss over the band and the disappearance made me nostalgic, I guess. I always felt it was unfair of me to keep the music from the world.

Not that anyone would care about it these days, but there's some amazing playing by Trina and Panda on those tapes. And Rollo. He was many things, not all good, but he was certainly a talented musician and producer." She put her arm around Sonny. "There's even a guitar track by this guy on there."

"And Clement, man," Sonny added. "That dude was out of dis world on percussion."

"You've just kept the tapes all this time and never done anything with them?" Meadow asked.

"Over da years, we collected bits and pieces for a home studio," Sonny said. "Better dan amateur stuff, but not da real high-end gear. Still, good enough so we could sort out da old eight-track recordings, back dem up, move dem to digital."

"We'd laid down eight songs," Louise continued. "Five were pretty much complete as Rollo had intended, and three more had most of the recordings done. They needed mixing, which included anything we'd recorded on the final few days here on the island."

"So what now?" Meadow asked. "Have you thought about making the music available?"

Sonny and Louise looked at each other.

"We talked about it," Sonny replied. "But it up to Louise. Tis her music. Dis whole ting a surprise to me. I thought we'd carry dis secret to da grave."

"Well, it's nice to know we can rule out the remains I found belonging to Luna Skye," AJ joked, then realised what her statement left unsaid. "Sorry, I know they could still belong to one of your friends."

Louise shrugged her shoulders. "They're just bones. The Lanterns are rocking the afterworld. Wherever that may be. But in truth, despite your efforts to dissuade that idiot Carlson from speculating about your discovery being someone from the band, it could be. Rollo or Trina, at least."

"Or the Kayo bloke," Reg pointed out. "Although you said he was a big fella."

Louise raised an eyebrow. "True."

"I presume you've had no contact with anyone from your old life?" Meadow asked. "No relatives of the other band members? How about your own parents?"

Louise's face fell at the mention of her family. "It killed me, but I had no real way of communicating with my mum and dad at the beginning. I didn't think I could simply call them and expect them to stay silent about me being alive. I had a plan to return to the UK to see them in person, but I had the problem of travel as my passport went down on *Soundwave* and I couldn't very well apply for a new one. Anyway, after a few months, they had a funeral service for me in London, and once I was officially pronounced dead, all my music rights went to them. Now, it seems silly of me, as I'm sure they would rather I'd come home than have the money, but my parents were working-class folks who'd never had money for anything nice. I was scared to death Thorburn would swoop in and take it all, so I kept quiet.

"Took us years, but we finally used a fake UK birth certificate we bought from this shady fellow to show the authorities in Cayman that Sonny was marrying Louise Palmer. It worked, and pretty soon I had a British Overseas Territory passport for the Cayman Islands. I've been Louise Watler ever since."

"I can work on tracking down relatives of the other band members," Meadow offered, "and we discussed earlier that my DNA should be a close enough match to my uncle's."

"I'm sorry, I took our conversation off on a tangent," AJ apologised. "But you were about to talk about plans for the music."

"I can't imagine anyone's interested in it these days," Louise replied.

The table erupted in keen assurances that she was absolutely wrong on that point.

"People used to go bonkers when Pearl played your songs," Reg said. "You'd be surprised how many people still remember."

Louise smiled. "I've seen your wife perform many times. She's an incredible talent. Why do you think Sonny's been bugging you over the years to have Pearl play here?"

Reg beamed. "You have no idea what that will mean to her, love. I don't think they'll be any problem with her playing here anymore. It's only been my stupid concerns which have stood in the way."

"I guarantee there are thousands of audiophiles and music buffs who'd love to hear what you have," Meadow said. "And needless to say, with your permission, the story I'd planned just took on a whole new angle. Don't underestimate how big this might go."

Louise winced and looked at Sonny. "Personally, I can't imagine who'd be interested, but if it does cause a fuss, then it doesn't just affect me, it's Sonny and Tee as well. They get a vote in this."

Sonny smiled at his wife. "I only been hidin' you 'cos you wanted me to, babe. I've always thought da world should hear dat music. You can ask Tee, but I tell you right now dat she feel da same way."

Louise turned back to Meadow. "Can we arrange something exclusive with you? I don't want to deal with a bunch of Sean Carlsons invading our lives."

"Of course, I'd love that, and I'll talk to my editor and see what we can offer you for the exclusive," Meadow replied. "But I feel Lahaina should be involved, too. I don't believe I would've made it past Tee to meet Sonny and therefore you without her and these two, of course," she added, indicating AJ and Reg.

Louise laughed. "I dare say you're right. However you want to work it out is fine with me, as long as we can turn everyone else away."

"I have a silly idea that might be fun," Reg grinned.

"He's not kidding," AJ interjected. "His ideas are usually silly even when he doesn't warn you first."

Reg gave her a frown, and the others laughed.

"Let's hear dat idea all da same," Sonny said.

33

Reg and AJ sat at their regular table near the stage in the Fox and Hare pub. In fact, they'd arrived early and shoved together two tables to seat everyone in their party. Now, as Pearl made her final preparations on stage for her first set at eight o'clock, the crowd pressed closely around them as the place had filled to capacity. AJ looked around at her friends and family. Her father smiled when he caught her eye.

"I wouldn't mind a bit more of this in my life," he said, and held up his glass.

AJ clinked her Seven Fathoms rum against his. "It doesn't suck, does it?"

"Nope," he agreed. "It doesn't suck."

Across the table, Meadow and Sonny were deep in conversation, and Nora's foster kid, Jazzy, was telling Lahaina about her track and field exploits at school. Nora and Thomas were negotiating dives she could cover for him on her days off. Reg was fussing like an old woman, as he always did before Pearl's gigs, up and down like a yo-yo, making sure she had everything she needed.

Beryl leaned forward past her husband and looked at AJ. "How much time here is too much time, in your opinion?"

AJ wasn't sure what she meant. "Come again, Mum?"

"I'm asking you, how much time with us here on the island could you tolerate?"

AJ was taken aback. The conversation she'd had on the boat with her dad had been in confidence, and she looked at him sideways.

He threw his hands up. "This didn't come from me, love."

Now AJ felt guilty. If her father hadn't said anything, it meant her mum had recognised her daughter's trepidation without prompting. Which probably hadn't been too difficult, as AJ was terrible at hiding her feelings. Which had to be difficult for Beryl.

"Whatever works out, Mum," she replied, and Beryl shook her head.

"Nonsense. This is your home and your life you've built. If we show up, we'll be invading that world, which will change things, won't it?"

As usual, her mum was direct and annoyingly accurate. AJ sometimes wondered if she'd been adopted and Nora was, in fact, Beryl's daughter. Although AJ was too much like her dad not to be related. Which she liked.

"It doesn't have to," AJ replied. "I think the bigger question is how long you could stay here without going stir crazy. Many people get island fever after a while."

"You're avoiding the question," her mother pressed, and AJ felt her anxiety building.

Her mother had an uncanny knack of applying pressure on the exact spot, which turned water to steam until AJ felt ready to burst. It wouldn't surprise her if she whistled out of her ears like in a cartoon. It was a brilliant skill for Beryl to possess at work, while less of an asset at home. But AJ knew this and tried to tell herself it was simply her mother's way. The woman wasn't trying to be overly assertive or insensitive; she was just after an answer to her question.

"You're right, it'll change things for me," AJ replied. "But that means things will be different, not necessarily bad. I'd love to see more of you both."

Beryl gave her a wry smile. "You'd love to see more of your father," she said, squeezing his arm.

"Yes, I would, Mum. But I'd like to see more of you, too. I just need you to understand that my life here is *my life* which I'm living the way I want to. If you're going to look down on my little dive op, or fuss over my love life, then there'll be tension and it won't be enjoyable for anyone."

Beryl nodded. "That's fair. Duly noted." She reached out to her daughter and AJ gently clasped her hand. "I promise I will do my best to tread softly in your world, my dear. Ultimately, I just want you to be happy."

"I know, Mum, and thank you."

The house music quietened and Pearl's voice came over the speakers. "Good evening everyone. How are we doing?"

Cheers erupted, and AJ couldn't believe the atmosphere inside the pub. A buzz of anticipation emanated throughout the place.

"You may have seen the papers today, both locally and throughout the world," Pearl continued. "Telling a very special story about a local resident who's been quietly playing other people's music for many, many years at her husband's place in George Town, Sonny's Soggy Wreck Bar."

Everyone at Reg's table cheered, joined by many in the room. Sonny had closed his place for the evening and brought many of his patrons with him.

"Here tonight, to perform her own songs in public for the first time in over half a century, please welcome Luna Skye."

Everybody stood and applauded as Louise, who decided it was okay to use her stage name once again, walked up to the microphone next to Pearl. Waiting respectfully until the applause finally died down, Tee and Sonny also joined them. Tee took a seat on a cajón drum, and Sonny picked up a bass guitar.

Luna looked radiant on stage. She wore jeans, no shoes, a white blouse embroidered with floral patterns, and a band of flowers in her hair.

"You're too kind, thank you," she said. "And thank you all for coming tonight." She paused to compose herself and let another round of applause die down. "This will be a first for me, playing without my wonderful friends who I dearly miss, The Lanterns." She turned and smiled at her husband and daughter. "But I'm incredibly fortunate to have my lovely family with me," she continued, reaching out a hand to Pearl, "and this talented lady beside me. This is a song some of you with very long memories may recall. It's called 'Time and Light'."

AJ marvelled at how quickly the four musicians had figured out an arrangement and seamlessly played together as though they'd always done so. Pearl knew the first few songs they performed, as she'd played them herself in the past, but they'd all had to either learn or remind themselves when it came to the songs which had remained unheard for over half a century.

"You may have read that we have the original recordings for what would have been Luna and the Lanterns' second album. We plan to release the album sometime later this year, which will be called *Path and Purpose*. The title comes from the original painting which I still have by my lovely friend and bandmate, Trina." Luna turned and smiled. "Who my daughter Tee is doing a fine job of standing in for on drums."

The crowd rose to their feet once more and clapped loudly. Sonny looked like he'd never stop smiling.

"The words to this next song were written by Rollo Fletcher, and the melody created by my husband with the rest of the band during an amazing day we spent on *Soundwave* right here off the shores of Grand Cayman. It was the last piece of music we recorded together. This song is 'Elastic Heart'."

I hope you enjoyed this story!
If you did, I have something extra for those interested in joining my newsletter... hear Luna and the Lanterns perform 'Elastic Heart'! Use this QR code for the exclusive bonus content!

For more AJ and Reg, grab the next book in series, *Destiny Island*

ACKNOWLEDGMENTS

My sincere thanks to:

My incredible wife Cheryl, for her unwavering support, love, and encouragement.

My wonderful friend James Guthrie for his advice, help, and encouragement regarding the musical aspects of this story.

Christina Rotundo and DyHard Productions for bringing Luna and the Lanterns to life in a spectacular way in the bonus song!

My family and friends for their patience, understanding, and support.

The Cayman Crew: My lovely friend of many years, Casey Keller. Chris and Kate of Indigo Divers for keeping Reg and AJ's dock in tip-top shape. My reporter friend who allowed me to use her alter ego, Lahaina Jones, as a character.

Jeffrey Garrison who won the opportunity at my AJ Bailey Dive Adventure event to be a fictionalised character in this story.

My editor Andrew Chapman at Prepare to Publish. I couldn't do this without him!

Shearwater dive computers and Dive Rite, whose products I

proudly use. Reef Smart Guides whose maps and guidebooks I would be lost without. My friends at Cayman Spirits for their amazing Seven Fathoms rum.

The Tropical Authors group for their magnificent support and collaboration. Check out the website for other great authors in the Sea Adventure genre.

My beta reader group has grown to include an amazing cross section of folks from different walks of life. Their suggestions, feedback and keen eyes are invaluable, for which I am eternally grateful.

Above all, I thank you, the readers: none of this happens without the choice you make to spend your precious time with AJ and her stories. I am truly in your debt.

LET'S STAY IN TOUCH!

To buy merchandise, find more info or join my Newsletter, visit my website at
www.HarveyBooks.com

Visit Amazon.com for more books in the
AJ Bailey Adventure Series,
Nora Sommer Caribbean Suspense Series,
and collaborative works;
The Greene Wolfe Thriller Series
Tropical Authors Adventure Series

If you enjoyed this novel I'd be incredibly grateful if you'd consider leaving a review on Amazon.com
Find eBook deals and follow me on BookBub.com

Catch my podcast, The Two Authors' Chat Show with co-host Douglas Pratt.

Find more great authors in the genre at TropicalAuthors.com

ABOUT THE AUTHOR

A *USA Today* Bestselling author, Nicholas Harvey's life has been anything but ordinary. Race car driver, adventurer, divemaster, and since 2020, a full-time novelist. Raised in England, Nick has dual US and British citizenship and now lives wherever he and his amazing wife, Cheryl, park their motorhome, or an aeroplane takes them. Warm oceans and tall mountains are their favourite places.

For more information, visit his website at HarveyBooks.com.

Made in United States
Orlando, FL
12 April 2025